"In an age desperately searching for meaning and wonder, L.P. Prince has penned a tale that slakes our thirst. A rousing globe-hopping adventure, Prince explores the mysterious influence of generations past, treads the darkest hells of human evil, and ultimately feeds our souls with glimpses of the very glory of God."
—*The Rev. David Booman*
Assistant for Pastoral Chaplaincy and Healing Prayer

"*Inklings* takes the reader on an exploration of the spirit that stretches from the charming coastlines of Charleston to the rolling grasslands of South Africa and includes the treacherous seas in between. The characters will woo you, test you, and surprise you with each page turn!"
—*Nicole Woolcock*
Consultant, San Diego, CA

"L.P. Prince has a sincere warmth that is evident in her illustrations, telling stories about the human condition. She offers a waltz in prose that is both elegant and meaningful, gently guiding the readers around the dance floor and leaving them filled with anticipation for the next chapter to unfold."
—*Charles W. Waring III*
Publisher, Charleston Mercury

INKLINGS

THE HEAVENS ARE
UP TO SOMETHING

L.P. Prince

E//ergreen
PRESS
Mobile, Alabama

Inklings: The Heavens Are up to Something by L.P. Prince
Copyright ©2019 L.P. Prince

ISBN 978-1-58169-709-4
For Worldwide Distribution
Printed in the U.S.A.
Evergreen Press
P.O. Box 191540 • Mobile, AL 36619
800-367-8203

CONTENTS

INTRODUCTION

The heavens are up to something, and you are invited to join in, to fulfill your reason for being, to know more and want more of what really matters. Come and taste the very real and mysterious workings of God in our day. Travel with Ntombi (pronounced Tom-Bye, the n is silent) from South Africa as she becomes a God sleuth, eyeing the interface between heaven and earth and uncovering the first signs of a clear and present, yet unique, outpouring.

Experience the iced ache of loss and the surrounding sense of an unseen presence guiding her toward her anointed future. In her struggles we experience the freedom of Truth amidst story. Along the way, consider your own calling and learn to see through the enemy's lies as he struggles to thwart your call and guide you anywhere but toward the future God has in mind for you—your highest good.

The characters are real and raw and as jumbled in origin and calling as the real world we inhabit. No Pollyanna's here. Just brilliant troubled souls on a spiritual quest.

Enjoy layers of mystery, more than you can grasp in a first read. The message is eternal. It began before the dawn of time and will continue beyond all we currently know. It is otherworldly. It is about a heavenly outpouring. It is about an army in formation. It is about the voice that guides us. It is about God.

To G. Dan Lumpkin

the world's greatest mentor

ONE

Black-backed Jackal

It's true what they say. South Africa even smells different. Fresher. Bare. Wanting, yet full. On this night, the air had an added stillness, as if the night animals had forgotten to stir.

Ntombi sat alone in a small cane chair against the back wall of the porch, the vastness of Kwandwe Game Reserve stretched out around her. The house was a long, one-story Dutch colonial, placed like proper punctuation amidst the poetry and mystery that is Kwandwe. Its whitish stucco coating and closeness to the earth would have made it blend in were it not for the gracefully curved abutments on each end. As the acacia tree adds an outstretched accent to an otherwise hard horizon, so sat the Homestead House.

The night was also filled with fear—the kind that comes from not knowing. The worst kind. The brightly lit room and open window to her right made ignoring the fear and watching the bush nearly impossible. She had full earshot to what sounded like an interrogation. The police had already questioned her, but she didn't know much. All she knew was that she was to wear his favorite dress tonight, the one with the bright blues and greens. She was to wait at the Homestead House. So, she had waited.

A policeman was now questioning Mandlenkosi's mother. His voice was stern and matter of fact. "Ma'am, I need you to tell me everything you know."

1

Her voice quivered. "He planned for months and made arrangements for Ntombi's father to be in the country." She paused, then added, "Mandlenkosi drove to Port Elizabeth yesterday to pick up—you know, the. . ." She paused again. Ntombi turned to catch her gesturing but missed it.

"He allowed plenty of time. Look, why else would a table be set for two? He arranged for the house, the dinner. He knows how much she loves this house."

From her perch, Ntombi could see the small round table covered in white linen. Ranger Todd, a fellow staff member and friend, was to be their waiter for the night. He was still there, in full tux and the formality of a white bowtie, standing erect against the wall and out of the way. He stood like a sentinel on duty, or as if sitting would signify a lack of hope.

Mandlenkosi's mother's description gave way to air gasping sobs. His father, in a shaky but stoic voice added, "He left the house at two p.m. on Sunday. I warned him about driving on a Sunday, but he's his own man. He's a good boy, works hard, enjoys the finer things. . .open spaces. . . the land."

"Pardon me, sir, what was he driving? And when did you expect his return?"

The conversation turned into a list of facts, all seeming to Ntombi a meaningless waste of time. Tata, her father, who was inside as well, had taught her a few things about tracking. Tata was the best there was. He would say, "You don't find a lion by knowing its height and weight; you find it by knowing its character, its likes and dislikes." It seemed to Ntombi that "people hunting" should be the same.

Her annoyance was interrupted by the sound of a car approaching. The slowness the dirt road required gave Ntombi ample time to imagine a cab with Mandlenkosi in the back. Surely he would rise from the back seat with an intriguing story on his lips. She stood and straightened her dress, then glanced down at her shoes, which were now in a pile beside her. They didn't matter. She could run faster without them.

As the car came closer, Ntombi became aware of a twisted knot in her gut entertwined with glittering threads of excitement lacing their way through frayed cords of angst. She struggled to see the driver clearly. The lights from the house didn't reach far. What she could make out was an old pickup truck coming to a stop at the front of the house. The driver leaned over and said something to the passenger, then turned toward Ntombi and rolled down the crank-handle window.

A woman's voice carried through the night air. "Sorry to hear about Mandlenkosi and so sorry I have to drop Zuri off with Todd. I have to be at work. I'm preparing the breakfast baskets for the morning rides." As she spoke, four-year-old Zuri ran around the truck and stopped to wave both arms. "Ntombi, I'm here."

Ntombi adored this little ball of energy. Yet, in that moment, a glob of disappointment stuck in Ntombi's throat. She couldn't speak.

Zuri began skipping her way toward Ntombi as the pickup drove out of sight.

Suddenly aware of the surroundings, Ntombi's voice returned, "Zuri, honey, don't dilly-dally."

Just then, something moved in the bush. Zuri must have heard it too for she stopped and turned toward the sound. Ntombi stood still as well. Part of her wanted to call out, and part knew better. This was, after all, a game reserve. Hope swelled along with a good measure of fear.

The cleared lawn in front of the house sat as a buffer by night and a dollop of groomed emerald green by day. Tonight it framed little Zuri.

There! The bushes moved again.

"Zuri, honey, you need to stand very still. Can you do that?"

"Yes, ma'am" came her tiny voice as she crossed her arms around her waist.

Ntombi slowly reached to retrieve the Ruger Hawkeye .30-06 leaning against the wall behind her. She brought it to her shoulder. As she did, her second worst fear materialized. A black-backed jackal stepped slowly into the clearing. It paused, then ran straight for Zuri. Ntombi shouted "Stop," and it did. Within striking distance, it made three turns, stumbled, then straightened.

Sure of the caliber she held, the distance between the jackal and Zuri, yet unsure of what lay beyond the jackal, Ntombi slowly took aim. As she did, the jackal noticed her and began to growl. With a fifty-foot clear shot and Zuri a short distance from the jackal, Ntombi squeezed the trigger. The shot was clean to the head. The impact threw the emaciated jackal backward to the ground, and the kick threw Ntombi against the wall. She bounced off and then landed back in the chair with a thud. Zuri was still frozen in place, her eyes fixed on the dead jackal.

The gunshot triggered a police response. "Get down!" they shouted. Instead, everyone ran to the front door.

Tata and Ranger Todd were first out of the house. The others stopped in the doorway. Tata ran toward Ntombi and Todd toward Zuri.

Tata called out. "Ntombi!"

Still a bit stunned, Ntombi answered, "Yes, Father. I'm over here."

"Are you okay?"

Ntombi placed her left hand on her right shoulder and moved it up, back, and around. "I'll be a bit sore tomorrow."

Todd, with Zuri now in his arms, approached the porch. "I knew I should have taken the shot when I had it yesterday. He was rabid."

"It was a clean shot."

"No, no. You did what you had to do. I am grateful, just a bit shook."

"That makes two of us." Ntombi handed the rifle to Todd. "Thanks for the loan. Glad I had it."

As he took the gun, Zuri reached for Ntombi. It was a good trade. Her little arms wrapped tight around Ntombi's neck. It was a hug—not the one Ntombi longed for, but a hug.

"Zuri, you were so brave and did just the right thing. Sometimes it is good to stand real still."

"I brave girl. Like you, I brave."

"Yes, Zuri, you are brave."

Todd stood with Tata by his side, the rifle in one hand, and rubbing Zuri's back with the other. "Five years here, and you get to take the first shot."

"Sorry."

"No, no, you did the right thing. We've been looking for him for days. Just wish I'd gotten him, and you and Zuri hadn't been put in harm's way."

"I hope he's the only one."

Todd looked squarely at Ntombi. "I'm so sorry about Mandlenkosi. I was looking forward to being your waiter. You know, stories to tell. He'll show up, like the jackal, but don't shoot him."

"Never."

"If it's okay with you, I think Zuri and I will go now."

"Yes, of course. I'm in good hands."

Cupping her tiny hands around Ntombi's face, Zuri added, "Yes, she in good hands. She in Zuri hands."

Ntombi kissed her little friend goodbye. "Very good hands. Thank you for taking care of me, Miss Zuri."

Zuri returned the kiss. "My p-weasure."

Todd smiled slightly. "Come here, Miss Zuri." He scooped her into his arms, then looked at Ntombi. "When that scoundrel finally shows, tell him I waited."

"I will."

Tata stood beside Ntombi while Todd carried Zuri to his car. The contrasts were striking: Todd's tall frame in a black tuxedo, a four-year-old in one arm, a big game rifle and starched linen tea towel in the other. He walked with his head slightly lowered and Zuri chattering away.

Ntombi and Tata watched in silence as they drove away. Tata spoke first. "Mind if I join you?"

"Please."

"First, I need to bag him."

"Be careful."

Tata flicked his right hand in the air as he walked away. "I have gloves in the truck."

Ntombi watched as Tata tagged and bagged the rabid jackal. He placed the bag on the front porch and pulled a second cane chair beside her. They sat with their backs to the wall and eyes on the bush.

"There's a full moon."

"Yes. The light helped with the jackal."

"And it will help Mandlenkosi as well."

"Tata?"

"Yes?"

"What do you think? What does your spirit tell you?"

"That he is alive."

"Me too."

"And he's not coming tonight."

"No, not tonight."

"What should I do?"

Tata took Ntombi's graceful hand and cradled it between both of his calloused ones. "Pray. Then do the next thing."

TWO

Breaking Fast

A month had passed since Mandlenkosi's disappearance. Ntombi read the warning sign as she stepped across the plane's threshold. MIND THE GAP. She nodded a silent greeting to a chipper flight attendant, turned down the aisle, and stopped. The massive aircraft had only one fellow passenger so far, a tall man with dark, glistening curls and deep blue-green eyes. It was the eyes Ntombi noticed. Watchful. She returned his stare with a slight cock of her head, prompting him to glance down.

Ntombi looked at her ticket stub and upward for a cue.

"Three A is by the window," the man said, pointing.

She was startled by the American accent and then surprised at her own surprise. She was flying to America. She'd have to get used to the accent. "Right. Thank you."

Ntombi found her seat, planted her backpack beneath the one in front of hers, and glanced back at the man. How had he known her seat number?

The plane soon filled with people and energy. There was a certain hustle of anticipation. Or was it fear-laden hurry? Ntombi found it to be a drumbeat of hurry up and wait. The rhythm was off.

As the stream of passengers began to slow, she removed the small, leavened loaf from her backpack, asked the flight attendant for red wine, and began to set her table. Just then, a barrel-chested man appeared with a big smile and a bellowing voice. His hair was thick, combed over to one side, the color of wet sand—preacher hair. His face was square and strong and a bit weathered. Africa weathered people, especially people not from there.

"Looks like we're seatmates," he said.

Ntombi's hopes of quiet communion to end her fast quickly vanished.

He continued, "Looks like you've set a communion table. Like me to bless it?"

"Thank you, sir. I had the bread blessed before I packed it, and the wine is airplane wine. It will suffice."

"Afraid of flying?"

"Don't know. Never flown."

"Then why the communion table?" He shrugged slightly and slapped both hands on his thighs with a solid thud. "Pardon me. I haven't even said hello. I'm Chip, and this here's my wife, Carly." He pointed across the aisle to a pale woman with long, reddish hair draped over her shoulders. Beside her was the man with the stare, who was now leaned forward, apparently listening in.

Chip continued, "We're missionaries in Zambia. I'm guessing you are Xhosan?"

"I am Ntombi. And yes, I am Xhosan. I was preparing to break fast with communion."

"We'll join you."

The man across the aisle piped in, "Me too," and Carly nodded her approval.

Group communion was not at all what Ntombi had envisioned. "Well, yes then," she said, as she peeled back the reused foil, releasing the sweet smell of leaven. She had found nourishment these weeks since Mandlenkosi disappeared by feeding her soul and, in turn, her soul had been sufficient for her body. She suspected the opposite was not possible.

The small loaf felt moist and spongy. She thought of bringing it closer to her face to smell. Instead, she simply broke it. As she did, Chip extended one large hand to Ntombi and the other across the aisle to Carly. Carly joined hands with the man next to her, and Chip prayed. The hustle of people settling in for the long flight seemed to join silently in the moment.

Ntombi couldn't recall ever holding hands with a white man. His prayer seemed real to her, like someone who talked to God on a regular basis. When he finished, she took a piece of bread and passed it to him. When everyone had received theirs, Ntombi lifted hers and placed it in her mouth. The flavor was unlike anything she had ever tasted. The slight sweetness brought forth moisture in her mouth and a sense of awe.

Ntombi leaned forward to watch her fellow worshipers receive the bread, each with their eyes closed. As she watched the man across the aisle, Ntombi saw a tear roll down his cheek and over his upturned mouth. He lifted his eyes to heaven, made the sign of the cross across his chest, and looked over at her. This time he didn't look away but displayed his tear-streaked face and soft smile. She returned the smile and offered a nervous, yet partly knowing, nod.

They continued their communion with the cup of wine. In thirty days, Ntombi had managed to tell no one she was fasting, and now these strangers knew her secret. The fast had not made the pain go away, nor had it provided answers. She had fought back hunger with prayer, walking, and praying. Or trying to pray.

At times, she pictured herself storming the gates of heaven, taking hold of the pearly gates and shaking them until the bars rattled. With each prayer, peace returned, hunger subsided, and hope sufficed.

The plane soon left the ground. Ntombi peered out the window and sensed a lift in her chest. Was it the altitude or fear?

"Where you headed?"

Ntombi turned, glanced at Chip, then forward at the seat back in front of her. "South Carolina. Charleston."

"We love Charleston, don't we Carly? What takes you to Charleston?"

Carly nodded from across the aisle and smiled, as if she could hear over the jet noise. The hubbub of flying seemed not to bother her. Her peace seemed thick, not easily disturbed.

With a glance toward Carly then Chip, Ntombi said, "I'm not really sure. I will be working as a research assistant at a college. It all happened quickly. Plans change. But mostly, I think going was easier than staying."

"How so?"

Ntombi took a breath, shrugged slightly, then turned toward the window. She had imagined feeling the bread and wine in her stomach and envisioned her time on the plane as solitude— long hours to think and make sense of her transition.

Chip changed the subject. "How'd you score an upgrade? Ours was free."

"My benefactor insisted my first flight should be enjoyable."

"We'll see what we can do to help with that too, won't we, Carly?"

Ntombi turned again and peered out the window, watching her homeland become smaller and smaller, finally giving way to nothing but ocean.

She had always liked the sea. It drew her. The sea was at the same time violent and holy. Many were drawn to it, but she suspected few knew why. Maybe God keeps the sea for himself, she thought. It is self-cleansing. All sin drowns in the sea and is washed away. And the voice of the Lord hovers over the waters.

Ntombi's flow of thoughts continued as she turned her attention to the land. Land can hold sin. It gets buried there and oozes up. But not all land. Surely some land was holy. And the air? She had never before thought of the air. Was it also God's? She doubted so. It was not pure. Words filled the air, and many words were evil, hurtful lies. And then there was darkness. Evil loved darkness. Maybe Satan ruled the air.

No wonder people were afraid of flying.

A smile spread across her face when she realized her thoughts were flying faster than the plane. Ntombi wondered if others pondered about such things as these, then quickly, her mind turned to words and their power.

About that time, Chip touched her arm. It startled Ntombi, and she jerked it away.

"Sorry, you seem deep in thought. Care to share?"

"Share what?"

"Oh, I don't know. How about your journey?"

"It's hard to explain. It's like that old movie, *Rebel Without a Cause*. I feel like a missionary without a cause. I don't know what I'm to do once I reach America or why. I only know the where. At least, I think I know the where."

A knowing smile came over Chip's face lifting his square cheeks and adding even more light to his eyes. "That sounds familiar. We went to Zambia only knowing where. Been there three years now and been graced with a few glimpses as to why."

"Really?" Ntombi turned toward Chip with newfound interest.

Chip sat back in his seat, folded his arms high across his broad chest, and stared straight ahead. "I grew up with a godly mother and, as you can imagine, I asked why a lot. She would say, 'Because I said so.' It's the same with God. 'Because I said so' is gracious plenty."

Ntombi studied Chip as he spoke. He had a way about him. She had met lots of missionaries in Africa. Most wanted to help—or simply needed to feel good about themselves for helping. Chip seemed different.

As Chip finished, Ntombi reclined her seat and pulled her blanket to her chin, which, in turn, popped the covers off her feet. Chip smiled and offered his blanket. "They're never long enough." Ntombi accepted it and spread it over her legs.

Her sleep was deep but much too brief. When she awoke, the man with the glistening curls from across the aisle was stretched out beside her. Ntombi sat up. "Where did Chip go?"

"I hope you don't mind. We traded seats so he could be by Carly."

Ntombi looked across the aisle. Carly was sleeping, but Chip wasn't there.

"I think he's in the back. He tells me this is your first flight."

"Yes, sir."

"Are you enjoying it?"

"I suppose. I don't know a good flight from a bad one." Looking to redirect the conversation, Ntombi asked, "What brought you to Cape Town?"

"I have some business ventures in South Africa, but I'm headed home."

"Where's home?"

"Boston."

"Hmm."

When the stranger returned to his book, Ntombi continued to size him up. She thought he was kind of handsome for an old dude. She liked his hair even though it was a bit unkempt like hers, though not as big. He was tall. She figured he was at least forty, but it was hard to tell white people's age. She wondered what he was reading but decided not to ask.

"Excuse me, sir. I think I'll go find Chip."

"Was it something I said?" He gave her a dimpled grin.

"Yes, try to do better next time," Ntombi teased, as she moved to step over his outstretched legs.

"I can get up."

"No need. I got it."

Ntombi's long legs easily cleared his. Her face passed near his as she bent to miss the low ceiling of the plane. He smelled good. Not chemical like most Americans. He gently took her leading hand, offering her firm support. The gesture reminded her of a gentleman helping a lady out from the back of a limo and onto a red carpet. It was helpful and felt good.

Ntombi found Chip leaning on a counter mid-cabin reading a Cape Town newspaper.

He looked up. "Did you sleep well?"

"Yes, sir, but not long. Will you tell me about your ministry in Zambia?" Ntombi's eyes were wide, and there was a slight tilt of her head. "When I get to Charleston, I'll be assisting a professor of religion in his research into calling. You could be my first interview."

Chip shared with Ntombi for over an hour. She learned of his and Carly's call and their obedience. First, obedience to the where. It was comforting to Ntombi to learn that she was not alone and to think of someone else's story for a while. She considered the sacrifice Chip had made, giving up a successful practice, their home, even time with their adult son. She was intrigued by the still, small voice and the sheer (or was it cloudy?) mystery of how God directs his called. She thought about whether the voice she'd heard was of God and wondered if she were running to or from her call or if she even had one. Or could it be she was only running?

When they'd finished talking, Ntombi returned to her seat

and found her new seatmate dosing, a book in his lap. She reached across him, placing one hand on the headrest of her seat, and stepped across, careful not to wake him. Her lagging foot brushed his thigh as she stepped through. The man stirred.

"Welcome back."

"Sorry. Didn't mean to wake you."

Ntombi watched inquisitively as he made adjustments to his seat, paying attention to which buttons he pushed. He must have noticed her watching him because he reached across her and pointed to a group of reclining options. Ntombi nodded her thanks, then turned toward her porthole window as the man settled his long frame back into his seat. She looked out, then up and around, to see as much as she could. The sun was setting, creating a pinky-orange glow atop the deepness of the sea below. It was a new vantage point, kind of like God's. She was seeing the earth from the heavens. Ntombi looked about the cabin to see if others were noticing the majesty just beyond, but no one seemed to notice.

With a slight shrug, she turned again toward her small earthward glimpse and pondered the magnitude and suddenness of change. The passing of a single month and the distance of a nineteen-hour flight put a chasm between her and everything she knew; her entire world was becoming unrecognizable.

Soon amazement gave way to sleep. When she awoke, her curly headed seat-mate was gone. Carly moved across the aisle and gently interrupted Ntombi's waking stretch with, "Hi. Chip tells me you're headed to Charleston. It's a beautiful place, as is your homeland."

"I will miss home. Though I am not sure why. The people are gone. Tata and now Mandlenkosi. Or maybe I miss the land."

"Is your father deceased?"

15

"Oh no. He's a missionary in Torrance, California."

"A missionary? And Mandlenkosi?"

"He was/is was to be…"

"Did he move as well?"

"Uh, no, or at least I don't think so."""

Ntombi told Carly how the detectives had found Mandlenkosi's car at the bottom of a steep ravine but had not found him.

Carly listened intently. "How long had you been engaged?"

"We weren't officially engaged, at least not yet."

With that, Ntombi contorted her long frame and reached beneath the seat in front of her, digging in her backpack until she retrieved the box.

"This was found near the crash site, beneath a bush."

The small, carefully gift-wrapped box now displayed atop a pedestal of Ntombi's graceful fingers made no attempts at hiding its content or Mandlenkosi's intent. It was a bit scraped and soiled, yet the once white paper and grosgrain ribbon were still intact.

At that moment, Carly had what sounded like knowing surprise in her voice. "You haven't opened it."

"I am waiting."

"Waiting is hard."

Ntombi nodded, lowered the box to her lap, and turned to look out the now blackened window. She could see Carly's reflection beside her. Together they peered into the tiny oval porthole, noticing each other's worried smile and the vast mystery beyond.

THREE

Charleston

Ntombi woke with a jerk and sat straight up in the hotel bed. She blinked to adjust her eyes and felt for the side of the bed, then swung her legs over the edge and slapped her hand about on the nightstand until she found the clock. 3:00 a.m. She fell back across the bed with outstretched arms and a thud, her feet dangling over the floor. She turned her head to one side, sniffed, and grimaced. The sheets smelled like bleach.

Ntombi looked up at the ceiling. "God, what have I done?"

On the ceiling were two thin streams of light forming parallel stripes. She studied the lines and wondered if they were somehow an answer. Maybe the life she had imagined for herself was the wrong path, and now she was on the right one. And maybe her host family would have better smelling sheets.

"Why am I here, God?"

She waited for a nanosecond, then continued, "I don't know anyone."

She thought of her host family, the Bayfields—Ben and Becca. They'd pick her up tomorrow and take her to their home where she'd stay the rest of her visit. Ntombi had met them a few times earlier, during their visits to Kwandwe. She wanted to be excited about seeing them again. She placed the crease of her right elbow over her eyes to shield them from the light and waited, hoping sleep would take her.

Ntombi soon gave up on sleep and made her way around the bed to adjust one set of curtains and then the other. Neither would close properly. Frustrated, she flung one set open and looked first at the brick wall on the other side of the narrow alleyway, then down at the streetlight below.

She placed both hands atop the lower half of the double-hung window and noticed the thin, wavy glass and the cool, damp sweat on the inside. She leaned in and looked down at the alleyway, then up and down as far as she could see. Not a soul. She turned and looked about her large, beautifully appointed room and then back at the street and decided America was backward. Inside was too big and outside too small.

And too many chemicals in the sheets.

She leaned her forehead against the cool, damp glass and prayed aloud. "God, do other people have all these questions? You must get tired of questions. I'm trying to be thankful. Thank you for the internship. Thank you for the room. Thank you for my benefactor." She lifted her head and looked up at the sliver of night sky between the buildings. "But isn't that a bit weird? I trust Tata, but it's just odd to be given money from some unknown source. I'm not complaining, just saying."

She quickly twirled around and settled down on the deep window ledge. Her long legs stretched out in front of her. She crossed one foot over the other with an exaggerated move, crossed her arms and dropped them. "And what about my life? Am I where you want me, or am I running away? How could I have been so sure I was to marry Mandlenkosi and be a teacher and now I'm here? And where is he?"

No answers came. In time, a foghorn sounded in the distance. It was a peaceful sound, like a whisper of assurance that safe harbor was near, and someone was on duty.

Ntombi stood and grabbed a pillow from the bed. She gave

the drapes a big yank, pulled them together, twisted their edges, and leaned the pillow against the bottom to keep them closed. She then repeated her curtain closing trick with the second window and climbed back in bed. This time she slept.

—

Ntombi dressed and headed out. Sometime after she fell back asleep, it had rained, leaving a hefty sweat on the bluestone sidewalks. A stubborn fog lingered across harbor and city alike. It was a Monday, making those "not from here" fewer in number and the lure of the city's beauty a more private affair.

Ntombi stepped through the front doors of the downtown Charleston hotel and into the soft, gray light of early morning, stopping to stretch as if she were alone in the bush. She folded herself in half with the grace of a ballerina, placing both hands on the cold stone in front of her feet. She straightened, lifting her arms high above her head. When she did, she noticed a man in a suit at the corner across the street watching her. Ntombi stared back at him at first, then he formed some word of admiration and shook his head. His attention made Ntombi suddenly aware of herself. She dropped her arms to her sides and looked away.

She had done her best to look American and blend in, but the fast had made her jeans hang lower on her hips. Her favorite green T-shirt rested an inch from the top of her belt. She felt for the gift card in the pocket of her jeans. Her mystery benefactor had once again thought of everything. Whoever it was had mailed the card to the hotel front desk. The note that came with it read simply, YOU WILL NEED SOME WARM CLOTHES. USE THIS. THERE ARE PLENTY OF SHOPS NEARBY.

Ntombi looked around for a moment before deciding which

way to walk. She noticed the soft, tastefully chosen colors of the buildings lining both sides of the street. Plenty was an understatement. Trash cans were lined up as far as she could see, yet there was no foul odor. Charleston seemed to her an old but clean city. Was it so clean that the trash didn't smell? Ntombi recognized the circular nature of her thoughts, shook her head, then turned and headed catty-corner across the street.

She made a beeline for a two-story, buttery-beige, stucco building. It stood proudly, despite—or possibly accented by— the occasional streak of blackish-green mildew and centuries of well-intentioned repairs.

The building's window display caught her eye as she neared, drawing her closer in. A box of old, broken tile was outrageously priced at seventeen hundred dollars, and a pair of carved, marble vases was marked twenty-eight hundred. Ntombi placed a hand on the broad window sill, moved her face an inch from the razor-thin glass, wavy with age, then cupped one hand around her eyes, as if the mist-covered sun cared to hinder her view.

There beyond the window sat room after room of randomly piled treasures: oil paintings in gilded frames, colorful rugs with century-old wear, small pieces of furniture, and countless fragile things. Ntombi smiled knowingly. The prices in the window were clearly a way of keeping the casual tourist out. She decided to return later.

There was a hustle in the streets, a rhythm made by those hurrying to work. Each had a different look—some in uniforms, some in ties or bow ties, and others with tool belts and fat-toed boots. Ntombi stopped occasionally and watched the interesting ones, thinking herself a researcher sent to study a new tribe.

Overwhelmed by the sheer number of stores and with no idea what she needed, Ntombi ducked into the first store she saw with raincoats in the window. With little effort, she selected a bright-green one with a hood and proceeded to the checkout counter.

After ringing her up and bagging the coat, the clerk took the card Ntombi extended and slid it through the credit card machine.

"Could you tell me how much is left on the card?" Ntombi asked.

The clerk punched a few keys, then Ntombi noticed her eyes widen. "Goodness! Need anything else?"

"What?"

"The remainder is nine thousand, eight hundred and twelve."

Ntombi raised her eyebrows at the clerk. "Maybe later. The coat is all I need at the moment."

Back on the street, the rain softly increased, leaving Ntombi wondering why she hadn't chosen a warmer coat. She looked about, removed a crumpled tourist map from her jeans pocket, then headed back in the direction of the hotel. She approached the antique store and noticed lights on and a gray-haired man putzing about inside. She watched through the window from a distance, hoping to go unnoticed.

He moved out of sight for a moment, then returned with a newspaper and a steaming cup. He placed both on a desk cluttered with porcelain statues, a stack of dishes, and about a year's worth of papers. Ntombi waited until he had a few sips and turned to page two of the paper before she made her way around to the front of the store and rang the bell. She could see the consternation on his face as he lowered the paper and looked over his tiny glasses at her. She looked straight at him and didn't flinch. It was a trick Tata had taught her—never let them see fear. He neatly folded his paper, which she found odd given the state of the rest of his desk, and made his way to the door.

Ntombi heard three locks release, then the door opened. A distinguished face appeared in the opening. "Yes?"

21

"I am from South Africa, and I know it's quite early, but with the jet lag…" The man studied her but said nothing, so she continued pleading her case. "I've been admiring your collection through the window and was hoping to get a closer look. I'm not a wealthy tourist or anything. I would be looking merely for the love of beauty and interest in the collection."

The man's harsh stare softened, and he opened the door wide. "Would you like a cup of tea?"

"Oh, yes, please. That would be lovely."

Ntombi took a seat in the chair across from the man's desk. In a moment he returned with a steaming cup placed on a delicate, matching saucer. Ntombi stood and received the tea in both hands. As she did, his eyes traveled the length of one arm to her face.

"Are you mixed?"

Ntombi jerked her head a bit, looked down at herself, and then back at the man. "No. Why do you ask?"

He gestured for her to have a seat. "Sorry, didn't mean to offend. Thought I noticed some English features. It's a hazard of the profession. I can be a bit of a snoop."

He moved around his desk and took a seat, placing one of the statues on the floor so he could see Ntombi. She kept her eyes on him as she took a long sip of her tea. The awkward silence quickly led to more questions. "So, what brings you to Charleston?"

"I will be part of a research project in the religion department at the university."

"Didn't know they were still researching religion. I guess it's a good gig if you can get it."

Ntombi laughed and shook her head. "I guess you're right." She placed her teacup back in its saucer, then looked up at the shop owner. "So, do you by chance have any old books?"

An hour later, Ntombi left the store, excited about the book she had found. A gentle shower fell once again so she tucked the neatly wrapped book under her raincoat and in the back waistband of her jeans. The paper wrapping and carefully tied twine were scratchy against her back, but the book made her jeans fit better. She hurried up the street with her hood up and her head down. As she neared Market Street, the gentle shower turned into a winter's downpour. Ntombi ducked into what she thought was another shop but was greeted by a broad walkway and what seemed like a mall. It was warm and brightly lit with a long line of shops displaying their finery and beckoning her to enter. The marble floors glistened with fresh polish. The wall in front of her hosted a larger-than-life framed poster of a plat-inum-haired, stone-faced woman displaying a handbag. All was well in here.

Ntombi removed her soaked coat and draped it over her arm, pulled her shoulders back and lifted her gaze straight ahead. It was a move Tata had taught her. "Look like you own the place," he would say.

The long hallway opened to an expansive room flanked by two gracefully curved stairways, each adorned with a freshly polished brass banister. A massive chandelier hung from the ceiling above. Ntombi smiled, threw her head back, and twirled slowly. As she turned, her own image flashed before her. The giant, gilded lobby mirror revealed her rain-freshened face sur-rounded by massive piles of damp curls. Ntombi reached into her jeans pocket to retrieve a hair-tie.

As she wrapped the tie around her hair, she caught some-thing else behind her in the mirror. The shock of seeing the image out of its context made it slow to register, but then it did.

It was him!

Ntombi turned quickly, and so did he. Although he was partly hidden by a cell phone, his face was dark, chiseled, and surrounded by mid-length hair juxtaposed against a crisp, white shirt and the finest blue suit Ntombi had ever seen.

She moved instinctively toward him. As she did, he slid the phone in his jacket pocket, turned, and bolted up the stairs, taking them two at a time. Ntombi gave chase, choosing the other curved stairway, hoping to meet him at the top. Her heart was pounding as she too leaped up two steps at a time, trying to be mindful of the curve in each stair. Her wet sneaker slipped on a tread about halfway up, but she caught herself.

He beat her to the landing and, without noticing her pursuit, bolted down a short corridor and quickly opened one of two heavily painted double doors and disappeared behind them.

Ntombi caught her breath, pleased she had not lost him. She looked around. At least a dozen people in business attire were scattered about, all with phones attached to their heads; some were in heated conversations, each pacing as they talked. She made her way to the double doors and threw one side open wide.

In front of her sat a large, mahogany conference table with twelve or so distinguished-looking people sitting around it, each seated in an oversized, leather armchair.

A woman of about seventy years sat at the far end. Her hair was white and brushed straight back, looking a lot like freshly spun silk. Her skin was a translucent porcelain, hosting nary a wrinkle. She was the first to speak.

"May we help you?"

Ntombi looked about the room and quickly found the man from the lobby right in front of her. His back was turned, but he was in arms reach. Realizing she had only a moment, she placed her right hand on his shoulder. As she did, he turned, revealing a friendly, yet puzzled face—one that could easily be Mandlenkosi's in twenty years.

Removing her hand, Ntombi bowed slightly. "Oh. Please excuse my intrusion. It must be the jet lag. I thought I had found an old friend."

Her pursuant responded with a smile. "Oh, that I were he."

Ntombi again bowed slightly and then backed out the door. "I am so sorry, please excuse me."

———

Back in her hotel room, Ntombi took a warm shower and wrapped herself in the hotel robe. She arranged her pillows just so and got into bed. She crawled back out and dug the small, white wrapped package from her backpack. She stood with only the dim light through the crack in the hotel drapes and inspected it, noticing the partly torn paper and the soiled ribbon. As she did, a wave of something came over her. She pulled the terry robe tighter around her body and up around her neck, trying to shake it off.

"You are safe, dry, warm," she told herself. "You are loved, and you have thousands of dollars in your pocket. Tomorrow, a new adventure begins."

But she couldn't get her heart to agree. Of course, she missed Mandlenkosi. Who wouldn't? Still, she couldn't get rid of the feeling that she could have prevented it all. She thought she could have done something differently, made some little choice that could have produced a different ending.

Ntombi placed the small gift on the nightstand then wrapped her arms across her chest, moved them down her torso and flung them to each side as if peeling the dark thoughts off and slinging them away. She sat on the edge of the bed and looked at the carpet.

She should have gone with him to pick out the ring. But, no, she had to be surprised. She'd had him jump through hoops and look what it had gotten her. At what it had gotten him.

Ntombi fell to her side on the crisp, white sheets. She pulled her knees up toward her chest, wrapped the robe around them, and gave into deep and mournful sobs.

FOUR

The Carriage House

Ntombi stood in front of the hotel wearing her new green raincoat. Passing cars were few at this hour, but, just in case, she waved a slight hello to each. Most returned the wave, though none were the Bayfields.

After a few minutes, a white Range Rover rolled into view. The Bayfields waved through the windshield as they approached. Ntombi remembered their faces from their visits to Kwande yet pondered their contrasting features. Americans were a mixed bag.

She recognized Ben's black, wavy hair juxtaposed with his sun-freckled face and deep blue eyes and Becca's dramatic, upswept hairstyle with its one silver streak.

Their car stopped in front of Ntombi, and Becca jumped from the passenger seat to the sidewalk in one quick motion. As Becca hurried toward her, Ntombi noticed her silver streak had not changed over the years.

"Oh, it's so good to see you. You remember Ben." Becca turned and realized Ben wasn't behind her and waited while he turned off all the necessary buttons and emerged from the car. When he reached the two women, he extended a hand to Ntombi. "Welcome."

"I am very pleased to see both of you."

"Ben will put your bag in the car. I hope your room was adequate. Sorry we couldn't be here when you arrived. Perhaps it gave you some time to become familiar with the city and campus. Your cottage is ready. Did you sleep well? Are you over the jet lag yet? It takes a while."

Ntombi watched Becca's mouth as if focusing on it could help her better understand the flow of American English. Capturing only bits of it through Becca's heavy Charleston accent, Ntombi simply said, "Yes. I slept well."

Becca threaded her arm through Ntombi's and led her to the car. "You ride up front now, so you can see."

Ntombi knew Range Rovers but mostly the kind with an open top. Her father had served as a tracker at Kwandwe Game Reserve for many years before his missionary call to California. He was the best tracker. The animals seemed to trust him, or at least his spirit, and at times would look for him. Even the white rhino, which eluded the other trackers, would occasionally show himself to Tata. Kwandwe was her father's land, the land of his youth and the land of Ntombi's ancestors.

Becca talked from the edge of the back seat, pointing out various sites along the way. Ben merely nodded agreement. Ntombi felt strangely at peace amidst the deluge of Becca's chatter and the comfortable silence of Ben at the wheel. It was as if she had known them for a long time.

The trio turned off the road and down a long, tree-canopied drive. Ntombi leaned forward and looked up through the glass into the trees. She enjoyed the sun flickering on her face. She had never seen trees like these so close together, covering the drive like netting over a bed.

"What are these trees and what's hanging from them?"

Ben glanced at Ntombi with a smile and then back down the drive. "They're live oaks, and that's Spanish moss."

Just then, the canopy parted, and there in front of Ntombi

sat a long flat house. Ntombi reached her hand to touch Ben's arm.

"Sir. Please stop."

"Why? What's wrong?"

"Nothing is wrong. Quite the contrary. I want to see it. It somehow looks familiar."

Ben pulled the car to a gentle stop in the clearing and gave Ntombi time to study what would be her temporary home. Becca sat unusually quiet in the back seat.

Ntombi studied the house and its long, lean welcoming lines and simple white paint in the cleared setting. It looked like the Kwandwe Homestead, Charleston style. It lacked only the Dutch Colonial scallop over the abutting ends and the second front door to be a near replica. Not knowing quite how to explain her thoughts, Ntombi nodded, and Ben slowly finished the journey down the long driveway. They stopped and got out.

Becca was the first to speak. "The carriage house is around back. I hope you'll find it to your liking. Ben will bring your bag. Come with me." Again, Becca inserted her arm in Ntombi's and this time elongated her steps as she led Ntombi around the back corner of the main house. There in front of Ntombi was a glorious white board and batten cottage. It had deep-green shutters and windows on all sides. They were large windows—the kind that blurs the divide between inside and out.

The carriage house door opened to a large room with soaring ceilings and a wall of windows overlooking the garden. In the bedroom sat a mahogany poster bed, intricately carved and neatly adorned with crisp blue and white linens. No netting. She supposed she wouldn't need it here, but she would miss it still. Bed netting did more than keep bugs out; it kept you grounded while you slept. It would be easy to soar without it.

The kitchen was small. Becca had added bright-green,

boldly patterned café curtains. Motioning toward them, she said, "I had these made so it would seem like home. The fabric is Kente."

Ntombi pushed back tears. She had never lived in such a place. It was like a Southern version of the cottages for the Kwandwe guests. She stood in awe of the fireplace, the art, the Oriental rugs, and...yes! She smiled at the sight of a large, hand-carved bowl brimming with ostrich eggs. Just as the iron kettle of ostrich eggs welcomed guests to the Kwandwe lodge, she now had a bowl of her own.

"These are beautiful. It's all beautiful." Ntombi lifted an egg from the bowl and gazed about the room.

Becca smiled. "I moved those from the main house for you; thought you might recognize them. They are one of my memories from Kwandwe, along with your smiling face. If you remember, you were the first person to greet us." Becca looked about the room, then straight at Ntombi and added, "Isn't it amazing that we are now standing here on U.S. soil? This time you're our guest."

"It is so kind of you and Mr. Bayfield to welcome me. I am grateful for all the work you did to make the arrangements for me with the college."

Becca shook her head. "Enough of that. You unpack, and I'll run to the main house and make some tea."

Within minutes, Becca returned carrying a silver tray with a lovely silver teapot and four china cups and saucers. Ben followed behind her. Ntombi greeted them at the door and exaggerated her welcome as if they were guests in her home. She extended an arm and motioned for Becca to place the tray on the coffee table. Ntombi and Ben took a seat on the sofa as Becca served the tea.

Becca joined them and began to explain the carriage house.

"When we built this, it was for mother. We made it one large room. Well, except for the kitchen and the bath. Mother loved to garden. We wanted her to have a full view all around."

Ntombi looked about the room. "The views are beautiful on all sides. And the ceiling. I love the vaulted ceiling and the beams."

"Yes, mother loved those too."

"Does she spend a lot of time here?"

"No, mother passed two years ago. And before that . . ." Becca glanced over at Ben and took a sip of her tea. "Actually, the first time mother came, I told her Ben would take her bag to the carriage house, to which mother quickly replied, 'I will be staying in the main house, thank you.'"

Ntombi laughed. "Really?"

Becca laughed. "Really. So, I guess we built it for you."

Ben nodded. "And because Becca likes a project."

Becca finished telling Ntombi about her new home, but Ntombi was only half listening. The other half was listening to her own spirit. It was at peace.

Becca spoke again, interrupting Ntombi's thoughts. "Tell me about your decision to come here."

Ntombi looked at Becca and paused. "There isn't a lot to tell. I just felt I was to come. Or maybe it was that all other doors were closed and then this one opened. I guess only time will tell if I have done the right thing."

Ben placed his teacup on the saucer and looked at Ntombi. "Perhaps you took the road less traveled."

Ntombi turned and looked squarely at him. "I love Robert Frost. Thank you for the reminder."

Ben nodded. "My pleasure."

Becca looked over at Ben and shook her head, smiled, and glanced back at Ntombi. "He likes poetry. I tease him and tell him he's the only poet laureate tree farmer in the land."

"Only need one. Once you hit perfection…" He winked at his wife, and they laughed. It was the kind of laugh a family shares, and Ntombi joined in.

Suddenly, Becca sprung to her feet. "I almost forgot. You have a message from someone." She hurried toward the main house, leaving Ben and Ntombi in a pool of silence.

After a moment, Ben broke the silence with a full rendition of Frost's words, with great emphasis on how taking the road less travelled made all the difference.

Ntombi looked up at him and applauded just as Becca reemerged through the door with a note in hand. "Benjamin Bayfield, what are you up to?"

"Just reciting a bit of poetry," he said, in a feigned British accent.

Becca peered at him over her half-frame glasses, smiled and shook her head, offering the message to Ntombi. "It's from a girl named Dominique. She called yesterday, and I wrote it down. Someone from back home?"

"Ah, Dom. I know her from school."

"A friend?"

"Not exactly, but I suppose it will be good to know at least one fellow Xhosan."

Just then, the hard slam of an old car door caught their attention. Becca smiled over at Ben. "Must be Mae. I'd know the sound of that Cadillac door anywhere."

Ntombi made her way to the window, assuming Ben and Becca would as well. Instead she watched alone as a woman emerged from the over-sized sedan, adjusted her clothes, and made her way to the carriage house.

Mae had on a red chiffon dress with a peach, flower-laden hat. The hem of the dress flipped out and swished in a semicircle motion as her hips created a figure eight in the opposite direction, first one side, then the other. Her walk was unhurried, though, like one who knew each shell of these paths and didn't care to hurry over them.

Becca went to the door and swung it open. "Well, lookie here!" She reached both arms around Mae's neck.

"Now don't you say anything," Mae said, making her way straight to Ntombi, and took her by the hands. "Let me look at this girl. My, ain't you the sight! God done went and made you the prettiest thing."

From across the room, Ben patted the cushion on the sofa beside him. "Mae, I like your dress. Come, sit down."

"Don't mind if I do. Thank you, Mr. Ben. It took all my energy gettin' dressed." With a flip of her hand, Mae dropped to the sofa and wiggled her way back, lifting her feet at least six inches from the floor. "Yes sir, this is my new Sunday dress. Y'all know I done got the spread since you got that cleaning service."

Ben smiled at Mae. "Well, I like it."

"Thank you, Ben." Mae beamed. Her teeth were bright white, with the lowers protruding just slightly beyond the uppers, giving her an impish smile that was impossible not to return.

Becca smiled at both of them, looked squarely at Mae, and asked, "Is that the only dress you got—I mean have—that fits? We need to go shopping. I'm picking you up tomorrow morning at ten."

Mae offered a wide-cheeked grin and raised brows, cupped her small hands and dropped them in her lap. "I love it when they're easy."

The foursome shared a laugh.

Ntombi studied Mae's face and her mannerisms. It was a cheerful face with chipmunk cheeks and a rich, chocolate color with some darker spots, like God forgot to stir it completely. "Miss Mae, do you have any Xhosan in you?"

"Oh child, I don't know."

"I was just noticing your high cheekbones."

Mae shook her head. "Child, my mamma always said that was the Cherokee. I don't think any of us really knows, even these white ones who thinks they knows."

Ben and Becca laughed and shook their heads. Mae chuckled at her own joke, leaned back, snatched a folded salmon-colored newspaper from the side table and began to fan. With the gusto of a Broadway actress, she launched into a story.

"Now about the dress. I wore it this past Sunday, and oh the ladies did stare. I knows they was fightin' back the sin."

"The sin?" Ben asked with raised brows and a grin to match.

"Oh yes. That most vicious sin—jealousy. You know the one when you sidin' with the devil. He jealous. That was the first sin." Mae kept fanning, took a breath, and pursed her lips before continuing. "Well. I knows what they thinking, you know, 'cause it's not even Easter yet, and, just then, the preacher—he young—he came up before the service started, put his hand on my shoulder, and said right out where all could hear, 'Well, Mae, that is a beautiful dress.'" She accentuated her description of his compliment with a slight wiggle beginning with the top of her head and ending with her hips, and planted her left fist on her hip. Still fanning with her right hand, she added, "Shut them right up."

Mae then placed her makeshift fan back on the side table and turned to Ntombi. "Now, child, if you need anything, you just ask Miss Mae. I'll get it for you. I don't own a thing on God's green earth except what matters. I got all what matters."

FIVE

Research

Ntombi sat on the slatted wood chair with an open book laid out in front of her on the library table. She leaned back in the chair and stared across the room as if studying the library stacks. The library was mostly empty. She could hear only the click, click, click of the librarians' sure steps on the plank floors. Ntombi thought of her ancestors, many of whom were called by God. Her grandfather had preached on weekends.

Ntombi turned her thoughts to the book in front of her.

"Are you an international student?"

Startled by the deep southern voice, Ntombi jerked her head and caught sight of the tops of two white feet in loafers. The feet met green corduroy trousers and led up to a small, wiry young man in an oxford button-down. He stood confidently with his hands in his pockets. His perfect smile conveyed his upbringing, as did his stance.

Ntombi was unsure if talking was allowed in the library. A quick glance to the librarian across the room assured her it was not, and so she whispered. "Yes, I am new here."

The young man responded at normal volume. "I'm Andrew. I've been here for three years." He grabbed the chair in front of him by the back, turned it around, straddled it, and crossed his arms along the back. "You're deep in thought. What are you studying."

"Calling?" said Ntombi with a lilt of uncertainty.

"What's calling? You mean like for preachers?"

"Something like that."

"Well, what have you learned?"

"I was just considering my father's call."

"Is he a preacher?"

"Kinda. He's a missionary in southern California. Or, rather, a tracker-turned-missionary."

Andrew cocked his head slightly. With his hands firmly grasping the back of the chair, he leaned back. "So how does one go from being a tracker to becoming a missionary?"

"Calling is like that."

"Touché."

"So, what are you studying?"

Andrew sat up straighter. "I'm an artist working on a project. It's a study of the face: You, my dear, have an amazing face. May I photograph you?"

Ntombi lifted a hand to her face and offered a questioning look. Amazing? "I am not sure I understand what you are asking."

"Natural light will be best. I don't have my camera today. Will you be here tomorrow?"

"Uh, yes. I'm doing research, and I expect I will be here in the morning."

"Great. I'll bring my camera tomorrow." With that, he stood and turned to walk away, then quickly pivoted back to Ntombi, offering his hand. "Sorry. Forgot to fully introduce myself. I'm Andrew DeSouza. And you are?"

"Mme Ntombikayise Tyunjwa."

"Whoa. What do you go by?

"Ntombi."

"Got it. I'll call you Ntombi. See you tomorrow."

Hours later, Ntombi left the library and strolled across campus. She couldn't stop thinking about Mandlenkosi. She believed him alive. Surely she would know if his spirit had departed, but there were so many whys. Why hadn't he called? Why hadn't he been found? Why was he on that road?

———

That evening, with the low winter sun beaming into the carriage house window, Ntombi settled into a chair to read a letter from Tata. She held it up to her nose. It smelled like Tata.

Letters were best. They required more time, and time was love. Ntombi knew Tata loved her. He always had time for her. When Mandlenkosi called and asked for her hand, Tata left his mission in California and flew to South Africa to be there for the announcement.

That was time. That was love.

Ntombi carefully opened the envelope and removed the letter, unfolding it and taking time to appreciate Tata's careful hand.

My Dear Ntombikayise,

I telephoned the Bayfields yesterday to learn of your safe arrival. I am pleased to know you are adjusting to your new home. I am proud of you and your courage.

My work in the Torrance Mission is doing well. Our homeless lunch group prays for Mandlenkosi each day as they say grace. It is humbling to see those who have so little show concern for one who had so much. Many ask how you are doing and if we have heard any news.

Please write when you have time and tell me about the research project. I have never met Dr. Whitting but know people who know him. He is an accomplished

scholar, known for his intellect, and is also well-pub-
lished.

It will be good for you to meet new people and to
make friends. I will pray and ask for just the right
friends for my beautiful Ntombi. No doubt the research
will help you to meet people, and the Bayfields know
lots of fine people as well.

Which reminds me. There is a quirky little coffee
shop in town, Corner Coffee. You should visit there.
Becca tells me all the students go there. It will be a good
place to meet people. Oh, and she said Dom had called.
You know, there is just something about that girl I don't
like. She has always been jealous of you. Best to keep
your distance.

Please give my best to the Bayfields. I will write
more when I have more to report. You and Mandlenkosi
are in my prayers daily. I know our heavenly Father
knows where he is and is caring for him—either in his
presence or yet on this earth. Mandlenkosi is not
beyond God's reach.

I also pray for your life decisions. This is a time
when you will be faced with many choices that will
impact the rest of your life. I pray for you and for your
choices.

I love you and miss you, my sweet daughter, and
hope to see you soon.
Your Tata,
Simon

Ntombi swallowed and lifted her gaze to watch the light
streaming into the room. Tears welled in her eyes, adding a
kaleidoscope of color to the rays of light. This was the first time

Tata had mentioned the possibility of Mandlenkosi being dead. A surge of feelings surfaced in Ntombi's chest. She loved Tata and missed him. Or was it Mandlenkosi she missed? Or home?

One of Tata's sayings came to mind, bringing a smile to her face: "Don't worry the mule is blind, just load the wagon." Tata had lots of sayings. This one meant just do the next thing.

With a deep breath and dogged determination, Ntombi laced her sneakers and went walking along the banks of the river. The path snaked through what was once a rice plantation. It now had an ancient, mystical feel. She had walked it once before and found she could lose herself there and focus on others she never knew.

What was life like for the slaves, for the plantation owners? She smiled as she thought of the way Ben said it: "plan'ation."

Just as the sun was beginning to set, Ntombi spotted movement in the water and moved in for a closer look. They were some sort of animals, but she didn't recognize them. Up and over, swimming around, they joined together to tumble again. Each had a shiny coat of slick, wiry fur and a whiskered face. She counted three or four.

"There you are."

Ntombi turned toward the voice. She had been so engrossed in the newly found animal life, she had not heard Ben approaching.

"Good evening, Mr. Bayfield. You startled me."

"I see you found the otters. They seem to be plentiful in these backwaters this time of year."

"It's like they're playing."

"They are. I came out to find you and see if you'd like to join us for dinner. Becca's collected something from the deli down the road. In about ten minutes it'll be homemade."

Ntombi and Ben walked together along the farm road back

39

to the main house, each in their own path, an axle width apart.

Ben was first to break the silence. "It's a beautiful time of day to walk these paths."

"Did you grow up here?"

"Only partly. My great grandparents once lived here. Then my grandparents lived in town and would come out during the summer months. I was only here for a month or so each summer."

"Where did you grow up then?"

"New York City."

"New York City? I'm sorry. It just seems that you are so at home here."

"That I am. My father went to New York to make his fortune, to be his own man, away from the family. It's different for me. He proved himself, and now . . . well, I guess now I don't have to. I watch pine trees grow for a living."

"Seems you're doing a good job. There are plenty to watch."

"Fifty-five-thousand acres in one tract of land. We'll thin some next week."

The lights of the main house came into view, and the pair walked the rest of the way in silence. Walking with Ben was like walking with Tata. Words were welcomed but not necessary. Sometimes two can listen at once.

Six

Waking

Mandlenkosi woke with a sharp, throbbing pain behind his eyes. He grabbed his head with both hands and pressed in, then uncurled from his side-lying fetal position and rolled to his back. Doing so made the pain worse.

He lifted his head with a groan and noticed some relief. He muscled himself partway up and leaned on his forearms. Darkness surrounded him, and the air was hot, sticky, and damp. He took a shallow breath and released it. Then another.

A queasiness churned in his stomach in an odd counter-rhythm with the pain in his head. He sat the rest of the way up, crossed his arms over his knees, and lowered his head, then thumbed pressure across his forehead. Doing so seemed to quell some of the pain. He kept the pressure there and blinked in an attempt to force himself to focus. There were such huge gaps in his memory. Blackout periods.

Slowly, his eyes adjusted to the lack of light. He stretched his legs out and leaned back on his hands. A single slatted ray peeked through a wall and revealed a three-high stack of crates to his right.

Mandlenkosi sat this way for a good half hour, fighting the spin of the room. Soon the pain subsided, and vertigo gave way to glimpses of the rough chipboard floor beneath him and of his only article of clothing, a pair of boxers.

"Hello?" he called out, then sat quietly and still. No voices, only a deep-throated humming sound of a large engine. "Hello, is anybody there?"

No response.

"Where the hell?" Mandlenkosi scanned the room. "It could be hell."

He pinched some skin on his arm and decided he was very much alive. "Surely, I'll go the other way."

With nothing else left to do, he decided to explore his surroundings. Mandlenkosi assumed he was in a warehouse of some sort. He stood slowly with the moves of a much older man, took four small steps, and did a full body plant into a wall. He stepped back and felt with his hands like a blind man looking for a light switch. It was steel, cold and hard, but not flat. Every few centimeters, a dip and then a rise. Mandlenkosi walked his hands along the metal wall for about four meters, then came to a turn.

The second wall was the same, only not as long.

Moving faster now, hand to hand to ensure he didn't miss anything, Mandlenkosi marked out the back wall in meters. Just over two meters, he thought.

The next wall was longer but proved harder to measure because of the crates stacked against it. Still, it soon led to another corner, but the next wall had a door. Its hinges were placed on the outside. It was designed to open out. The door gave Mandlenkosi the final evidence he needed.

He was locked in a shipping container. But where?

Mandlenkosi stumbled toward the only source of light, squinting against its brightness. He stood with his face against the slatted opening and kept his eyes closed. He could feel the sun's warmth and the smell of sea spray. Once he'd adjusted to the light, he pressed an eye against the opening.

All around him, stretching as far as he could see, were ocean waters. He was seemingly high above the ship's deck, possibly at the top in a stack of containers, and all the way at the back. His view pointed directly behind the ship, so he could only watch where it had been. The ship's frothy wake was below him, constantly parting the ocean and leaving behind a whitish streak.

Mandlenkosi stood ever so still at his porthole perch. His breathing became labored. The air, the only fresh air, was just beyond the porthole. He gasped for one rapid breath after another. He then reached his fingers through the porthole's slats and moved them about as if they could breathe for him. For a moment, he thought he would pass out.

But then a calm voice entered his spirit. Do the next thing.

"The next thing?"

Yes. Do the next thing.

Mandlenkosi wiped sweat from his eyes with the back of his hand and began to hiccup. He began to laugh between hiccups, and then he laughed at how he sounded. Soon, his breathing returned to normal, and he made a decision.

He would do the next thing.

Turning from the window, he noticed weakness in his legs. He grabbed each quad in his hands, and they felt strong to the touch. Walking told a different story.

He fought the urge to focus on the weakness and began feeling his way around the container. In one corner, he found a crumpled pile of clothes. He dug his trousers from it. He shook them a few times for good measure and put them on. Mandlenkosi laughed to himself, wondering if he really needed them.

Turning his attention to the cargo, he took a crate from the stack and yanked on one of its thin boards until he pried it loose. He repeated this move until several crates were open.

Some contained a goodly supply of South African red wine while others held bags upon bags of macadamia nuts.

In another corner sat three large, work-crew-sized containers of water—fresh water. Beside it, a plastic grocery bag held bags of dried meat and dried fruit. He puzzled over it all, but then decided it was intentionally left for him.

Mandlenkosi used his hand to bring water to his lips and gave thanks.

—

Days passed until, one morning, the air felt somehow less sticky. Perhaps the winds had shifted, or the ship had changed course during the night. Mandlenkosi sat in his freshly washed and air-dried, dingy-white boxers atop a pile of flour bags full of Macadamia nuts. His arms were behind him, his hands firmly planted on the rough wood floor. His legs were outstretched and crossed at the ankles, accenting his mismatched footwear. On one foot he wore a fine, deep-brown, Italian leather dress shoe; on the other, a smelly, old Nike sneaker with its sole partly peeled from the bottom. Mandlenkosi sat and enjoyed the early hour.

A ray of light pushed through the porthole and formed a rectangle on the wall. Mandlenkosi had managed to remove the slats with a shoestring and plenty of time. He leaned slightly to his left, allowing the warmth of the sun to grace his face.

He closed his eyes and imagined the scratchy bag beneath him to be the sands of a tropical beach. When the sun's rays moved off his face, he stood, stretching both hands up until his fingertips felt the top of the container. He held the position until he felt his muscles loosen, then bent at his waist and touched the floor between his feet.

Mandlenkosi's once white shirt hung on a loosened rivet, as

did his deep-navy, Italian suit. Looking at it, he remembered the car accident and the rituals of the remote hillside tribe. When he remembered the tribesmen in the canyon, he smiled for they had worshipped him as someone sent from the ancestors or the gods.

Mandlenkosi squinched his forehead and patted the pile of twists on top of his head. "The girls. The little girls in the tribe twisted my hair." He wondered how he looked in twists, not that it mattered.

Mandlenkosi returned to his porthole view and passed the time by stretching first one arm then the other through and waving at the nothingness. Suddenly he smiled widely, revealing perfectly formed white teeth with a gap between the front two.

With brows lifted and the look of an idea dawning, he pulled his arm back through the porthole and followed the streaming light to the one lit spot in the container, pointed at it, outlined it with his hands forming an imaginary box in space. Next, he positioned a large crate as a table and a smaller one as a chair. Both now directly in line with the light, he stepped back and dusted his hands. He then removed a tiny spiral notebook and a pen from beneath a pile of nuts and wondered why he had hidden it.

Mandlenkosi sat on his crate-turned-office chair, his legs on either side of the makeshift desk, and his knees at nearly shoulder height. And he wrote, "I lacked prestidigitation, and the chief sold me."

Then he closed his tiny notebook and placed the pen beside it. It was what he remembered. It wasn't much, but it was a start.

Mandlenkosi spoke into the air. "This is a good day. There are far worse fates than a free ride on a ship. I have dried meat, dried fruit, three containers of water, and the cargo. I expect if they had wanted to kill me, they would have. Why feed me if they want me dead?" With that, he stood from his desk and resumed his porthole perch, watching the wake for hours more, studying it as the ship plowed its frothy oceanic path.

From his vantage point, he could see where they had been. Conversely, he had no idea where he had been or even who he was. He could remember some recent things but not much from before the car accident and capture. A new life was emerging, one not of his choosing, and one he suspected he wouldn't want.

Returning to his desk, Mandlenkosi decided to write all he could remember of his life. He looked down at himself and then wrote.

I am young, strong, and obviously handsome. Why else would the tribesmen worship me?

Mandlenkosi sat and stared into space for a bit and then wrote some more.

It must have been a good life. I am (or was) wearing a suit. It is now tattered, soiled, grossly inappropriate, and a bit oversized. But it is a suit. The fabric is of good quality, and I know quality when I see it. The tie is fine silk and obviously I knew how to tie it. It is an unusual tie with its scintillating blues set against a dazzling vermillion background.

Perhaps the accident was on a special day.

Mandlenkosi glanced at his feet. "And, at least I have shoes." At the sound of his voice, he pushed his makeshift desk aside and stretched his long bare legs out, displaying his mismatched shoes. He placed his hands on his knees and, for a moment, pondered the symbolism of shoes with a sole. Surely the dress shoe was who he was, and the other could very well be who he was becoming.

"Right Foot, please meet Left Foot."

"I am pleased to meet you, Mr. Right Foot." His left foot spoke with a South-African-infused cowboy accent. "You are quite distinguished. What is your name?"

Mandlenkosi's right foot responded in its best Queen's English. "I am Sir Richard of Cape Town. And you are?"

"I am known around these parts as Left Louie, the gun-slinging gambler full of grit and getty-up."

"I hesitate to say it, but you are either an unlucky gambler or an abysmal dresser."

With that, Mandlenkosi feet began to battle. Mandlenkosi watched on, amused. He laughed at his ability to entertain himself and the poignant symbolism of this, his Battle of the Soles.

At dusk each day, Mandlenkosi sang. His memory was filled with songs—the words and the melodies. On this night, he stood with head held high and outstretched and upturned arms. He swayed side to side in a counter sway with the ship and sang. He sang in a baritone voice, surprising for his girth. He sang the words of a slave ship long gone:

Amazing Grace, how sweet the sound, that will save a wretch like me. I know I am lost, but will be found. 'Tis Grace will set me free.

SEVEN

Odd One

During what seemed like a quick drive to town, Ntombi smiled as she recalled her photo session with Andrew. She had enjoyed his company in an odd, cousin kind of way. She had found it hard not to laugh at his antics and even harder to say no to his creative genius.

Ntombi turned into the Corner Coffee parking lot. The smell of old coffee wafted into the street. She wondered if coffee drinkers liked the odor.

The building's façade was old and worn with peeling gray-green paint. It was virtually untouched by a remodeler's hand. The two stories matched the architecture of the attached storefront but somehow had more character. The old wood and glass door, with layers of vermillion paint, opened in. A long, narrow space with raw, dark wood and wide plank floors introduced the path to the counter while a dozen conversations echoed about the room.

The countertop was also a display space, with a small gap for the brewmaster to greet customers. She stood in line for her turn and noticed a glass case filled with sandwiches and quiche, a bin full of scones, and a basket of homemade cookies. Behind the counter sat a cooler filled with wine, imported beer, milk, and juice. Beside it was a large, stainless box with beer taps protruding from the top.

Ntombi had apparently arrived just in time—the line quickly grew from three to thirteen. She watched the brewmaster work and decided he alone was worth the wait. His long, sandy hair hung in decade-old dreadlocks, yet they were shiny. His expression and dialogue didn't seem to fit the hair. Or was it the dreadlocks that didn't fit him?

When it was her turn, he greeted her. "I've not seen you here before. New in town?"

"Yes, I am Ntombi."

"Ntombi? I'm Daniel."

He quickly wiped his hands on the pink-and-white linen towel tucked at his hip and reached across the counter to shake hers. "I'm pleased to make your acquaintance. What would you like?"

In shaking his hand, Ntombi felt something was not right. Or maybe it was too right.

"Tea, please. Do you have rooibos?"

Daniel raised his brows and smiled. He placed one elbow on the glass display counter and planted his head in his hand and looked straight into Ntombi's deep, blueish-green eyes. "Ya! You're South African! I know your country well, but not well enough. We must talk. I'll take a break shortly, and we can talk. But first, I will make for you Daniel's best cup of bush tea."

Ntombi nodded her agreement and looked around for a place to stand. Moving just three steps to the left, she made room for the next customer and found herself once again peering over a small gap in the tall counter's clutter.

Moments later, Daniel slid a cup of steaming rooibos toward Ntombi. "There. That should be to your liking. There's more seating upstairs. I'll be up in a minute."

Ntombi zigged and zagged through the crowd of chattering people. They seemed to all know each other. This was no doubt the gathering place like the watering holes at Kwandwe, a place for God's creatures to gather and find nourishment.

She found the stairs tucked away behind another doorway. They were dirt laden, foot-worn, and leaned forward and to the left. Then again, the entire building leaned. Maybe the stairs were straight, but either way, they seemed sturdy enough.

At the top was an open space full of worn sofas, café tables, and a hodgepodge of upholstered, discount furniture store chairs. Each one was placed as the last guest felt best. Three students studied in one corner with a fourth asleep on a nearby couch.

Ntombi selected a pair of chairs and a small coffee table. The chairs needed only a slight adjustment to create a conversation space. She sat and crossed her long legs, then uncrossed them, leaned back in her chair and felt the tired springs. She sat up straight again before choosing a posture somewhere in between.

The tea was the first familiar taste since leaving home. Ntombi sipped and watched the activity around her. A few times since she'd arrived in America, she'd felt invisible. This was one of those times. So many people were there—all so close, and yet everyone in a world of their own. The three men to her right were discussing Scripture. Across from her was a middle-aged man with a younger woman. They sat really close to one another, and he alone wore a wedding band.

Daniel arrived with a steaming teapot on a tray, interrupting Ntombi's thoughts. She stood.

"Thank you for indulging me and my fascination with South Africa." He looked across the table at Ntombi. "People watching?" He carefully placed the tray on the table and motioned for Ntombi to have a seat. She lowered herself to the chair with the grace of a prima ballerina. Daniel, on the other hand, dropped dramatically into his chair. When he did, his dreadlocks bounced up and then forward. With one quick swoop of his hands, he tossed them back over his shoulders.

Ntombi leaned toward him and whispered, "This is a marvelous place to study the culture. I feel like a cultural anthropologist."

"The scene changes hour by hour. You should join us—well, not join us—watch us for live music in the evening. Depending on the band, one sees quite a different crowd." Daniel watched as Ntombi took a sip of her tea and then asked, "Howzit?"

"It's as good as hearing someone say 'howzit.'"

"You'll find I speak some of the language."

Ntombi grinned and took another sip of tea. With a lilt in her voice, she asked, "So. Howzit you know my country?"

"It's a God thing. I traveled with my grandparents for many years. They are getting older, and I carry their bags, so to speak." Daniel paused to sip his tea. "Okay. Now about you. What tore you away from South Africa?"

"I am here as a research assistant for one of the professors at the university, Dr. Whitting. Actually, I have only just begun."

"Ya. Whitting. What are you researching?"

"Calling. Dr. Whitting's expertise is church history."

"Calling? What sort of calling?"

"The call of God and, more specifically, the voice of God. Not necessarily what people are called to do, but how they know it is of God. And then, collectively…" Ntombi's voice trailed off, and she stared into the space in front of her.

"Collectively?"

"I just had this thought. What if we pieced all the calls together? Maybe then we could see what God is up to."

"Yebo yes!"

"Yebo yes? I love it."

"Hearing more words from your homeland or your idea?"

"Both!" Ntombi took a sip of her tea and added, "But I haven't even met Dr. Whitting yet. He's been out of the country. I think I'll be interviewing people. At least I hope so, seeing as I have already scheduled my first interview. It's with Miss Mae who works for the Bayfields. She volunteered."

"Whitting is an interesting sort."

"You know Whitting?"

Daniel tilted his head back and then cocked it slightly toward Ntombi, looked down his nose and over imaginary glasses. In his best erudite tone and South African accent, he said, "Dr. Ntombi, I presume?" He sat up straighter. "Seriously, though. It's like you're a private detective, following God around to see what He's up to."

As Daniel spoke, Ntombi matched the angle of his head and smiled. She liked the idea and wondered if Whitting was up to a bit of God sleuthing.

"You need a business card with the title KINGDOM SPY." He pressed an index finger against his mouth and squinted, then his eyes widened as if he'd had a revelation. Daniel took a sip of his tea, nodded, and raised his brows. "It's a good gig."

They sat quietly for a moment, as if on African time. She could usually read faces, but it was harder to do lately. White faces were harder to read.

For the rest of their time together, they sipped tea and talked of lesser things. At one point, Ntombi wondered if Daniel needed to get back to work, though he seemed unconcerned about time. Maybe the tea had filled the holes, and he had more now.

Ntombi found Daniel's stories interesting and aglow with insight. Then there was that hair. It too was shiny. How does one have glistening dreadlocks? She had never been close to a white man with dreadlocks. She tried not to stare but had questions.

"I suppose it's time for me to get back to work. When will I see you again? I'd like to give your research project some thought. Who knows, I may come up with some ideas. That is if you care to turn over a variety of rocks."

"Oh yes, please. I like rocks."

"Good. I work Tuesdays, Thursdays, and Fridays."

They said their goodbyes. Daniel went back to work, and Ntombi left the coffee shop. As she walked to the car, she couldn't help but think of the dichotomies: a thirty-year-old with shiny dreadlocks in a Blues Brothers tie working at a grungy coffee shop but interested in her, in South Africa, and in her research into calling. And at times speaking with the voice of an angel.

Then again, all seemed a bit askew at that shop. Perhaps Daniel was normal.

EIGHT

Miss Mae

Ntombi sat on the edge of Mae's sofa displaying what Becca called her "lady-like posture." The sofa looked like soft velvet but felt stiff like Velcro. She studied the room. A large, mahogany secretary with wavy, paned glass doors and a pull-down front was adorned with a vase of pink silk flowers and a plastic, molded plaque which read THE LORD IS MY LIGHT AND MY SALVATION.

A lovely, mostly coral, Oriental rug adorned the floor and provided an incongruent backdrop for the olive green Naugahyde recliner and the tin TV-tray turned side table with worn creamy paint and the remnants of hand-painted flowers. A single framed photo of a young lad provided the only hint of family.

Ntombi found the inconsistencies of the room puzzling and the harmony of her hostess beautiful. It felt good to be here. Mae was her people—with slight modifications.

The kitchen was mere steps away, and Ntombi could hear Mae humming as she worked and the soft thump of Mae's bare-footed steps on the wood floors. Ntombi looked up to see her push the swinging door open with one hip and twirl through it, tray and all. Mae brought freshly baked cookies and a pitcher of iced tea. Ntombi stood to greet her and reached her hands out to help with the tray.

Mae smiled softly and shook her head. "I gots this. Now I know you like your tea hot, but you ain't had tea till you had Mae's sweet tea. I am meaning to convert you to the ways of the South, at least in the tea category. They is many ways down here you don't wants to get caught up in."

Mae placed the tray on the coffee table, handed Ntombi a cold, sweaty glass, and took one for herself. They both sat down with Ntombi on the sofa and Mae on the green chair.

Ntombi smiled and took a sip of her tea. "Mae, your home is lovely."

With hands gesturing at various things around the room, Mae described her little house. "Oh, it's a mishmash. Becca done gone and give me so much stuff, I hardly have room to walk. Just look at this rug."

Mae pointed toward the floor behind the sofa. Indeed, the beautiful Oriental rug was a bit too large for the room and turned up the wall a few inches behind the sofa. Mae continued her description. "You know Ben thinks she likes to shop. It ain't that. She just has in her how things ought to look, and she can't leave it alone until she gets it right even if it ain't her own house."

Mae cackled at her own joke and lightly slapped the top of her thigh. As she did, her hand sunk in, producing a jiggle instead of sound. "Laudy, she had her work cut out for her with me. But, look at us. We both sittin' here all prim and proper-like, and she ain't even here."

The pair laughed at themselves and leaned back in exaggerated form, demonstrating their best slouch. Yet, as the conversation continued, each of them returned to their erect pose, as if it had become normal.

"Child, I know you doin' some research. Call of God, right?"

"Yes, ma'am."

"Thank you for including me in your interviews. I knows a lot about how God talks to people. You see, we been talkin' for nigh on forty years, and He been tellin' me to talk to you and make sure you know about His voice."

Ntombi quickly set her cookie on the napkin, dusted the crumbs from her fingers, and pulled her notepad and pen from her backpack. "Go ahead. I'm ready."

Mae leaned forward, set her tea down and went to teachin'.

"The Bible says the sheep will know His voice. Now I don't know nothin' about sheep, but I knows the voice. You see, to know His voice, you have to know the other one. Well, not know him but know his voice. Know when he's lyin' to you. He is a liar. Everything he sayin' is a lie."

Ntombi wrote as quickly as she could to catch up, then encouraged Mae to continue.

Mae folded her hands atop her midsection, wrinkled her brow, and pursed her lips over her teeth. As she did, her eyes grew intense, like tiny, dark portals. Ntombi wondered if she could see through them to her soul, but instead of staring, slid back on the sofa and rearranged her skirt, prying it from the grasp of the bristly fabric underneath her. She straightened her dress and positioned the notepad just so in her lap, giving her the look of someone who had done hundreds of interviews. "Tell me about both voices. God's and the enemy's."

Mae took an uncharacteristic pause and then pinched the fingers of her left hand and brought them to touch her mouth. Releasing them, she said, "You might as well just name him. He's Satan, the devil, and he is real." She shook her head. "Shoo! He is sure enough real."

Ntombi jumped in. "What does he do?"

Mae looked at her quizzically. "Talk."

"What does he say?"

"He all the time tellin' people things that ain't true, ain't never been true, ain't never gonna be true. Thing is, people—good people even—they don't know when it's the devil talkin' to 'em."

Mae looked away and then back at Ntombi and continued, "You see, he's tricky. Real tricky. He even make people believe it's just they own thoughts, or, worse yet, he make them believe he God. You know he wanted to be God. That's how he got thrown out of heaven." Mae folded her hands neatly in her lap, lifted her head, and lowered her eyes, looking over to watch Ntombi write. She waited.

Ntombi finished writing and looked up from her notes. She took a deep breath and released it. "Well then." Ntombi placed her pen carefully along the spiral edge of her notebook. She looked down at it for a second, then released it and looked up at Mae. "Tell me about God's voice."

Mae gave one quick nod and began. "Well, I wanted to talk with you since you's planning to interview all those PhDs and the like. Not that they ain't good to interview, but my experience has been, they intellect can get in the way. You know, become their god." Mae paused for a moment and grinned. "You might not want to write that down."

Ntombi smiled back at her. "I've decided it best just to listen for a bit."

"Okay. You see it's best when you knows you need God." Ntombi nodded her agreement, and Mae continued. "Anyway, you see, I done been through so much. Me and God, we's tight. We just talk and talk and talk."

Mae moved one hand across her lap and smoothed out the fabric on her dress and added, "I used to pray. You know, like other folks. Tried to pray those big prayers. You ever heard one of those?" Mae shook her head and laughed. "You can sure enough tell a lot by how someone prays. Some folks, they sound like they givin' God a lecture. They tellin' and tellin' and tellin'. Bible says to ask but ain't nary a question in their whole prayer. You ever heard that? Listen next time. So when I say me and God, we tight, I don't mean we's equal. Lordy no! I does the asking, and He does the tellin'. And sometimes I ask again."

"Like what?" asked Ntombi as she jotted notes.

"Sometimes I say, You want me to do what? Not that He would ever tell me to do something bad. He never goes against His own Word—that's the Bible. But sometimes what He say to do don't make logical sense. That's 'cause He's all about eternity and what's good for His kingdom, not just here."

Ntombi smiled to herself as she realized that through Mae's words, the heavens were open and spilling out. Not wanting to stop the flow, she said, "Give me an example."

"Well. Like when he put on my heart—you do know he talks to the heart, not to the head?" Mae pointed one finger at Ntombi's notes and shook it slightly. Ntombi got the point and picked up her pen.

Mae waited until Ntombi finished writing. "Well, when he told me to call you and ask for an interview, I said to him, 'What, Lord? She done got her interviews and they big people.' But I know'd before it came out of my mouth, his definition of big people and ours is total opposite."

Ntombi offered a knowing grin. "How so?"

"How so? Well, I don't know everything. But seems to me, thems that know he's big and they in great need of him is the big-uns. Those that's big on earth have a harder time lovin' him, you know, for himself, not for the stuff he can do for them."

Ntombi kept writing, and Mae continued. "Oh, and that reminds me. Our preacher. Shoo! Now he is both—big on earth and gots a big, big heart for God. Anyway, in one of his sermons, he talked about how different people love differently. You know, in how theys love God. He said, some love themselves for they own sake, and others love God for they own sake. You see, it's selfish about what they's gonna get from God."

Ntombi looked up from her notes. "That's interesting, I think he's quoting—"

"Wait, that's not all. Let me think." Mae glanced up, then continued. "They is two more. Yes. Two more. Oh yeah, then there's the ones that love God for God's own sake. For who he is, not what he can do for them. I think I be in that category most of the time. Everybody slips."

"What about the fourth?"

"Oh yeah, the fourth. It's something like loving oneself for God's own sake. That one is hard for me, but I am sho' enough working on it. It's different than the first. It's not self-centered. It's all about God and being grateful for how he made you."

Ntombi quickly caught up with her note taking and said, "Give me an example."

Mae scrunched her brow then grinned and sat up straight. "I think it's like when I'm thankful God done give me these curves instead of making me skinny." As she talked, she slid both hands along the sides of her waist. "No offense. But, you see, he made me, and he's highly creative; and on the day he was makin' me, he was in a curve makin' mood. So I come out all curvy with lots of jiggly bits." Mae started laughing and couldn't stop. It was contagious. Ntombi then laughed at Mae laughing. Before long, the laughter brought on tears for Mae, and she pushed herself to her feet to demonstrate her "jiggly bits."

Ntombi placed her notebook on the sofa and stood. She followed along and matched Mae's every move, at least as best she could. Her long, slender frame created different lines, but each dance was beautiful. The two laughed as they moved, God's daughters dancing and twirling before their Creator. One with a drum beat in her head and reverberating movements; the other as if the air bowed and parted before her uncommon grace.

The dance ended and a flood of peace settled into the room. The two sat and looked at each other. Ntombi looked at Mae and saw a different kind of tears welling in her eyes and flowing over her smile. There was a sparkle in her eyes that Ntombi hadn't noticed before. She smiled back, but neither spoke.

Then, Mae began to pray.

Ntombi watched and wondered if it was okay to watch. It was as if Mae left this world for a bit and traveled to the throne of God. Her facial expression was a glob of otherworldly peace mixed with all-consuming joy. It was the face of one who loves.

When she finished, she looked over at Ntombi. "I have one more thing to tell you. God told me to tell you about the cloud."

"The cloud?"

"Yeah, the glory cloud. Like the one that traveled before the Israelites. Those of us—and you in that group—-who are called for a special purpose. We have a glory cloud. And sometimes it moves. When it moves, we are to move but never get ahead of it! That's where people get tripped up. They all the time movin' out and then sayin', 'You hoo, God over here.'"

Ntombi interrupted. "Or the cloud moves?"

"Yeah. Sometime it moves, and we try to stay put. Ain't no peace unless you and glory are in step—him out front and you following just as close behind as you can."

"And some people's clouds move a lot and others not so much."

"You gettin' it!"

NINE

Swamp Talkin'

Ntombi clenched the bar in front of the passenger's seat of the Ben Bayfields' old open-topped Jeep Wrangler, trying not to bounce out as the two of them sped along the deeply rutted road.

"Hang on!" Ben said, then whipped the Jeep off the road, nearly flipping it as the dry-rotted tires lost traction over the sand.

Ntombi jerked halfway out of the jeep and then back in. As she landed back in her seat, she shouted over the noise. "This is like riding an unbroken horse backward."

"Sounds like the voice of experience," Ben said with a smile and a glance in her direction.

"Except for the backward part." They hit a deeper rut, and Ntombi bounced straight up out of her seat.

They crossed a field with tall, grayish-green grass, which skirted along the underside of the Jeep. Ntombi remembered an old car of Tata's with a tailpipe partly held on by tape and wondered if the Jeep's tailpipe was in better shape. Before she could ask about the pipe, Ben turned and headed straight for a large swamp. Ntombi's eyes grew wide, and her grip on the handle tightened. Just feet from the shore, where the sand turned to mud, Ben jerked the wheel to the left. The Jeep slid sideways until it stopped.

Ben glanced over at Ntombi and dusted his hands proudly. "We're here."

Ntombi cocked her head to one side. "And where is here?"

Ben opened his door and jumped to the ground. "Come with me, my friend," he said, then headed out without waiting for Ntombi to follow.

Ntombi jumped down from the passenger's side, quickly caught up to Ben and tried to match his stride.

Ben took a deep, loud breath and stretched his arms above his head, then out to his sides, barely missing Ntombi with his swing. Ntombi looked down. With each step, the mud seemed to squish and release beneath her boots. She heard a distinctly Southern voice in her head say, "This sure ain't Kwandwe."

Ben pointed out in front of them. "Look."

There, squarely in front of them, was a gigantic, dual-tracked Komatsu excavator. Bits of rust showed through its yellow body. To Ntombi, it looked like a giant, steel insect.

"We're going for a ride."

Ntombi's eyes widened. She looked back and forth from Ben to the heavy-duty machinery, making no effort to hide her intimidation. Ben met her look with a grin and climbed up the five-foot-high track like a pro. Ntombi shook her head and took a deep breath and followed behind Ben, paying no mind to the amount of mud she accumulated on her jeans along the way.

Ben slid past the operator's seat, stood and moved around behind it. He gave it a good slap. "You sit here."

Ntombi looked at him askance and then at the seat. "You want me to drive?" She looked about the open cabin, surveying the controls, shook her head and took a seat.

Ben leaned across her and started the engine. He gave Ntombi a few instructions over the loud rumble. Once she knew the basics, he grasped the steel handle above his head, separated his feet, planted them and leaned back. "She's all yours."

Ntombi pushed the pedal, and the dozer lunged forward. Ben laughed as she adjusted her speed to match her skill level. They were off, zigging and zagging their way along the bank of the swamp.

"You got it. I won't let you fail."

Ntombi laughed. "Unless you were looking for a straight line." She sat straighter in her seat, trying to get a feel for the dual-track movement.

"Straight doesn't matter. Now turn left."

"Left? I'll go into the swamp!"

"That's right! How else we gonna get to the other side? Straight in is best."

Ntombi shrugged, slowly pushed one lever forward, and pulled the other one back.

They went straight in.

"Give it a little gas. The swamp responds better to confidence."

The large dozer seemed to know what to do. The giant, yellow beast powerfully divided the black waters. Ntombi smiled. "Wow! This is amazing." Suddenly, they hit something on the bottom, and the dozer lurched sideways, splashing some mud into the cabin. Ntombi smiled wider. She didn't bother to wipe the splatters from her face.

"Will we get stuck?"

"Probably not."

Ntombi scrunched her brow, turned her mouth up on one side, and turned to look at Ben. As she did, the controls went with her, turning their huge machine to the right.

"Oops." Ntombi swung back around, and this time glanced up at Ben while keeping the controls steady. "So where are we going?"

Ben swung his left hand from behind the seatback and

pointed toward a clearing in the distance. "Over there, aim for that clearing," he said, then returned his grasp to the seat.

Suddenly, the tracks let go, and the dozer began to float sideways.

Ntombi clinched her hands around the controls. "Yikes! We're floating! What do I do?"

Ben spoke calmly. "Just go with it. Slowly. Wait . . . Wait . . . You're fine."

They floated nearly sideways for about fifty feet until Ntombi felt a slight tug beneath them. The tracks had touched the ground again.

"That's it," Ben said. "Now, carefully feel your way out."

Ntombi accelerated slowly. She could feel the tracks grab the bottom of the swamp, lifting them up a few inches. She exhaled and wondered why something as strange and foreboding as a swamp bottom could bring such a sense of relief.

Ben glanced down at her and back toward the shore. Then, with his best Southern gentleman's voice, he continued, "Now, hon, do you remember that fixed point we were aiming for?"

"You mean the clearing?" Ntombi said, as she looked up at Ben and then all around them, realizing the clearing was no longer in sight.

"You only missed it by a few hundred yards."

"Sorry, sir," Ntombi said, with a shrug and a clenched smile. "What do I do now?"

"Just take her straight for the shore."

Once on shore, Ntombi could see a group of construction workers in the near distance.

"Head toward the workers."

"What are they doing here on a Saturday?"

"They're constructing transmission lines. Got a little behind. I made a deal with them. They needed to work on Saturday, and I wanted a Komatsu ride."

Ntombi laughed. "Sweet!" She drove forward a bit more but stopped the amphibious machine some fifty feet from the workers. "Don't want to get too close."

Ben laughed with her. "As the saying goes, this is close enough for gov'ment work."

———

Later that afternoon, Ben and Ntombi arrived back at the house, each splattered with mud and smelling of swamp water. Ben stopped at the entrance to the front porch and gave each boot a good swipe on the boot scraper. Ntombi did the same and followed Ben onto the porch. Ben extended a hand toward the wicker sofa before falling back on a chair. Ntombi plopped down and leaned back.

"Kick your boots off if you'd like."

Ntombi looked at her boots, caked with dried mud, and wiped her hands on her pants. She crossed one leg over her knee and grabbed the toe in one hand and the heel in the other and gave a tug. The boot released, slinging mud across the porch. Ntombi looked at Ben, her lips pulled in a straight line, eyebrows raised. "Sorry."

"Hey, it's all right," he said as he stood in his socks and headed toward the screen door. "Becca, you in there? Hon, we sure could use some sweet tea. We're too dirty to come get it ourselves."

A couple minutes later, Becca came through the doorway with a pitcher in one hand and two glasses of ice in the other. She set them on the table. "You may want to stir that," she said. "I was late in adding the sugar." Becca turned and headed back in the house. As she did, the screen door caught the tail of her dress. With one graceful sweep of her arm, she retrieved it.

Ben poured two glasses of tea, then leaned back in the chair and called to Becca over his shoulder. "Hon? You not joinin' us?"

Becca called back through the screen. "Seems I'm not dressed for the occasion."

He sat back in his seat and looked at Ntombi. "Guess it's just me and you, kid."

Ntombi leaned back against the sofa and took a long drink from her glass. "Shoo! Good day!" she said, nodding her head. "Thank you."

"Glad you liked it. So, what did you learn today?" Ben asked as he leaned back in his chair and crossed his feet atop the coffee table. He took a long sip of tea, looked at Ntombi, and waited.

Ntombi straightened a bit. "Uh, well, I learned how to drive a Komatsu."

Ben nodded. "And?"

Ntombi twisted her mouth slightly to one side and looked out across the front lawn. Turning back toward Ben, she said, "I learned that I don't have to know where I'm going to enjoy the ride."

Ben cocked his head to one side. "Good one. Calling is like that. What else?"

"I learned I don't have to know how deep the swamp is."

Ben raised his brows, then nodded, this time smiling slightly. "What else?"

Ntombi thought of the two fixed points Ben had pointed out. One was where they had been, and one was where they were going on the other side of the swampy river. She wondered if a fixed point behind mattered in discerning God's call. She decided it did and continued. "I have a question."

Ben took another long sip of tea and set it down. He swallowed and wiped his mouth with the back of his hand. "Shoot."

Ntombi took a sip of her tea before she began. "Well, my question is more about life than about driving construction equipment."

"Good. That's the whole point."

Ntombi leaned back into the sofa. She placed her stocking feet on the coffee table, cradling her glass between her knees and talked with her hands. "You know how you told me to look at a fixed point on the other side of the bank?"

"Yes."

"Well, don't I need a fixed direction for my life? You know, to know where I'm going?"

Ben leaned back again and placed his hands behind his head. His answer came in the form of another question. "Tell me. What happened to the point on the shore today?"

"I missed it."

"That you did. But what did you notice about where we came out of the water?

Ntombi's eyes widened. "We were still in the right place."

"Precisely. Don't you think God factors in some float time?"

Ntombi glanced out at the yard and quickly back at Ben. "You knew I would miss the mark. You had me aim at one point, knowing I would end up somewhere else."

Ben sat quietly smiling at her as she let it all sink in. She stared at a spot just over Ben's head, as if the answers she sought were floating in space. She was learning. This was like one of her interviews, except with mud and machinery. Perhaps God also knew she needed to learn this lesson, maybe not for now but for later.

Turning her focus back to Ben, Ntombi continued, "God does the same thing. He factors in our missteps, gives us room to make them, so we can still arrive at the right spot. He gives us time to learn."

Ben turned his palms up and raised his shoulders in a knowing shrug. "I reckon so. At least he has with me."

"Then it could be that Mandlenkosi wasn't the wrong person but the right person at the wrong time."

Ben grinned. "Or maybe you're asking the wrong question."

Ntombi sat her glass down on the coffee table, stood, and took a few steps. She turned back quickly. "Yeah, maybe I need to be asking "what." That's it. What. I need to ask God what it is I am to do with my life instead of with whom. I should be asking where I'm headed. Once I know what and where, then God will reveal how, right? And who I marry is part of the how?" She turned back toward Ben and waited for his response.

Ben took a slow breath and released it. "Or, the better question may, in fact, be the who question."

Ntombi folded her arms and peered down at Ben incredulously. "What? I mean, who?"

Ben stood, met her gaze, then turned with a boyish spring in his step and paced the floor between the chair and the screen door. "Well, seems to me we enter this world—the swamp in our analogy—with a little nudge from God."

Ntombi stood still, cocked her head to one side, and watched Ben pace. Then, with raised brows, she said, "Oh, I know! Like when Jochebed placed her son, baby Moses, in a basket and floated it on the river."

Ben stopped pacing and turned toward her. "Jochebed? Well, yes, now that you mention it."

Ntombi nodded excitedly. "And the pharaoh's daughter was on the other shore."

"Great parallel," he said. "But…" Ben placed a hand out giving a clear and overly dramatic halt signal. "But was Pharaoh's daughter the purpose of Moses's life?"

Ntombi stepped toward Ben. "No," she said, making a chopping gesture with both hands. "Leading the Israelites was."

Ben's face lit up. "Somewhat. But where did he lead them?"

Ntombi tilted her head to one side. "To the Promised Land? The long way around?"

Ben bent his head and looked Ntombi in the eyes. "I can tell by your use of Jochabed's name that you know something of the Word of God."

Ntombi nodded.

"It is time to learn the God of the Word."

Ntombi thought for a moment, allowing his words to settle in. "So. Was I right? Was that the right answer?"

Ben placed his hands on her shoulders and looked her squarely in the face. "He tried to lead them to their highest good. To God—God was their destination. He's our destination as well."

TEN

Getting Out

The late night air in Charleston was oddly calm. Not one leaf moved. Yet the glow around the lampposts revealed a slightly inland fog. Most of the city slept. North King Street was the exception.

Dom walked backward in her stiletto heels, facing Ntombi. She moved both hands up and down like a conductor. "Come on. The night is young."

Dom had a different look about her, one Ntombi hadn't seen before. Her blouse was low-cut, sheer, and flowy, with a black-and-brown snake print. It hung off one shoulder and was clearly designed to show off the wearer's bra and most all of its contents. Her heels were so high and spiked so thin, Ntombi wondered how she could walk the uneven stone sidewalks forward, much less backward.

"So, midnight is young?" Ntombi asked, then exaggerated her slow, laggard pace.

Dom twirled back around, then swung one arm up and over, motioning forward. "Aye, things don't start hopping 'round here until after midnight. You've been cooped up way too long. A little fun will do you some good."

Ntombi felt like excess baggage that Dom insisted upon dragging up and down the streets of Charleston. She supposed Dom was right, and this was a good way to acclimate to her new environment. She decided to consider it an exploration of the local culture. She would study it like an anthropologist studies a newly found tribe.

Ntombi yawned loudly. Dom chided her without turning around to look.

"Stop it."

"Oh. Sorry," Ntombi said, as she exhaled the last of the yawn.

"Let's go in here and get you a little pick-up."

Dom pulled Ntombi into Corner Coffee. It had taken on a new vibe in the late hour. The crowd was even thicker than the morning crowd, and Ntombi marveled at how so many people could fit in such a small space. She paused to enjoy the fact she could see over most of the heads.

Ntombi realized Dom was no longer in front of her and walked deeper into the crowd to find her. A few moments later, Ntombi watched the crowd part and the top of Dom's head, her hair straightened and bleached to a dingy, orange color, move toward her.

"Here." Dom handed Ntombi a steaming mug. "That should restart the evening," she said, then crossed her arms under her chest and lifted herself back into her ill-fitting bra. She rearranged her blouse to recreate the seemingly accidental bare left shoulder. Ntombi watched the preening gesture with wide eyes as she sipped her brew.

Music started playing, and bodies immediately moved with the beat. Ntombi thought of home and the beat of drums. Movement and drums had long been a part of her life. She had learned to distinguish good movement from evil. This was on the edge, and Ntombi wondered how wide the edge was.

When the first song ended, Dom looked up at Ntombi. "Seems the coffee's working. I'm going for a beer. I'll get you one," she said, then cocked her shoulders back, stuck her chest out, and disappeared into the crowd.

Ntombi stood with both hands around her mug, partly to keep it from spilling and partly to give her hands something to do. She bent her neck to take a sip. When she did, she felt a strong hand rest on the small of her back. Ntombi turned and found herself eye-to-eye with a handsome stranger. He was too close. She started to say something, but he raised a finger to her lips to silence her. Without taking his eyes off hers, he removed the mug from Ntombi's hands, then turned to place it on a nearby table. When he turned back, he began to dance, locking eyes with her once again.

Ntombi felt the music and bodies on every side. Who was this guy? It didn't matter. She was, after all, exploring the culture. Her body became one with the beat and with the bodies around her, especially her new dance partner's.

She leaned in to be heard. As her mouth neared the side of his face, he obliged, touching his right ear to her lips. "Will you tell me your—"

Ntombi pulled her head back, and he put a hand behind her neck and pulled her back in to whisper in her ear. "No."

Suddenly, all the lights in the room came on. The crowd flinched and then cowered and groaned at the sudden light.

"Sorry," a voice from the back of the room said. "Looking for the fan switch."

But just before the lights went out again, Ntombi caught a glimpse of her dance partner's hand and the shiny gold wedding band it wore.

Amidst the sudden loss of light and the confusion, Ntombi managed to slip away from the man and into a far corner. She stood alone there for a few songs, wishing she could retrieve her mug of coffee without drawing attention.

Then, she heard Dom's voice from the middle of the room. "Ntombi!"

"I'm over here." Ntombi gave a less-than-enthusiastic wave.

Dom bent slightly forward and wiggled her derrière side to side as she moved through the crowd. Bystanders laughed and parted to give her the berth she needed.

"Who was that? The guy you were dancing with?" Dom asked when she reached Ntombi.

"Uh, I don't know."

"You have got to learn to get a name. Anyway, he's a cutie. Here." Dom held up a tall glass. "It's draft."

Ntombi took the beer, hoping it would settle all that was stirring inside her. She struggled to sort through what had just happened on the other side of the room and hoped Dom wouldn't ask any more questions. Then she caught sight of him moving through the crowd toward them.

"Let's go outside," Ntombi said.

"Sure." Dom turned and motioned toward the door.

Outside, the two were met by a policeman on foot.

"You two had better pour those out or go back inside."

Just what she needed. On top of everything else, now she was a lawbreaker. But sensing Dom wouldn't be happy seeing the beers poured out, Ntombi reentered the coffee shop turned bar turned dance floor turned wrong. Dom was close behind.

"Just a little longer, and we can go," Dom shouted over the noise. "You met your Prince Charming and let him get away. I'll do a better job of hanging onto mine."

Ntombi just smiled and took a sip. The beer was cold and smooth, and much needed to make the swell of hot, sticky bodies and loud music "fun." She found a small unoccupied space just inside the door and stood watching the crowd, her back to the front window. Dom, for a moment, stood beside her.

Ntombi sensing Dom would rather be elsewhere, leaned down and said in a voice loud enough to be heard, "You go ahead. I'll just stay here."

Dom nodded yes and moved quickly into the crowd.

Ntombi stood and watched the room, trying not to look like a bystander at a circus. Her thoughts seemed less troubling as the beer glass emptied. She wondered if people noticed her standing there alone and then tried to decide what was worse— to be noticed or to go unnoticed.

Her answer came when she saw her mystery man moving through the crowd again. The scene played out as if it were slow motion on the silver screen. His eyes were fixed on her while women stepped one by one, directly into his path. He encountered each in a different way. Ntombi watched. He seemed to want something from each encounter and to leave each woman wanting something.

Ntombi dropped her gaze to the floor, turned to set her beer on a small table pushed against the wall, and made a beeline for the door before he could reach her.

Outside, the fog had thickened, bringing a cool dampness with it. Ntombi looked up and down the street, then sat on the Charleston-style park bench in front of the coffee shop's window. She crossed her ankles and tucked her feet under the bench. Then she uncrossed them. She put her hands under her thighs and pulled in her elbows with a shiver. She wished she had brought a wrap.

Ntombi sat looking down at the bluestone sidewalk until a pair of shiny, black loafers stepped into her gaze, causing her to flinch.

"May I sit?" a man's voice asked.

Ntombi looked up, dreading what she would find, but was surprised by a friendly face. "Dan-iel! Of course. Please join me."

Daniel moved to the other side of Ntombi and lowered himself onto the bench. "Night's not going so well?"

"To say the least. I don't even know why I'm here."

"I do."

Ntombi leaned her head back and offered a sideways smile. "Please. Enlighten me."

"You had good intentions."

"When was that?"

"When you decided Dom doesn't have many friends, and you don't know many people here. You started thinking about how you should have been nicer to her growing up and how you didn't want to hurt her feelings." Daniel tipped his head and turned slightly to look at the side of Ntombi's face. "Am I getting close?"

"Yeah." Ntombi stretched her feet out in front of her and bounced them a couple of times. She kept her eyes on them when she spoke. "And the road to hell is paved with—"

"Good intentions. You got it."

"I didn't want to hurt her feelings."

Daniel took off his black suit jacket and placed it around Ntombi's shoulders. It wasn't very warm, but it smelled like him. Ntombi looked over at Daniel and smiled. "Thanks."

He continued, "Good can be the enemy of the highest good."

"How's that?"

"It's one of the enemy's tactics. He'll even use a good trait like tenderheartedness to lure someone."

Ntombi bobbled her head side to side then back to the center. She reached over and placed her hand atop Daniel's. "I'm glad you're working tonight."

Daniel paused for a moment, then stood. He stretched one arm out and curled the other in a big yawn. "Yeah, if I could just figure out those light switches."

75

Ntombi looked up at him and grinned in surprise. The street light behind him seemed to create a halo around his head. She thought the look fitting, smiled softly, and handed him his jacket.

Daniel took it and threw it over his left shoulder. "I'll send Dom out. You need to go home."

ELEVEN

Eyes

Ntombi gathered her backpack from the back seat of the Bayfields' rusty, white Volvo, pulled its straps over each of her shoulders, and hurried toward the student center. This morning she would meet with her new boss, Dr. Whitting. She felt a nervousness in her chest and wondered if it was the aftermath of the weekend or fear of meeting Whitting.

A tall guy with earphones was walking toward Ntombi carrying a gym bag. When he got closer, he removed one earbud from somewhere within the mass of wet curls that fell from his head and gave her a thumbs-up. "Great photos." She had no idea what he meant but shrugged it off as yet another American oddity.

She walked to the student center, figuring it would be a good place to prepare for the meeting. But when she stepped inside, she found herself surrounded by herself. Directly in front of the door, the first photo to catch her attention was a massive horizontal closeup of her eyes. Just her eyes. Each was large enough to walk through.

Ntombi walked slowly toward it and stopped. "I'm staring at me, staring at me."

She glanced sheepishly around. Various elements of her face were blown up and beautifully displayed in black-and-white all over the room. A couple students joined her to view the image of her eyes.

A girl with one thick, reddish braid hanging over her shoulder spoke first. "This is marvelous."

"Thank y—" Ntombi caught herself and recovered. "I mean, do you know who did these?"

"No, but I heard there are more in the Adams Building."

More? How could there be more? Why had she let Andrew photograph her? Ntombi backed away from the exhibit and stepped outside. She'd have to find another spot to prepare for her meeting.

Ntombi found Dr. Whitting's office door open. She stood first in the doorway, unsure if she should enter. His large leather chair was turned toward the window. Light streamed in but oddly seemed to part before reaching him. He turned as if he'd somehow sensed her presence.

Ntombi puzzled over Dr. Whitting's face. It was oval, or, rather, a collection of ovals—his eyes, his glasses, even the top of his shiny head, all oval. He looked up at her with light blue eyes, hardly raising his head. As he peered up at her, his mouth formed a straight line, and his cheeks widened. His large, madras bowtie sat slightly askew beneath the broad display of cheeks. Ntombi tried not to smile but found his look almost comical.

"You know I didn't choose you," he said, still without fully lifting his head.

"No, sir. I didn't know that." She stood in the doorway, unsure of what to say next. The offer to work with Dr. Whitting had simply arrived. She hadn't thought to question it. She knew Tata had called the Bayfields and then they had made some phone calls, but the other inner workings were just that, inner workings. She knew nothing of them.

"My research assistant was to be a young man from Pepperdine. Graduated first in his class. His father has an endowed chair at Harvard. Comes from a long line of scholars."

Ntombi's first thought was to plant her fist on her hip and proclaim, "Well, you da man." Her second thought was to say, "My father has a chair at the homeless mission in Torrance." But somehow she held back, deciding it best not to reveal her cheeky side.

"So what went wrong?" she asked instead.

"For another time. And we should both hope it isn't wrong. Now, tell me what you have to offer. Suffice it to say, I haven't read your vitae."

Ntombi moved from the doorway to just inside his office. "I don't know what I have to offer, which is precisely why I am here. I am glad you didn't read the vitae. Who I am cannot be contained on paper."

Ntombi heard the annoyance in her voice, but Dr. Whitting showed a slight appreciation for her spunk. Perhaps he'd decided what she lacked in intellect might at least prove entertaining.

They talked—or rather, he spoke—for nearly an hour. Ntombi moved about the room, from plaque to plaque, like she was visiting an art gallery. She inquired about each accomplishment. Occasionally she'd glance his way while he spoke. He was softening. He seemed at home in this office. Ntombi was pleased with her ability to steer the conversation. Not one lull.

As his lecture-style presentation about himself came to an end, Ntombi reached in her backpack and pulled out an old book. "I brought you something," she said, but realized she may have overstepped her bounds and added, "though I doubt it will add to your collection."

"What is it?"

"I found it in an antique store in town."

"Antique store? They are grossly overpriced."

Ntombi's voice turned stronger and more matter-of-fact. "Nonetheless, one of them has an intriguing religious book collection tucked away in a cubbyhole."

Dr. Whitting stood and moved toward the window as if plotting his next move. He gestured toward his desk with one hand.

"Just put it there."

Ntombi, now incensed by his arrogance, laid the book on his desk. It was a gift for God's sake—literally.

"I will look at it later. It's good you have some room in that backpack now. If you are to be of any help to my research, you will need some background. Tyler began his prep work a year ago and was gracious enough to return these." Dr. Whitting turned and handed her a heavy box.

"Don't you want to open it first? There might be a note or something."

"Must you question everything? The note, my child, was sent separately, and I have kept it. Tyler will no doubt be of import some day. I have retained it for posterity. Now, read these before our next meeting. Some are my work. Others are classics."

"I have read everything I could find of yours but will gladly reread them."

Whitting's eyes lifted, and Ntombi thought she noticed a slight upward turn to his mouth but then decided it was more of a smirk than a smile.

"Great," he said. "And it will be good for you to reread them. I have more when you finish these. Oh, and I almost forgot to give you this."

Dr. Whitting turned and retrieved a notecard from atop a pile on his credenza. "As part of the project, you have a host—a seminarian. Her name is Emma. It's up to you to contact her." Whitting shoved the card at Ntombi, then returned to his desk and sat, as if to say, "Our meeting is over."

Ntombi lingered a bit too long. Perhaps it was her awkwardness with the new culture or maybe her desire to study him. Was there not more to be learned by studying the author than the author's works? As she stood there looking down at him, he donned his reading glasses, picked up some papers, and began to read. Ntombi missed the message. She just stood there. It was only for a second or two, but in the nuance of professional etiquette, it was clumsy.

"Don't you have somewhere to be?" Whitting asked.

Ntombi nodded quickly and bowed slightly, then looked Dr. Whitting in the eyes. "Yes, sir. I really appreciate the opportunity to work for you. It is an honor, sir."

Ntombi extended her hand, and Dr. Whitting looked at it for a moment. She didn't flinch. He then offered his hand, and she gave it one firm shake, released it, then turned and left.

Once outside his door, Ntombi exhaled. She had imagined a different first meeting. She left not knowing how to take him and wasn't sure she wanted to. Her first thought was, who does the old coot think he is? But then she smiled as she remembered just how much she liked a challenge.

⌒

Motoring down the Bayfields' tree-lined drive, Ntombi felt the muscles in her neck relax. There was something about the land that she craved. When she reached the shell lane leading to her cottage, her tires making crunching noises beneath her, she saw Becca waving to her from the porch of the big house. Ntombi stopped and rolled down her window.

"Ntombi! Dr. Whitting is on the phone. Sounds urgent."

Ntombi entered the house through the sun porch. Becca followed behind her, and the screen door slammed behind them. She found an old-fashioned wall phone hanging off the hook. She smiled. The Bayfields lived simply. She liked that about them.

"Uh, hello?"

"Ntombi, this is Dr. Whitting. I picked up the book when you left."

"Yes, sir. Do you already have it?"

"Have it? This is a first edition. Museum quality. Very few copies ever printed."

"I read through some of it. It seems to be about The Great Awakening. I was thinking—"

"Oh, yes! It is a compilation of original writings by ministers who witnessed The Great Awakening."

"Yes, sir. I thought it might be of interest to you as a church historian."

"Where did you find it? We must go there."

Go there? Did this mean he liked it? Go to the store with Dr. Whitting? Yikes.

Whitting continued, "Now I will go to the library and borrow one of the velvet stands they use for viewing rare works. We mustn't cause any damage to the book. I will not tell them what I have. They would insist it be kept in one of those dimly lit, temperature-controlled rooms. That can wait. Meanwhile, we need to read it. It will be pivotal to our research."

Our research? She liked the sound of that. It would indeed be more exciting to have a partner in her research. But instead of a partner in crime, a partner in good. They could spy on the holy together. She realized she liked Dr. Whitting better on the phone. Maybe it was the absence of those icy-blue eyes.

"Now, about the book store."

"Yes?"

"Call me Whitting."

"Yes, sir—Whitting. I found the book at an antique store. It's only open a few days a week. Seems the owner is not much into commerce."

"Not into commerce?"

"He has a fine store. Overstocked. Describes himself as a hoarder with impeccable taste. I get the sense he only opens to share his collection and have some company. He lives upstairs from the shop."

"Pray tell, when is the next time he opens?"

"Thursday."

"Good. We will go on Thursday. Meanwhile, can you come this evening? Most of the students are gone by four. Better yet, I'll come there. It will be better to work from there. We'll turn the pages of this great work together. Put Becca on the phone. I shall get directions and be there by four-thirty."

Ntombi looked up at Becca, then realized she'd only raised her eyes to do so. Was she adopting Witting's habits so soon? At least her eyes were round and dark. Dark eyes were friendly, easier to trust.

Twelve

Control Central

Ntombi stood close behind Becca as she opened the back door for Whitting. Whitting nodded his hello as Ntombi moved around Becca and offered to help him with his load. Whitting tightened his grip. "I've got it."

He shuffled past them with a stack of books under one arm and an overstuffed, doctor-style bag in the other hand. Just inside the door, he turned to garner some help. "Just take the top one, the one you found. And please, be careful."

Becca led the way through the kitchen and toward the dining room. Ntombi followed last, watching the way Whitting shuffled across the clay tile floors. He seemed different here. More normal.

Whitting entered the dining room. He looked about, then turned to Becca. "I think it best to close the shades."

Becca shrugged, then moved about the room lowering each of the grass blinds partway, just enough to block the sun.

"It is for the good of the book," Whitting explained. "Natural light can be destructive to the pages."

Ntombi doubted a book whose words had traveled across centuries could be destroyed so easily by God's created light. Surely if the book was worth consideration at all, it contained uncreated light.

Whitting looked over at Ntombi as Becca nodded goodbye and backed out of the room. He pulled out a dining room chair and gestured for Ntombi to have a seat. She followed his cue and allowed him to help her with her chair, the book still perched atop her fingers as if she were presenting an offering.

Whitting pulled out a chair beside her and sat, then gently crossed one hand atop the other and placed them on the edge of the table. Glancing first at the book and then at Ntombi, he said, "Let's look at it together."

Ntombi set the book in front of Whitting. Before touching it, he reached in his briefcase, removed a velvet-covered book-stand, put it on the table, and ever so gently placed the book onto it. Ntombi watched his hands open the cover of the book. His skin was almost transparent. Maybe some white people were sheer.

Whitting reached in his shirt pocket and pulled out a pair of horn-rimmed reading glasses, flicked them open with one hand, and placed them midway down his slightly upturned nose. "The works contained in this book were collected in the mid-1700s, and what you have here is the original collection. The best I can tell, this copy belonged to Thomas Prince himself."

"Thomas Prince?"

"The author. Or, rather, the editor." Whitting kept his gaze on the book and continued. "He was pastor of Old South Boston before the Revolution. He was a friend of Jonathan Edwards and George Whitfield. Prince had the likes of Sam Adams and Benjamin Franklin as children in his church. He pastored Old South for forty years and was a prolific writer. He had a particular penchant for history and knew he was to capture it for future generations. His most noted work is his *Chronological History of New England*."

Ntombi lowered one eye pensively. She wanted to understand Whitting's intrigue with the book as much as, if not more than, she did the content.

Whitting continued, "He was also a great collector of books.

One of his undertakings was to collect and publish firsthand accounts of the work of the Holy Spirit during what is now known as The Great Awakening."

Ntombi leaned over to get a closer look. As she did, she felt a different spirit enter the room, like a guide leading them along an unmarked path. Soon, the old English lettering and the absence of the s faded from consciousness. The pair huddled side by side over the book, silently reading the first few pages until Ntombi felt the giant wave of truth cresting about them. She shuddered and sat up straight.

Whitting broke the silence. "This is written like a discernment guide, a key to a puzzle. The Great Awakening is not my area of expertise, but still it is clear what Prince was intending."

Ntombi raised one hand to her mouth and paused. Her eyes grew wide, and she lifted one finger in the air as she spoke. "Yes, but maybe the puzzle had other pieces mixed in. Like someone had taken two puzzles and mixed them all together, and the pastors of the day were trying to sort through the pieces."

Whitting looked at Ntombi and raised his slightly unkempt brows. "And this is the picture on the cover of the puzzle box," he said, pointing to the book. "So they could tell which pieces belonged." He turned back at the book. "Yes, God was doing a new work among them."

"But where do the wrong pieces come from? And who mixed them up in the box?"

Whitting stood, brought his right fist to his mouth, lowered it, and began to pace. "Throughout history, with any outpouring of the Spirit, there have also been false signs from the enemy. Or, as Edwards would say, when revival begins, the first one to revive is Satan. Prince's reason for collecting these stories must have been to help fellow ministers know the difference."

"And for us as well. Look at this bit." Ntombi pointed to a paragraph but stopped short of touching the page.

Whitting bent down and leaned in to get a closer look. "I see," Whitting whispered and began reading aloud. His voice was different—it was his preacher's voice. Ntombi smiled. Tata had a preacher's voice too.

> It would be a contempt of these wonderful Works which God hath made to be had in Remembrance, if they should be buried in Oblivion so as not to be known by those who live in after Ages.

Ntombi looked over at Whitting. "That's us. We are those in the after Ages."

Whitting pointed at a line in the book as he slid back into his chair. "Look, here. He concludes his preface with a prayer.

> May the Holy Spirit whose work upon the Souls of many is to be narrated, accompany the Narrative with His powerful Influences, that it may promote the Redeemer's Interest, and make every Reader feel by his saving Operations that he is indeed come in an uncommon Way of Grace. And may this whole Church, and all the Ends of the Earth see greater Things than these. Amen. July 29th, 1742.

Whitting leaned back in his chair with a thud and stared straight ahead. Ntombi did the same. A deep silence entered the room and Ntombi's soul. She knew they had indeed come upon the book by God's grace, "in an uncommon way."

Time ceased existing as they bathed in the silence. Ntombi felt the words of the book and suddenly knew "powerful influences." She wondered if Whitting felt it too.

Whitting crossed his arms over his chest and spoke into the air in front of him. "I cannot imagine a prayer like this going unanswered."

Ntombi nodded her agreement. After a few more moments of silence, they both leaned forward and continued reading. Whitting carefully turned each page with his wooden page turner. Ntombi enjoyed the crisp, amber pages, and the crackly sound they made as well as their musty smell. She thought of the dichotomy. The pages were old, their message long-forgotten, but the need for such truth and hope for another awakening were never more present.

Suddenly, Whitting closed the book and placed his hands atop it. Ntombi flinched, thinking she had done something wrong.

"Sorry," he said. "It just came to me. Maybe we should approach the research separately."

"Separately?"

"Yes, I could peruse the historical works, and you the works of the Spirit in our day, and then we merge." Ntombi sat with the words forming in her mind yet not a single word came out of her mouth. Whitting, apparently taken with his new idea, held up one finger and simply said, "Wait." He stood and looked down at Ntombi. "I have something in the car. I'll be right back."

From where she sat, Ntombi could see Whitting's car through the dining room window. She watched for him to come into view. When he did, there was a spring in his step, one she didn't know him capable of. She watched him fiddle with the lock on the trunk of his pale-green Citroën for a moment before lifting it. He held it up with one hand and searched inside with the other.

Soon, a long wooden dowel served as a makeshift rest so he could reach in with both hands and retrieve two long rolls of paper. Whitting quickly tossed the dowel back inside, steadied the lid about a foot above the car, and turned it loose. It closed with a solid thud, and Whitting gave a quick nod of satisfaction before disappearing from view.

Whitting reappeared seconds later in the doorway, looking like the cat that ate the bird. Ntombi smiled back as she welcomed this new side of him. She stood and crossed the distance between them. "Now, what have we here?"

"They're charts. Large charts. Well, not yet. At the moment they're blank slates waiting to become charts."

"What?"

Whitting smiled, undeterred. He went over to the table and set the rolls on top, turning back to Ntombi. "What if we each created a timeline?"

"I'm listening."

"Mine would be a historical look at the condition of the church at the time of the Great Awakening." He paused and looked away in thought for a moment before continuing. Ntombi watched intently as he continued unfolding his partially thought out plan. "I'll need to consult a few subject matter experts. Yes. I know who to call," he said, speaking almost to himself. Turning to Ntombi he continued, "You see, we must first consider all the angles of the Awakening and then draw parallels to our day. No, not parallels. That will be last. Second, we need to capture what God is doing in our day. But we must be completely open to the possibility there are no, absolutely no, parallels.

"You see," Whitting said again, and Ntombi wished she did see, "this scroll is for you. I got it from the art department. You are to capture your findings completely separate from mine. The scroll is made of vellum paper so that we can use it as an overlay. You know, just in case there are parallels."

"So I am to create a timeline?"

"Yes, don't you think? You could capture the last twenty

years and as much of the current day as you can glean from the data."

Whitting turned quickly and reached for his briefcase. Lifting it up to the table, he said, "You'll likely need some supplies. I have some sticky pads and markers, but use whatever you think best." Whitting dug in his scuffed, leather case and, after a bit of untangling, extracted a jumbled pile of twine, sticky pads, markers, and various other items. "Sorry for not sorting through this before I came."

Ntombi looked at the pile of supplies and felt her heart begin to pound. The task suddenly seemed enormous and, at the same time, vague. Squishy. "Where will my data come from?"

"Interviews mostly. I'll make the arrangements. It would also be good for you to pursue contemporary church writings. I'll engage a team of students to help as well. I have funding to pay them. They will collect, read, and analyze materials from churches, seminaries, and other ministries throughout the country, but they will need a team leader."

Not sure of what else to do, Ntombi sat at the table and began sorting the pile of supplies.

Whitting pulled out the chair across from her had a seat. He leaned in. "We need to go back to that antique store—the one with the books." Whitting leaned back and brought a fist to his mouth and released it. "The shopkeeper may have other books we could use—you know, from the same collection. When did you say the shop is open?"

Ntombi finished untangling a small, lime-green sticky pad from a ball of shiny, fuchsia ribbon. "He has sporadic hours, but he said he is usually there on Thursdays."

"Great. We'll go on Thursday."

THIRTEEN

Room with a View

The sun was up, but Mandlenkosi saw no need to rise with it. After all, there was no hurry. He swung side to side in his makeshift hammock and counted the corrugated steel stripes on the ceiling, using the motion to make them harder to count. Suddenly, there was a strange movement, like a flash through the window or a darkening. A shadow, but from what? Mandlenkosi flipped out of the hammock, pulled on his trousers, and walked gingerly on his bare feet to the porthole.

Mandlenkosi could already feel the sun's warmth on his face. He looked out his window but saw nothing out of the ordinary. And then it hit him.

"Birds! We are near land!" Excitement gave way to anticipation, and anticipation to fear. Where am I? Will we be stopping? Is this the end?

More birds appeared, flying around and back and forth. Mandlenkosi watched them for hours. He waved and smiled at them. One bird looped back around and tipped a wing as if to say hello. Mandlenkosi could almost smell the land growing closer. But what land was it? He knew the day would unfold with adventures—not just the ones he created in his mind lately, but real experiences—and he found himself eager for anything new.

The ship began to slow. Everything in Mandlenkosi wanted

to run to the front to be the first to glimpse land. But he was trapped in the stern, watching everything backward. He decided to enjoy the unfolding mystery, even if it was secondhand. Needing someone to share it with, he put his shoes on and conversed with Right Richard and Left Louie.

"Okay, guys. Clue Number One. This new land has many birds."

He walked back to the window. Just then, the color green, lots of it, crept into view. Just a bit at first, coming from both sides. Before long, Mandlenkosi could make out layers upon layers of lush and vibrant greenery climbing the hillside. To his right, the green was punctuated by a bright yellow dot. He leaned in and squinted to make it out.

A tropical bird.

Mandlenkosi stood with his eyes wide open, his mouth parted, enjoying the majesty of color. He hadn't thought he missed it until this moment when color returned to his world in a kaleidoscope of newness. He stepped back and slapped the wall of the container. The cold, steel surface didn't make much of a sound. He looked down at his feet. "Clue Number Two, the vegetation is dark green, and I see a hillside." He placed both hands on the edge of the porthole and peered out again. "And it is lush. Or at least partly so. And tropical. There are tropical plants and birds." The nearer to the land they came, the more it spread along the right side of Mandlenkosi's little window until he felt he was being swallowed up by the color.

"Wait." Mandlenkosi's brow furrowed. "It seems we are entering the land. How can a cargo ship have land on two sides?" This time his shoes didn't have an answer.

And then it hit him.

"We are entering a canal! The Panama Canal! It must be the Panama Canal. All the clues fit." Mandlenkosi spun in a circle, placed a hand on each side of the porthole, and kissed the air outside. Like a child at the start of a long-awaited vacation, Mandlenkosi felt only excitement to see new things. And he was quite satisfied with himself for solving the mystery.

He continued to watch the hillsides come into view. The right was terraced, forming a pyramid-like structure of dirt and green. Everywhere he looked was beauty.

An ache entered his chest and sat somewhere at the base of his ribs. He stepped back from his perch and dropped to the floor of the container with his head in his hands. The sight of land had awakened in him an emptiness, a longing for home. This wasn't his home. This land was an imposter.

Mandlenkosi's memory bubbled up.

"I am from South Africa! I don't know who I am or what I do, but I know where. Of this I am sure." He stretched his legs in front of him and leaned toward his feet. Then, as if needing an audience for his declaration, he lectured Right Richard and Left Louie. "This land is not my land. I am like a Bedouin or a drifter, just passing through. I will someday return to my land."

Neither shoe responded, so Mandlenkosi stood and returned to his porthole perch.

Once the initial excitement was over, it was a slow day. Mandlenkosi considered yelling to those on shore but knew he would not be heard over the whistles and clanging and screeches of cable car escorts.

—

Mandlenkosi found it hard to sleep that night. The ship was docked, and a city loomed in the distance where there were people, surely thousands of people. Loneliness crept in. He wondered if it was raw envy, imagining free people smiling and laughing, and crowds, and the smells of a fine restaurant. He even pictured the hundreds of fish swimming beneath the boat, knowing he could eat none of them.

He imagined the people in the city and decided that if they knew, one of them—certainly one of them—would care about him, his captivity, his condition. Surely if they knew, they would care.

Mandlenkosi tipped up a bottle of fine South African pinot, swirled it in his mouth, and swallowed. He imagined it was better than any wine in all of Panama. He welcomed its effects and fell asleep against the cold, hard container wall, his makeshift hammock swaying overhead.

Fourteen

Thursday

Thursday came. Ntombi found Whitting waiting outside the pale stucco front of the antique store. He smiled as she approached. "The sign says only people who are planning to buy antiques are welcome."

"That's true. I got in by telling the man I was visiting from South Africa. He likes South Africa. Hopefully, he remembers me." Ntombi's eyes ran the height of the antique store's textured front. There were windows on either side of the door, their frames adorned in layers of Charleston-green paint. Probably a century's worth. The door, as was often the case in Charleston, opened in.

Numerous handwritten signs hung on the door warning the casual tourist of the precious nature of the collection and the persnickety nature of the proprietor. Ntombi rang the bell. Whitting stood just behind her. She found his nervousness strange and hoped it wouldn't cause a problem for them but felt confident in her ability to overcome his oddity with poise and appreciation for the collection.

Ntombi peered through the glass-paned door. She saw a man rise from a desk near the entrance and shuffle toward the door. But it wasn't the man she'd met before. There was a resemblance, but this man's face was longer, his hair was somewhere between yellow and gray, oily, and tossed messily to one side.

He paused at the door, sizing up his visitors through the glass.

"Hello, sir. I was here a couple of weeks ago, and—"

"Ah, yes," he interrupted, his face lighting up. "You're the girl from South Africa."

The deadbolt clicked, and the door parted just a bit. Ntombi seized the opportunity to explain. "Yes, sir. I was here and very much enjoyed my time with your collection. The art is magnificent."

"It is my brother's collection. Come in. He spoke of you. And who is this with you?"

Ntombi introduced Whitting as they stepped in. The door closed behind them, and Ntombi heard the deadbolt turn and click into place.

The two followed their guide from room to room, admiring the art. It wasn't hard to do. Many of the paintings were as old as the 1700s and rivaled some of the classics. The pine floors beneath them were carpeted with overlapping oriental rugs, making the floors as worthy of adoration as the walls.

"The collection is quite remarkable," Ntombi said, pausing to take in a still-life painting. The deep browns and huntboard motif of game and fruit indicated an early Dutch artist. "You say it's your brother's collection?"

"Yes, I did say that. A few of the pieces are mine, though."

Ntombi strolled from one painting to the next, stopping to genuinely study the ones of interest. She turned over a dangling and faded price tag on one of them. It read, original oil on canvas, circa 1789, artist unknown, likely Dutch, $22,500. She dropped the tag and brought one hand up to her chin as she stepped back a bit to view the painting from a distance. Ntombi turned slightly toward the shopkeeper. "When I was here a few weeks ago, I spent some time with the books."

"Yes. The books." The shopkeeper nodded, turned and headed down a short hallway. "They're this way."

Ntombi followed, with Whitting close behind. The man shuffled slowly ahead of them.

The book section was small and down three wooden stairs. Its floors were less worn than the others. Another oversized Oriental rug adorned the center of the space, its edges upturned along the kick plate of the bookshelves. The shopkeeper extended a hand, gesturing for Ntombi and Whitting to enter the small room. They stepped down into the space, and both looked up and around at the mahogany bookshelves overflowing with old books. Ntombi, with her eyes open wide and barely hiding her excitement, turned toward the shopkeeper.

He read her thought. "My brother said you bought one of the religious books. Those are mine. He doesn't know the religious books." He paused for a moment, then asked, "Is the light sufficient?"

"Oh, yes, sir. It is quite sufficient," Whitting said. "Too much light would harm the books." Ntombi looked over at Whitting. It was the first thing he'd said since they'd entered the store.

The shopkeeper bowed slightly. "I'll take my leave then. Enjoy."

Whitting and Ntombi each took seats on small mahogany stools. The stools were slick with wear and seemed to have been crafted of the same wood as the shelves. Each had a hand hole in the center, allowing it to be carried about. Together, they sat, peering up at the rows of shelves tucked into six-by-eight cubbyholes of wonder.

Ntombi thought about the little man and his collection. Why had he gathered so many old works of faith? Was he searching for something? Perhaps searching for God? What about his brother? Was he not interested? And no mention of wives or families? Had their lives been devoted to collecting, drawn by beauty and fueled by wealth?

Whitting stood and studied the stacks. "I'm looking for a pattern," he said. "Some sense of order. But I see none." He began in the top left corner and had Ntombi start on the other side. Hundreds of old books filled the shelves. Some were neatly placed, and others were in haphazard piles. The smell of mildewed pages filled the space. The two worked mostly without talking.

Whitting was peering through his spectacles at eye level and Ntombi atop the library ladder when, out the corner of her eye, she noticed their host standing in the darkened doorway. She wondered how long he had been there.

"Charles forgot to give you these when you bought the book on The Great Awakening."

Whitting stood frozen as Ntombi came down from her perch to receive the gift.

"I doubt he knew where to look for them. I took them out of the book to protect them. You know, most people who buy these want them only for decoration. I assume you're reading yours."

Whitting straightened. "Yes, sir."

"Anyway, these were stuck in the book when I bought it. Most of it is handwritten, but you can make it out with a little scotch and a lot of time." He smiled slightly and extended to Ntombi a small, jumbled stack of papers, browned with age around the edges.

Ntombi bowed slightly as she accepted them. "Thank you," she said, as she carefully held the brittle pages atop the palms of her hands. She smiled inwardly, imagining Whitting behind her, doing all he could to contain himself.

Thursday

Once outside the shop, Ntombi placed the stack atop Whitting's outstretched hands. Both moved from the sunlight into the shadow of a nearby building to see what they had. There before them, penned in his own hand, were the words of the Reverend Thomas Prince, the eighteenth-century preacher and scholar, who himself was awakened and called—to document The Great Awakening.

FIFTEEN

Emma

The next morning, Ntombi sat alone in the crowded student center waiting for Emma, her host. An unexplained excitement pulsed in her chest.

Emma arrived just a tad late for their scheduled rendezvous, a rolling bag zigging and zagging behind her. She stopped and took a deep breath when she reached the table. "Sorry I'm late." She settled into the chair across from Ntombi and fidgeted a bit to find the sweet spot.

Emma was a bit older than Ntombi but not by much. Ntombi had enjoyed their time together the last time when they met. She was like a wise aunt or older sister. She had a level-headed way about her, a way Ntombi trusted.

"So," Emma said after they'd shared some small talk and pleasantries. "How are you settling in? Made any friends yet?"

Ntombi thought for a moment. There was the dreadlocked guy from the coffee shop, Dr. Whitting, the photographer who exposed her to half the campus . . .

"A few."

"Well, you have me now too," Emma said matter-of-factly, then sat back in her chair and unwound her floral, cotton scarf. "If you'll have me." Emma lifted her eyes to Ntombi and smiled.

Ntombi laughed. "Yes, I'll have you."

"You know, I'm one of the rolly-baggers. Too old to carry

my books. Sure you're not ashamed to be seen with me?"

"I may join your ranks soon. The further I get into the research, the heavier my bag becomes." Ntombi paused, then chuckled. "In more ways than one, I guess."

They talked for a while about the weight of the call. Ntombi was pleased to have a listening ear, even if she found herself skirting the edges of full disclosure.

Emma leaned back in her chair. "Have you read Lewis' work on the weight of glory?"

"Not yet. I'll have to get it. I've been reading this book on the anatomy of the soul. Dr. Whitting mentioned it, and I think I picked up the wrong version. The one I am reading quotes several ancient rabbis. Anyway, the imagery is marvelous. They describe the soul as shaped like the body but residing mostly outside the body—above the body, actually."

Emma moved her eyes up and around as if looking for her soul. "Fascinating. It certainly feels above the body—like how they say 'lift your spirits'—but still rooted somehow. Tethered to the body."

"Let's walk," Emma said, springing to her feet. She gestured with one hand toward the door.

They strolled along the sidewalk, Emma's rolly bag bumping over each crack. As they rounded a corner, Ntombi found herself face to face with the tall jock with the curls, the one who had commented on the photos Andrew had taken of her. This time his hair was dry, but it shone still and framed his chiseled face. His face was different than the others Ntombi saw, with cheekbones kind of like Mae's, except white.

They passed with the requisite southern nod, then Ntombi felt a hand on her shoulder. She turned, and it was him.

"Hey. You're the girl in the photos, right?"

Ntombi smiled up at him and nodded. She tugged Emma's

sleeve to get her to move along, but Emma didn't budge.

"You could be a model, you know," he said, then turned and left.

When he'd walked far enough away, Emma pulled Ntombi toward her. "Do you know who that was?"

"No, I've only seen him once before. He must be an athlete of some sort."

"That's Steve Caldwell!"

"Who is Steve Caldwell?"

"Only the star of the basketball team and one of the best-looking men God ever created."

"Oh." Ntombi turned around as if reconsidering him or perhaps just to get another look. She questioned how she'd missed it, but he had already disappeared into the crowd, so Ntombi shrugged, turned around, and took Emma by the arm. This time, she quickened her steps as she pulled Emma forward, and the pair rejoined the pace of the crowd.

Just then, Ntombi sensed someone walking behind her. She turned. It was Steve Caldwell, looking down at her quizzically, almost timidly. She looked in his soft, brown eyes, and he smiled mischievously.

"You think we could talk sometime? Tomorrow, in the union?"

"Uh, sure," Ntombi said quickly and then just stood there. She could feel Emma's eyes boring into her and suddenly became aware of others who had stopped briefly to witness the exchange.

"I finish practice at eight-thirty. How about nine?"

"Okay" was Ntombi's only reply as the voice in her head said, Words, Ntombi. Where are your words?

"Great. See you then." Steve rocked back and pivoted with that extra bounce Ntombi had noticed before. Her heart raced.

Emma locked her arm in Ntombi's, and they continued walking. "Talk about lifting your spirits."

"His face is different."

"Yeah, if by different you mean beautiful."

Ntombi released Emma's arm, leaned against her, and gave her a little nudge with her forearm. "You can't say that, you're married."

Emma returned the nudge. "Well, seemed you needed a little help with your perception skills. I'm just saying."

Ntombi laughed. "He has high cheekbones and a wonderful smile."

"If I were to venture a guess, I would say he has some native-American in him."

"Yes, but—"

"But, nothing! As we say in the south, that dog will hunt!"

SIXTEEN

Breathe

The ship was still. Mandlenkosi awoke to a peaceful silence, eerily juxtaposed with the reality of his situation. He stretched against the raw twine of his hammock, then flipped out of it with uncommon grace and made his way to the porthole. The city lights were beginning to dawn, one by one, until they were like lightning bugs on a summer's night.

Mandlenkosi watched eagerly. He decided he too would walk to work. He restacked the freight, creating a track of sorts, and began circling inside the container. With each lap, he stopped at the porthole to see how the day was coming along.

In what he thought was a stroke of genius, he reversed course and walked counterclockwise. This path seemed odd to him. After just two counterclockwise laps, Mandlenkosi stopped at the porthole to ponder why one way seemed better than the other. After all, neither went anywhere.

He stood with his hands resting on the ledge of the opening and his chin on his hands so that his forehead pressed against the top of the porthole. Suddenly he jerked backward and turned to the corner where his shoes sat. "Hey, Right Richard! Left Louie! You there? Wake up. I've got it."

"Got what?" Mandlenkosi said, on behalf of Left Louie.

"The directional challenge."

"Well? Yeah? What did you figure out?"

"It is because we drive on the left."

"What?"

"Yes. You see, I naturally turn left to start. Or, wait, maybe it's a hemisphere thing." Mandlenkosi wrinkled his forehead and turned back to his view to further his contemplation. Soon he thought of the ship and wondered if it would set sail again today.

He turned back to his shoes. "Hey, guys. Maybe the view will change. Who knows? If we keep going long enough, we might end up back in South Africa."

Just then, an engine started. It was a new sound, not like the ship's engine, and suddenly there was a loud clank. Mandlenkosi flinched. He knew that sound. All at once, he remembered. It was the sound of a new container being lowered into place. He remembered the sound made when his own snapped into place. He smiled. He was remembering more and more each day now.

"When I was loaded, I was loaded. And, whatever it was I was loaded with, I don't care to have it again." He remembered the syringe and wondered how long he had been unconscious.

Mandlenkosi eventually found the mechanics of the loading process interesting and the newness a welcome distraction. He listened as the crane engine idled and then revved. A swishing sound—that must be the crane moving. Containers were hoisted up; others lowered into place. At one point, a container passed by the window. Mandlenkosi flinched and stepped back from his perch. Then, without warning, there was another loud clank, and his corrugated steel home went dark.

"No! Not there!" Mandlenkosi cupped his face in his hands and bent over from the waist. Pressing his hands against his knees, he tried to breathe. "My window!"

Mandlenkosi straightened and began to pace back and forth frantically. "Oh, dear Lord, please, please, please make them

move it. I will not survive without the light. I need more air."
He paced faster, gasping for breath, then stopped and began
fighting the air. "Why, why, why?" His fists swung wildly.
Mandlenkosi slapped his forehead with both hands and dragged
them slowly down his face. He stumbled his way to a crate of
wine bottles. His eyes narrowed, and his teeth clenched. He
grabbed a bottle and weakly slung it against the wall.

Glass shattered, and wine spewed. The second toss was
harder and more forceful. The third even more so.

He began to scream, this time not into the nothingness but
actually hoping to be heard. He felt his way to the porthole and
screamed. "Help! Fire! Fire! Anyone! Help!"

Mandlenkosi cried until his strength waned. He stepped
back from his darkened porthole and began kicking the glass
aside before dropping to his knees, landing in a pool of wine
and glass. One shard cut deep. Somehow the pain helped. It
gave him new focus.

Mandlenkosi gave in and fell into a fit of gasping sobs. He
dug his nails into his thighs. Tears streamed down his face to his
neck, soaking his sweat-stained shirt collar. When he felt he had
no more left inside, he stretched out prostrate on the floor.
Wine soaked deeper into his clothes as he raised a weak fist to
heaven and shook it.

"O God! Where are you?"

At that moment, peace fell around him like a blanket of
oxygen, filling the dark steel space with silence. Complete, holy
silence.

Then, something unseen entered his dark world.

Mandlenkosi knew—instantly knew—that the Presence was
standing over him, looking down. At that moment, a new and
different fear engulfed him.

I AM here.

Mandlenkosi froze and squeezed his eyes shut. The Holy One's feet were standing at his head. The feeling was so real that Mandlenkosi thought if he turned, he might even catch a glimpse. He felt caught in a place where time and space had ceased.

The voice continued, not aloud, but piercing Mandlenkosi's soul. I AM here.

After several moments, Mandlenkosi felt the weight of the Presence leaving. He laid still for a minute longer, then stood and brushed away his tears. He wiped his hands on his trousers and looked around. He knew his Visitor was gone but needed to look just the same. He took a breath. This time, his lungs filled with peace, the kind that passes all understanding.

Mandlenkosi understood he was still in container hell. But he also knew he was not alone. He decided that true freedom was not dependent on a set of physical circumstances.

Mandlenkosi turned and blinked several times to clear his sight. He glanced over to the porthole and what was once his view to the world beyond.

And then he saw it.

There, past the darkness, was another porthole, one just outside his and mostly aligned. He moved closer to inspect it.

Two eyes stared back at him.

SEVENTEEN

Bells and Voices

Ntombi stood outside a towering, old, cathedral-looking church where her next interview was scheduled. She hoisted her backpack higher on her shoulder and gazed up at the imposing structure. The building was handsome, made of carefully cut, precisely placed, and artfully mortared stone. The bell tower rose high above the trees and sat silent. Ntombi looked down, noticing the gray, bluestone steps. Each dipped in the middle and was rounded toward its edge with wear. A good sign. Church steps should be worn.

She climbed the three stairs slowly and opened one of the tall, mahogany doors. As she stepped through the doorway, she oddly recalled the Mind the Gap signage on the transatlantic plane. This was a space where all gaps were welcome, even the big ones—the ones between God and man.

The sanctuary was empty. She chose a pew near the front, sat on its edge, and rested her arms on the back of the seat in front of her. She prayed, and as she did, she noticed her prayer was different. For the first time, she didn't feel she needed words.

She sat in silence with her eyes closed for a while, her spirit communing with God's until the most heavenly voice sang out and filled the air around her in perfect pitch. Second soprano. "Praise God from whom all blessings flow, praise Him all creatures here below."

Suddenly she was engulfed in worship. It was as if her soul were high and lifted up, in a worshipful dance of sorts. As the song ended, Ntombi stood and turned to see a lovely older woman in a corduroy jumper, standing mid aisle with her hands in her pockets. The woman smiled ever so softly and nodded. Ntombi returned both and headed toward the pastor's office, thinking of the aerodynamics of God's kingdom on earth and how one can lift another just by being themselves.

She sat in the pastor's outer waiting room and felt jittery, but how could she possibly be fearful of meeting the pastor?

She smiled as she remembered one of Tata's teachings. He often said, "It is impossible to experience fear and gratitude at the same time." This, she thought, is the perfect time to put his words into practice.

Thank You, Father, for the dance, and for Your presence in this place. Thank You for the soloist who sang, and the upcoming interview, and for a quiet space to meet. Thank You for this day, and for leading me to the book, and for Whitting's turnaround. Thank You for Tata and for Becca and Ben—

"Good morning. You must be Ntombi."

Ntombi looked up and found Reverend Doty standing over her, his hand extended. She stood and shook his hand.

Reverend Doty had a serious face with soft lines. He just looked smart. She then wondered how she knew what smart looks like.

"Yes, sir. I am Ntombi, and I'm most grateful for your time."

He nodded quickly and extended his arm, inviting Ntombi to go first. She realized she liked this part of American culture where women go first. At home she was often left to toddle along behind.

109

In front of the reverend's desk was a seating area centered around a low coffee table. Ntombi gestured at the stately camel-backed sofa opposite two wing-backed chairs. "Is this okay?" she asked.

"Absolutely." Reverend Doty walked over to one of the chairs and gestured across the coffee table toward the couch. "Please. Have a seat."

Ntombi pulled her interview notes and three pens from her backpack and placed them neatly on the table. Next, she pulled out a small tape recorder she'd purchased at a resale store after Mae's interview. It was her way to make sure she didn't miss anything. "Is this okay?" she asked, holding it up.

"Of course." Reverend Doty pressed his hands into the arm-rests to lift himself and shifted back farther into his seat. He looked comfortable and relaxed as if he were at home. It made Ntombi relax a bit as well.

Ntombi pressed the red button on the recorder and set the device on the table. She picked up a pen and notebook and sat up straight. She occupied only the front half of the sofa. She had rehearsed the interview in her mind many times. With the first question, the dialogue flowed and very seldom ebbed. She quickly found her notes useless and allowed the conversation to progress naturally.

After a few minutes of dialogue, he tilted his head back against the tall wing chair and looked up at the ceiling. He took a breath and released it. "It's an odd time for Christendom." Ntombi wrote his statement in her notebook and waited. He continued, "People ask what they can do to get closer to God, but when I tell them to read their Bible, I know most won't." Again Ntombi wrote and waited. This time he looked over at his overstuffed bookshelves and continued, "But our time is only a piece of this larger thing."

Ntombi followed his gaze to the bookshelf. It was packed, floor to ceiling. She thought of how wonderful it would be to spend a week alone with his collection. She looked back at him and asked, "Dr. Whitting talks of an awakening? Do you think we're in another awakening? Another reformation?"

Reverend Doty chuckled. "Ah, yes. Whitting. We have had many long debates, sped along by a goodly pour of scotch." He paused thoughtfully and softly dropped both his arms on the arms of the chair. "I don't believe we are in a reformation—yet. Well, not fully. It is coming." He lifted his hands and perched them in a triangle against his chin, paused, then folded them in front of his chest. "There has been a lot of activity such as churches trying new things. I don't think becoming more like modern culture is the answer though."

Ntombi raised both brows at him and noticed a slight smile. He raised one finger in the air. "Ah, music is a good parallel. Take Beethoven's Fifth. It goes bom, bom, bom—bom, and then there's the pause."

Ntombi was not writing. She watched. He closed his hand in front of his face and pulled it slowly to the right to show the pause. "Do you feel the pause? It is important to feel the pause." Ntombi nodded a slow and attentive yes, and he continued. "You see, the pause is very much a part of the music. I think much of the Church is still in the pause. We will come out of it, though. As we say at baptisms, the church is preserved to the end of time."

Ntombi looked down and started to write again. Reverend Doty waited.

As she described the pause in her notes, she thought about the concept of a pause. Was there a pause before the Great Awakening? At that moment, Whitting's plan of separate but parallel research seemed wiser than she'd realized. An eagerness rose inside her. She longed to know what he was uncovering. She looked down at her notes and continued with one of the questions she'd underlined.

"Tell me about your call."

He smiled. "Well. I tend to back into my call. I find myself following my call before I realize I am—before I even realize what my calling is or that I have one." He rested his head back against the chair. "I went to seminary because I found my religion classes interesting. I began writing because I like to read." He paused again, smiled and looked over at Ntombi. "Come to think of it, I accepted my first pastoral position to have something to do until I could find a real job."

Ntombi thought of the large church he now pastored and smiled. She expected God smiled too.

Her thoughts turned to herself. She wondered if God smiled at her trip across the Atlantic. She wondered if God knew where she was headed in her life and just wasn't saying. Or maybe her glory cloud had indeed moved.

Reverend Doty interrupted her thoughts. "I have a life mission statement. Do you want to hear it?"

"Sure."

"It is to love God with my mind. I want to think good thoughts about God. I want to know things that God knows."

"Cool. I love that." Ntombi looked down and wrote quickly, Love God with my mind. "But how did you arrive at your mission statement?"

"For me, it's been a gradual process. Not one big thing but lots of little ones. Loving God with my mind really came clear to me when my son decided to test me with his end of term history questions. I knew all the answers. I realized, at that moment, God had given me this mind, and I am to use it to love Him."

Ntombi wrote quickly, and to keep the interview focused, returned to her pre-written questions. "In mentoring others about their call, what are the common patterns you see?"

Reverend Doty thought for a moment. "For many, there is a restlessness, a dissatisfaction with life as they know it."

Ntombi looked again at her question list. "And what are the common mistakes people make in discerning a call?"

He laughed. "The hunch method."

Ntombi returned the laugh. "The hunch method?"

"Yeah. Sometimes people say to me, 'This idea just came to me, so it must be from God.' Yet when I get behind it and ask more questions, it turns out it is something they want to be or do, and they really want God to bless it. They're doing it for the wrong reasons."

"Like what?" Ntombi asked without looking up from her note taking.

"A yearning for affirmation. Or sometimes it's confusion about God, so they think they'll become a minister to figure it out. Sometimes they just want to help people and do some good on earth. But often it's more about them than it is about God. They're missing the fact that a calling is about God."

Ntombi lifted her gaze and stopped writing. "Tata has often said that some serve a cause and others serve Christ."

He looked straight at her. "Indeed. I expect you see a lot of people coming to Africa with a cause."

"Africa is full of those who want to help or feel good about themselves for helping. And some are clearly there for Christ." Ntombi softly placed the pen against the spiral edge of her notebook and looked straight ahead. "I think what I'm saying is, I agree. The why matters."

"Yes, it does matter. Actually, he matters."

EIGHTEEN

More Eyes

Mandlenkosi moved slowly toward the porthole. The eyes staring back at him were dark, wide set, and young. Very young.

"You okay?"

Mandlenkosi's breath caught, and he took a step back. The voice was maybe seven or eight.

Mandlenkosi's heart thumped in his ear as he spoke. "I am fine. Who are you?" He moved in close, and she hopped from a small crate and bowed slightly as if needing to offer a proper introduction.

"I am Annika. This my sister Keiko."

Mandlenkosi blinked twice to adjust to the sliver of light passing between the containers. Slowly, he could make out a girl—Asian, possibly Chinese. She had on a school uniform. Her shirt was soiled with what looked like dirt, and her plaid skirt hung loosely. The girl standing behind her, the one she called Keiko, had on the same uniform, but hers was neater. Both girls were barefoot. They looked alike, except Keiko was smaller. Each had long, thick, black hair and, even in the dim light, it had a sheen. Keiko was frail, like a flower. Annika was small as well but occupied more space with her presence.

In the far corner, three more girls huddled together. Above them and to the right, Mandlenkosi saw a second porthole. He took a breath and released it. They had sunlight and a view.

114

Annika's eyes followed Mandlenkosi's stare. "They afraid. Just caught."

Mandlenkosi looked at them and offered an awkward smile. "Do you know their names?"

Annika nodded and then pointed to each girl. "They are Jasmine and Loma and Manuela. Manuela speaks some English."

She turned back to Mandlenkosi. "Why you here?"

Mandlenkosi slowly met her stare. "I don't know."

Annika climbed back up on the crate, put both hands on her hips, and looked straight at Mandlenkosi. "You strong. You need make idea so we get out."

Mandlenkosi didn't know what to think. He had known the day would hold adventure, but this was not what he'd expected. "O—okay. I make idea."

Mandlenkosi stepped back into the darkness, bent from the waist, and wiped both hands on his trousers. All he could think of was that he was glad he had dressed today. He glanced back to the porthole several times, each time half expecting there'd be no one there. Maybe he'd imagined it. But each time her wide-set, dark eyes were there, following his every move. Several more minutes passed. He sat on the floor but was instantly filled with hate for the raw wood and cold steel around him. He stood and repositioned his macadamia nut "beanbag" chair.

He plopped back down and placed his head in his hands and searched for ideas but found only questions. He rose and returned to the porthole. She was still there. Watching. Waiting. Mandlenkosi found her calm curiosity...curious.

"Annika?"

"Yes, sir."

"Please call me, uh . . . Bill."

"Right. Bill-san. You make idea?"

"I have some questions. Do you speak Chinese? I have only heard a few words from the crew. I expect they are mostly in the front of the ship. Anyway, I think they are speaking Chinese. Can you understand them?"

Annika turned and pointed toward Keiko, who was now sitting with the other girls. "No. Me, my sister Japanese. These girls new."

"Where are they from?"

"We just met them in Panama. This is second ship for us. We were unloaded in Panama. Big city. They put us in a hotel room. We were locked in with bad guys next door."

Mandlenkosi grimaced. "Did they hurt you?"

Annika answered rather matter of factly. "No. They bring us food."

"Did you get a look at them? Your captors?"

Annika narrowed her eyes slightly and paused before she spoke. "I do not know word captors. Bad guys were different in Panama. In Japan, they Japanese. They bring these girls yesterday. They from Panama."

"Do you know why you are here?" Mandlenkosi asked, then wished he had worded the question differently.

Undaunted, Annika described the day she and her sister were captured, and the string of cars, a tractor trailer, and two ships that brought them to this cargo ship. She spoke proudly of her ability to fight back. "On day they take us, they use needle. They grab Keiko first. We on our way home from school."

Mandlenkosi furrowed his brow as he listened.

Annika continued, "Man in passenger seat go for Keiko first. I grab her. We fight back. Then another man come out of back seat with needle. I fight him and he stab my arm with it. I bite the spot fast and suck hard, then spit. But some got in. When I wake up, we locked in house. Keiko with me."

She stopped there. Mandlenkosi looked at her, and his face softened. He allowed his thoughts to settle and his inner voice to calm before he spoke. "Did you hear them say why they caught you? Or where you are going?"

"In Japan, bad men laugh and say, 'big money.' They call us vu-gin. They say 'vu-gin big money in America.'"

Mandlenkosi couldn't believe what he was hearing. These girls, these young, innocent children, were sex slaves. Two of them still wore their school uniforms. They should be in a schoolyard somewhere inventing new games, not on this ship looking to an equally hopeless man for a way out to save them from unspeakable acts to come.

Mandlenkosi was enraged. He hated these men even more than he had hated them for himself. Surely hell had many levels with special places for those who would do something like this.

He swallowed to hide his fear, nodded at Annika, then slowly moved to the right of the porthole into a corner Annika could not see. He placed his face against the steel and pounded the side of the container with open hands. His plea was simple, whispered, and pained. "Oh, God."

He stood there for a moment, first with tears. Then he gagged, but nothing came up. In time, he noticed the sweat of humidity on the wall and the ache of his wrists. Somehow it felt better than the ache deep in his gut. He wondered if one pain could replace another.

He breathed in and released it with the shudder of held back tears. He knew what he must do. He must come up with a plan.

Mandlenkosi wiped his mouth with the back of his hand and quietly moved back into Annika's view. He looked her in the eyes and spoke firmly. "Bill will make idea."

"Thank you, Bill-san. Thank you. You make idea."

Mandlenkosi settled onto his macadamia nut chair. He had promised an idea, but he had none. He could share his wine and nuts, but what about escape?

The cargo loading stopped, and the ship's engines started churning. He was suddenly thankful for his geography classes. He was glad he knew the sun rises in the east and sets in the west and that he'd studied the Panama Canal. He even smiled slightly as he thought of a term paper he wrote in primary school about the construction of the Panama Canal. He remembered drawing the map and showing the oceans connected by the canal. His thoughts then turned to the gaps in his memory. How could he remember a ninth-grade term paper and yet so little about how he got here?

He took a deep breath and released it with a sigh. He knew the ship would soon be at sea, but this time it would be on the Pacific. He leaned back against the side of the container, but before rest could bring comfort, jerked up straight. The truth of his situation finally hit him.

He was for sale...

NINETEEN

Walking with Whitting

Ntombi stood at the dining room window with her arms crossed, watching as Whitting's Citroen made its way through the canopy of oaks. She smiled softly at the thought of Whitting's arrival. Somehow, she was glad to see him. He was, after all, an intriguing old coot. Her head tilted slightly as one who can converse while quite alone, and at that moment, decided that exploring the depths of Whitting's mind was worth the transatlantic flight.

She was still wrapped in her thoughts when Becca called to her from outside the dining room.

"Ntombi. Whitting wants to go for a walk. Get your jacket, hon."

Ntombi raised both brows at the thought of a walk. She loved the quiet, sandy paths that surrounded the Bayfield home and decided their family land needed a name. She wondered if it already had one as she hurried to the mudroom. She grabbed her jacket from the hook and her sandy sneakers from what Becca called her "muck boot tray."

"Coming."

Ntombi greeted Whitting and ushered him onto the back porch where she plopped down on the wall seat and dusted her sneakers together a couple times before putting them on. They shared the usual niceties and set off walking.

Whitting seemed different, more at peace. She thought perhaps it was the walk, the fresh air, or just maybe the newly found truth from the book settling into his soul.

Suddenly, Whitting raised both hands in the air and took a deep breath. "It's a glorious day. How can one not believe in God on a day like today?" He dropped his arms with an exaggerated thud.

"Indeed it is a beautiful day." Ntombi wondered why Americans began conversations with the weather and then quickly segued. "I'm excited to hear about the pages we found."

"And I about your interviews. But first, the pages." Whitting's tone turned serious, and his stride slowed. "I am not sure I have adequately conveyed the gravity of your find."

Ntombi slowed her pace to match and moved in closer. "Gravity?"

Whitting responded with a flick of his wrist. "Grav-i-tas, my dear."

Ntombi elbowed him. With the height difference, her gentle nudge hit him just below his shoulder. Undeterred, Whitting continued. "Seriously. Do you recall me mentioning the recent auction of *The Bay Psalm Book*?"

"Yeah, you said it sold for fourteen million."

"Right. It was a part of Thomas Prince's collection. As you know, he was a pastor and historian, but he was also a voracious book collector. And he bequeathed his book collection to the church he pastored."

"Old South, right?"

"Exactly."

"And the Psalm Book?"

"Yes. Well. Likely part of his collection. There are only eleven known first editions in the world. The church owned two of them. One was put up for auction by their current leadership.

The other remains in the Rare Books Department of the Boston Public Library, along with more of Prince's collection."

"And the book I found?"

"Well, obviously not as old. The Bay Psalm Book may have originally belonged to one of Prince's grandparents. His maternal grandfather was governor of Plymouth Colony, and his paternal grandfather was known as the Reverend Elder John Prince, a colonist and preacher who would have no doubt used the psalm book in worship. The book you found was compiled by Prince, and clearly part of his private collection."

Ntombi looked down at her feet as their walk slowed under the weight of conversation. "So how do you think the book I found got separated from the rest of his collection?"

Whitting nodded. "It's hard to know exactly. But this brings us to the incredible part. During the Revolutionary War, the Old South Meeting House—where the Old South Church met—was occupied by British troops. It's thought that British soldiers took many of Prince's books from the church bell tower. Some were used as kindling, but others . . ."

Ntombi touched Whitting on the arm and turned him toward her. "So, God allowed soldiers to steal the books then. Wow. What better way to disperse truth. That is so cool."

Whitting grinned up at her, turned and continued walking. "I suppose you're right. But still there is great mystery and beauty behind your finding this book."

"How so?"

"I don't believe it's by accident you found the book and right now of all times."

Ntombi attempted to skirt part of Whitting's meaning. "Of course. God must have wanted us to have it for our research."

"Yes, of course, but what I am trying to point out is how amazing it is that you found it."

"Why is that a big deal?"

"Okay, let's trace it out. It was likely stolen by soldiers, traveled across an ocean after the war to live on someone's shelf, was collected by who knows how many over the years until it ended up with our shopkeeper. Meanwhile, you're a continent away yourself. So there it sat for decades, apparently, awaiting your arrival, and, eventually . . ."

Whitting's voice trailed off. Ntombi turned and looked at him, trying to grasp the fullness of what he was saying. They walked awhile in silence until an unexpected clearing revealed a small, swamp-like pond. The morning mist was late in lifting, giving the water an ethereal softness punctuated by cypress trees rising from the haze. Their limbs dripped with dew moistened moss. The stillness of the moment filled Ntombi with awe.

She took a breath and released it. "So, what about the extra pages? What's in them?"

"It appears they're pages from Prince's personal journal. They're penned in his quill-and-ink hand, and, with the exception of some Old English lettering, quite discernible."

Ntombi turned toward Whitting. "So you're telling me we have his notes? That's incredible."

Whitting kept his gaze on the swamp. "With what I've been able to learn about him, I expect at one point he had the pages carefully and chronologically placed to coincide with specific articles in the collection."

Ntombi looked down and slid some sand back and forth with her sneaker. As she did, she thought of how nice it would be to be barefoot. "So, what'd he write about?"

Whitting glanced at her and grinned. "I'm not that easily tricked."

Ntombi slumped her shoulders dramatically. "Let me guess. After my interviews?"

"Precisely."

Ntombi nodded her agreement and returned her gaze to the sandy shore. She reached down and picked up a dried twig and gave it a toss. The two watched as it spun its way across the narrow edge of the swamp and onto the other side. It landed softly and silently on a thick bed of pine needles.

"I've come to like the smell of pine."

"I expect there's not a lot of it in South Africa."

Ntombi smiled. "No, there's not. Actually, I'm enjoying many new smells here. You know, my father is a tracker—or was a tracker. He taught me to pay attention to the air and use all of my senses."

"They will certainly come in handy with our research, which brings me to a new twist I'd like you to consider."

Ntombi again dropped her shoulders. "I was just thinking how I needed another twist."

Whitting laughed. "It's my job to torment students."

"But I'm only a lowly research assistant."

"All the more sporting. Besides, you're obviously an assistant with connections."

Ntombi furrowed her brow. "Connections? Me? What kind of connections?"

Whitting responded with a chiding tone. "How else do you think you ended up here on such short notice? Not that I'm complaining."

Whitting gestured with an outstretched hand. Ntombi followed his lead, turned, and began walking back toward the house.

"Seriously? You think someone pulled strings? For me?"

"All I know is the order came from on high."

"You mean the president?"

"Nope, higher."

"Who's higher?"

Whitting gestured in midair with his left hand, symbolizing the president, and placed his right hand a few inches above it. "Over the president is the board, many of whom are donors, but I digress."

Ntombi thought about the board and wondered how on earth someone on the board would put in a good word for her. Whitting must have misread the politics, or maybe Ben and Becca knew someone on the board.

Whitting returned to his previous thought and instruction. "So back to the twist. From now on in your interviews, I want you to ask about the battle we're in—the enemy's efforts to keep us from our call."

Ntombi's mind quickly tracked, and she surveyed options for this new twist. The dark side could be interesting but scary. What if she got too close? Is there a way to know about it without experiencing it like a scientist and not a lab rat? Then it came to her. Whitting's call. She'd ask about his call. Ntombi stopped walking and looked around. She pointed to an old picnic table at the end of what Becca referred to as her cutting garden. "How about over there?"

Whitting eyed the picnic table. "For what?"

Ntombi gestured toward the table. "I'll start with you. Would you tell me about your call?"

Whitting laughed and shook his head. "Checkmate. Sure. I'll go first."

The two went over to the table and took seats opposite one another. As they sat, Ntombi noticed the age of the table. The wood grain had dried to a creviced surface. She sat carefully, and Whitting did the same. He first placed his elbows on the table and then lifted them gently and placed his hands in his lap.

He began, "It was 1967. I was in college, and I never really did anything halfway."

Ntombi placed her elbows on the table and rested her head atop her hands. "Go on."

"You have to understand. It was the 60s."

Ntombi lifted her head from her hands and nodded once.

Whitting continued. "Anyway, I used to do LSD with a friend, and we'd practice telepathy."

Ntombi's eyes grew wide and then she caught herself and put on her neutral face.

Whitting pursed his lips, put his hands against the table, and leaned back. "One night we decided to read Scripture while we were high." He leaned forward again. "That's when I was converted."

Ntombi crossed her arms on the table, lowered her head, and looked up at Whitting with just her eyes. Whitting smiled. "I should back up a bit. I was baptized at age five. My father would drive my sister and me to church but would never go himself. Most of my childhood we attended a Bible church about a mile from the house so we could walk. I learned a great deal of Scripture and had several excellent mentors. At one point, when I was thirteen and participating in the Christian version of the Boy Scouts, they asked if anyone wanted to go in this side room and pray to receive Christ. I did it, but only because my friends did. In hindsight, it wasn't real for me. More of a head thing."

Ntombi nodded as if she understood.

Whitting went on. "As an undergraduate, I put my Bible on a shelf. I was a science major, and I became more of a secular humanist. But then came my conversion at USC in 1967, right in the middle of the Summer of Love."

"What happened?"

Whitting lifted first one palm up, then the other. "With my call or the Summer of Love?"

Ntombi laughed. "Skip the Summer of Love stuff."

"Yes, well, as I was saying, my conversion happened—and I don't tell this to many people—but my real conversion happened that night on LSD. That night, the friend and I led each other to Christ. We were reading Scripture, and the same image appeared before both of us. We saw a road that divided, and we had to choose a path. We knew Jesus was one of the paths. We chose Christ." Whitting paused then continued. "That same night it came clear to me that I was to marry my girlfriend and go to seminary. I also stopped doing drugs that very night and never did them again."

"Wow!" Ntombi grabbed the splintered edge of the table and leaned back. She paused there for a moment and then sat up straight. "So. Obviously you went to seminary. Did you marry your girlfriend?"

"I did. She became my wife. I called her the next morning and told her God told me to marry her. She said, 'Well, okay then. If God told you.'"

Ntombi threw her head back and laughed. "Are you serious?"

Whitting returned her laugh. "I am serious. You can't make this stuff up."

Ntombi leaned forward and gently slapped both sides of her face. Then folded her hands on the table. "Did you leave USC immediately?"

"Pretty much." Whitting's tone changed to a matter-of-fact cadence. "So I applied to seminary because I wanted to learn what the Bible had to say. I didn't know why, other than the fact that I viewed the Bible as a blueprint for life and wanted to understand it. Then there was this mysterious thing that happened."

Ntombi's eyes grew wider. "Another one?"

"I left USC and drove with a friend to the seminary. Why I didn't call, I don't know."

As he talked, Ntombi's mind wandered to the passage of scripture that says the Lord works in mysterious ways. This was indeed mysterious. Whitting was right. You couldn't make this stuff up—but Jesus could. He made everything up. If all else failed, he could reveal himself during an LSD trip.

Ntombi's focus returned to Whitting just as he was finishing his story.

"When we arrived, I walked straight to the registrar's office. I didn't know where it was, but it was as if I was led there without even thinking about it. It was lunchtime, and no one was around. I remember walking in, and there on the counter was my acceptance letter."

Ntombi jerked her head back. "No way!"

"Yeah. I know. And it was facing out, toward me. I took it as confirmation that I was in the right place."

Ntombi's lips parted, and she shook her head. "That's amazing."

"It truly was. Now listen. Please be careful where you tell my story. The part about the LSD is not on my vitae."

"I expect not." Ntombi lifted her head up and to one side and looked at Whitting through one eye. Then she turned square toward him. "So what about your wife?" As soon as the words left Ntombi's lips, she thought better of it. "Or is that a conversation for another day?"

Whitting took a deep breath, held it, and blew it out. "Yes, I think that's enough about me for one day."

"One more question, if you don't mind. The roads you saw in the vision. They remind me of Robert Frost's poem.

"Precisely. We all must choose. I merely saw the two roads."

Ntombi looked across the table at Whitting and then into

127

the space beyond him. It was all about choices. She wondered if God would have given him another chance. If he had chosen the other road, would Jesus have given him another fork in the road? Or had there been numerous forks in the past that he'd ignored? Her thoughts turned to her own choices, and, at least for the day, it felt like she was on the right path.

Ntombi was first to break the silence. "Speaking of roads, let's head back to the house."

With that, the two carefully stood and drew their legs from under the picnic table and over the bench, and headed back toward the house.

Whitting interrupted the silence of the walk. "Don't forget to learn about the dark side of calling."

"Oh yeah, the dark side."

"Yes. That which keeps us from being and doing all that God had in mind when He created us. If the call comes from the Voice, surely there is a competing voice. The enemy always tries to thwart our call, even interjecting his voice as if it were God's."

"I'll be sure to ask about the dark side as I interview. Speaking of—"

Whitting silenced Ntombi by placing a hand on her arm. He turned her toward him, looked up at her, and shook his head. "Yes, there is a dark side to my story. And it is for another day."

TWENTY

An Idea

As the ship gained speed, one of the girls became seasick. It was misery for her and secondhand misery for everyone else. Mandlenkosi could smell and almost taste the agony as he called out to Annika.

"Yes, Bill-san?"

"I have some ideas."

"She very sick."

"Have her look out the porthole. Stare very far out, on the horizon." Mandlenkosi wondered how he knew that.

"Hor-i-zon?"

"Where water touches sky."

"Yes, Bill-san."

Mandlenkosi watched through the aligned portholes. Annika first demonstrated the instructions and then helped her up to the window on the other side. Mandlenkosi grinned and nodded. At that moment, he decided Annika was a good leader.

Mandlenkosi spoke loudly to be heard across the container. "Good job. Now here is a pad of paper and a pen. Get everyone's full names, first and last, and try not to waste any pages."

Annika hurried over and climbed up on the crate to receive the pad and pen.

"Give them the pen so they can write their name. I've put a line on the top of each page. Have them write it on the line."

"Okay." Annika jumped down and scurried back to the group of girls to complete her assignment. In a few minutes, she returned. "Here." She handed the notebook back to Mandlenkosi.

Mandlenkosi took it from her and studied each page. Keiko, Annika, Jasmine, Manuela, and Loma. These were his charges. His burden somehow felt more real as he studied each name.

He looked up from the pages. Annika watched him. He took a deep breath and handed the notebook back to Annika. "Perfect. Now ask if anyone can draw."

"Okay. My sister draw some."

"Have her draw your face beside your name and show the other girls what she is doing."

Annika stepped away without a word. When she returned, she held the notebook up for Mandlenkosi to see. "The sick girl. Her name is Jasmine. She draw good. She is drawing each face. Very careful. She no longer sick when she draw."

"Wonderful. Now have two girls work on removing the slats from the window in the back. Here are some tools. I used my shoestring. And here is a slat from my vent. It may help."

Annika and her sister went to work on the vent. After some wiggling and tugging, the first louver gave way, sending the pile of girls to the floor with a thud. Their giggles and cheers melded into a chorus as Mandlenkosi gave a shout of victory. The remaining louvers proved easier than the first.

The girls took turns peeking their heads out of the opening. Mandlenkosi found himself envious of their small view, but he quickly and purposefully turned his thoughts to the task at hand—escape.

After a while, Annika returned and handed him the sketches.

Mandlenkosi smiled, nodded, and handed it right back to

her. "Now, write a description of each girl on the back of her page."

"In English?"

"Yes."

"What do I include?"

"Height, weight, hair color, eye color, any birthmark or distinguishing feature. Include where they are from, names of parents and their phone numbers, addresses, email addresses. Anything you can get."

"Okay. I make list." She jumped from her crate and got to work.

Mandlenkosi creased his forehead and turned around, surveying the cargo in his container. In the midst of his bottle-throwing rage, Mandlenkosi recalled seeing a plastic baggy among the nuts. He decided to find it. It would be useful to store the girls' information—his list of precious cargo. With some rearranging, he felt around between the stacked bags and pulled out the small baggy. He was careful not to tear it.

Mandlenkosi opened the bag and puzzled over its contents. A velvet bag was neatly tucked inside the plastic one. He rolled its contents between his fingers. It felt like tiny bits of gravel. Mandlenkosi moved toward the secondhand light from the girls' container and opened the velvet drawstring bag. He looked inside. Rocks? Why would anyone ship rocks?

He lifted his head and noticed a tiny ray of light. The two portholes had, for a moment, aligned with the sun. He ran toward it and quickly reached in the pouch. He pulled out three stones and held them in the light. They glistened, then all went dark again. He folded his hand tightly around them. They were diamonds!

Mandlenkosi's mind raced. Were the diamonds being smuggled just as he and the girls were? Contraband. They were all

131

contraband. There were probably price tags on each of them already. Mandlenkosi heart sank as he realized the tiny bag of rocks was likely worth more to the captors than he and the girls were. He grimaced and placed the rocks back in the velvet bag and the bag in his pocket. At least for now, the plastic baggy was of more value to him than the diamonds. Amazing how values change.

Annika called for him from the window. "Bill-san. I make lists."

Mandlenkosi took the notebook from her. He read each page before removing it from the notebook. He placed the stack in the baggy and dropped it into the collar of his tucked-in shirt. The feel of the plastic against his hot sticky skin was a close reminder of his charge.

"Annika?"

"Yes, Bill-san."

"Do you know where we are going?"

"I only hear America."

"I suspect we'll dock in California." As he spoke, his face turned from confident to surprised. He didn't know how he knew that, but somewhere deeper than the surface layer of reason, he knew.

He lifted his eyes in deep thought, trying to wake his memory. Eventually, he remembered.

"I have been to California!"

Mandlenkosi sat down and drew the outline of California. He then began to list the things he remembered. Tall buildings, vineyards, airport, sunshine…his father!

TWENTY-ONE

Lessons of Another Sort

Ntombi crawled into bed early and nuzzled into the freshly laundered sheets. She pulled them up to her chin and looked at the ceiling. The day had been a full one: a walk with Whitting, his interest in the book, a stop at Corner Coffee. She liked the new Whitting. And Daniel? There was just something about him, something not quite right. Or maybe too right.

She turned on her side and reached for the lamp. She felt the round notched edge on the switch and paused to look about the room. Her cottage home reminded her of the homestead house at Kwandwe. A soft turn and solid click of the switch and the room went mostly dark. Without notice, fond memories of Kwandwe ushered in thoughts of Mandlenkosi. A ball of grief formed in her chest.

Ntombi flipped quickly onto her back. The ceiling was now lit only by the garden lamppost just beyond the arc of the palladium window, which created a sculpted shadow. She found studying the shadow was not enough to quell thoughts of Mandlenkosi nor fear of his demise. She decided to pray, and, before words came, a tear formed and rolled from her right eye, across her temple, and around her ear, disappearing into her hair. She wiped the wet streak, took a deep breath, and whispered a prayer.

"God, Mandlenkosi is either lost or dead, and I am here in

this strange city. This guy named Steve." She brought both hands to cover her face and breathed through them. "Father, should I even mention them in the same sentence?" She dragged her hands down her face and crisscrossed them atop her chest. She pushed her head deeper into the pillow and tilted her face upward. "God, should I have come? Am I where You want me to be, or am I running? Did my glory cloud come to Charleston?"

She waited for an answer, but none came. Another tear formed, and this time she wiped it with the side of her hand before it reached her hair. "Father God, if being here is all wrong, will you show me? And if my calling is to study calling, will you give me a sign? You gave signs in the Bible. I need a sign."

She inhaled and released it. Strangely, a peace entered her soul, and soon sleep swallowed her.

Then he came in her dream. It was Daniel, the guy from the coffee shop. And he was standing over her bed, as if hovering. The Blues Brothers' tie hung from his neck, and one hand was stretched out to her. Ntombi stretched her hand toward his.

The moment he took her hand, Ntombi found herself standing at Daniel's side atop Corner Coffee. Ntombi looked out over the rooftops of Charleston and saw a hodgepodge of sculpted peaks amidst the damp fog and coolness of the night air. The only light was from the moon and a few lampposts below. It melded with the recently settled dew, giving each rooftop a sheen.

Ntombi spoke first. "I didn't know there was an upper deck."

"Most don't," he said. He stood beside her, enjoying the rooftop view. "By the way, this is our classroom."

Ntombi turned quickly toward Daniel and back toward the view. "Classroom?"

Daniel stayed focused on what was in front of them. "We are learning to recognize the voice of God. If we are to understand the call, we must first know the voice of the One who calls."

Before the idea could settle in, Daniel pointed to a rooftop. It was flat, one of the tarred roofs, and among the least interesting.

Ntombi looked, and an image formed, but not a rooftop scene. She saw a woman sleeping in her bed. She was on her back, and her husband was beside her, curled on his side. Ntombi wondered how she knew it was her husband or how she saw a bed for that matter. With her eyes fixed on the scene, she asked only, "Who is she?"

Daniel crossed his arms and gave one quick nod. "Just watch."

Ntombi blinked and then somehow peered through the woman's body and saw her soul wrapped tightly like a cocoon. Ntombi's mouth opened slightly and her brow creased. She watched as slowly the woman's spirit lifted from her body. As it rose, the woman began calling out defensively, insisting she had been a good person. In the middle of her plea, a pair of folded hands appeared above her. The hands paused in the air, then opened as a rose unfolds.

A voice spoke clearly, calmly, and rather matter-of-factly. "You never knew my Son."

With a jerk, the woman sat straight up in bed and shook her husband to wake him.

Ntombi jerked too and raised both hands to her mouth. She turned to Daniel, her eyes wide. "What was that?"

Daniel continued to look forward with a slight smile. He spoke softly. "It was the dream that led to her conversion. It was the beginning."

"But what was the cocoon?"

"Sin."

Ntombi nodded, looked back, and the vision was gone. "What became of her?"

"She met Jesus. Later, she obediently wrote a book for those who would lose their jobs."

Just then, Ntombi could see one person perched on each rooftop, reading a book. "What's that?"

"She was obedient. She wrote it in God's timing."

Ntombi turned toward Daniel. "How so?"

He shrugged slightly. "Well, in this case, she finished the book just before a season of massive layoffs. She wrote it as an act of obedience. She had no idea what lay ahead or that the book would help so many people."

Ntombi looked at the side of Daniel's face. "Kinda like Noah with the ark?"

Daniel smiled. "Kinda. Except Noah knew a flood was coming." He turned toward Ntombi, gestured behind her and across the rooftop balcony, and ushered her to the other side. Ntombi saw a middle-aged man stretched out in a recliner. It was the middle of the night, but the man was not asleep.

Daniel explained. "He's pastor of a home church. The church is growing, and he feels it's time to buy a building. Watch what happens."

As she watched, a vision appeared in front of the pastor. Ntombi's eyes widened. In his vision, the pastor stood shackled in chains. Gradually, one at a time, they fell off.

Daniel quizzed his student. "What do you think it means?"

Ntombi thought for a moment. "Something about his church?"

Daniel nodded. "Precisely. He took it to mean he was on the wrong path. He was to do church differently. And he did."

"How so?"

"In many ways actually, but mostly by focusing on teaching the Word instead of finding a building. As a result, the construction that went on happened in hearts and minds, not on a plot of land."

As he spoke, Daniel walked to their right and Ntombi followed.

Daniel stopped a few feet from the ledge and again pointed in the distance. "This image was on top of an old, raised-seam, metal roof. It was a wife's dream."

Ntombi watched as one peering through walls and time. A man and his wife lay in bed, and an image of a house appeared over the woman. Ntombi somehow knew it to be a house in another city. The woman smiled as she slept.

Ntombi kept her eyes fixed on the woman's dream. "Why is she smiling?"

"She knows they're to live there—in that house."

"Do they?"

"They do. Not until several years later, but eventually they live in that exact house in that exact city."

Ntombi turned quickly toward Daniel. "That's amazing. But why did God call them to a particular house?"

Daniel glanced at Ntombi, then back at the scene in front of him. "So many reasons really. But among them was that it gave them the change of pace that allowed them to live out their call. The house was not the call; it was the place where they would live out the call."

Ntombi turned back toward the scene and saw it vanish as quickly as it appeared. She thought of her own call as she took a deep breath of the night air. She thought of how the air felt and wondered if she was dreaming. Surely one doesn't feel air in a dream. She thought of her prayer asking for a sign. Maybe this was it.

She closed her eyes and reopened them. The scene had not changed, except now the myriad of Charleston rooftops glistened with even more dew. A massive live oak with draping moss reached like long arms along two adjoining red clay tile roofs. Ntombi smiled at the unexpected beauty and thought of God and how He reveals beauty. Would it be beauty if it all came at us at once? Maybe that's why the call sometimes comes slowly so we appreciate the beauty.

Daniel waited in silence.

Eventually, Ntombi smiled softly and nodded. "It is a beautiful night. I never knew rooftops could look like this."

"Indeed. God has layered this city with beauty."

"I wonder why."

Daniel raised both brows. "Hmm? I've never thought to ask him, but I expect it has something to do with the amount of prayer."

Ntombi replied with a simple, "Hmm," as if she could understand who he would have asked.

Suddenly, in the distance, a couple walked along a rooftop holding hands. Ntombi looked at Daniel and quickly back at them. They walked up the steep angles of one roof and slid down the other side and across a flat roof. They seemed to float.

Ntombi couldn't see their faces but paid close attention to her hair. It was long, almost black in the moonlight. It cascaded part way down her back in a pile of ringlets. "Look at her hair."

"It looks like yours, doesn't it?"

Ntombi tilted her head slightly. "Yeah, but she's white."

"Yes, and with beautiful hair just like yours."

"I always thought mine a bit odd, but it looks good on her. So what was their call?"

"Too much to show in one scene, but in their early years as a couple, God called them on an around-the-world mission trip."

Ntombi's eyes grew wide. "All the way around?"

"Yes, without them knowing why, they bought around-the-world airline tickets, stopping in country after county, city after city, spending months ministering as the Spirit led."

Ntombi turned toward Daniel. "Wow, their cloud moved a lot. And now?"

Daniel looked at Ntombi with an impish grin and rolled his eyes up and over. "Well. I'm not sure I can say this yet, but he becomes an Old Testament scholar and teacher and develops a Bible teaching app, used by millions around the globe."

Ntombi turned back, and their image was gone. She looked at Daniel. "I want that app."

Suddenly, another image appeared. There before her were Chip and Carly from her flight to America. "It's Chip and Carly!"

Daniel laughed. "Now watch closely."

Ntombi watched Carly in front of a classroom of fourth graders. Then she was speaking in a hallway to another teacher who needed encouragement. Ntombi listened carefully to their conversation. "I'm not surprised. It seems just like her to be teaching and encouraging and loving everyone she meets."

"Precisely. Only now Carly teaches and encourages and loves everyone she meets in Zambia."

"Amazing. How did that decision come about?"

"Much is wrought in the heart's desires." Daniel grinned. "Let's rewind the tape so to speak."

Ntombi watched as Chip sat reading his Bible. Next were scenes of him teaching.

Ntombi creased her forehead slightly. "That isn't Zambia."

"No, it's before they left or even knew they would go."

"I see. Chip's job hasn't changed much either. Only the place and the eagerness of those he teaches."

Ntombi pointed to another scene forming. "What's that over there?"

"You tell me."

"It's a boy preaching on a street corner. He can't be more than thirteen."

"From a very young age, he knew he was supposed to preach."

Ntombi turned from the young preacher to look at Daniel. "It seems like something is missing, though. His words are right, but it's like he's angry or something."

"Great observation." Daniel held his hand up for a high five. Ntombi smiled and slapped the palm of his hand. She felt nothing though, and it made no sound.

Daniel nodded his head back in the direction of the boy preacher. "Now look. Do you recognize him?"

Ntombi looked. She could tell it was the same boy but much older. He was inside a church tent meeting, only he wasn't the one doing the preaching. He was at the front of the rows of seats, on his knees. And he was sobbing.

"It's him."

"That's right. Twenty-seven years later. This was the night he met Jesus."

"I don't understand. He's been preaching for twenty-seven years?"

"Yes, he has. And he's a good example of John Wesley's mentor's words, "Preach faith until you get it, then preach it because you have it."

"Wow! So how does that fit with his calling? Seems out of sequence."

"True, but calling usually doesn't follow a straight line. Seems the One who calls isn't real fond of straight lines."

Ntombi thought of her intended marriage to Mandlenkosi,

his disappearance, and the nineteen-hour flight across the Atlantic. There was nothing straight about her line, except maybe the plane that flew straight. She thought of how the Bayfields had visited Kwandwe and how their visits led to her visit. She wondered if all the sharp turns weren't actually headed somewhere.

Ntombi took a breath and again focused on the rooftops. The beauty, she thought, is in the changes. If they were all the same, all perfect, all the beauty would be lost. Maybe calling is God's art.

Daniel looked around a bit before focusing in one direction. "Ah, here's an example of a not so straight line. Look over there." Daniel gave a quick nod and looked straight ahead.

Ntombi followed his gaze. There before her, as clearly as if she had transitioned in both time and space, was an image of Tata perched out on the tracker's chair on one of Kwandwe's Land Rovers. Behind him was a guide at the wheel and a full load of guests. Tata sat up straight in the chair with binoculars up to his eyes as the Rover crept slowly over the dry crevices of what once was a riverbed. Ntombi smiled big. "It's Tata!"

"Think of his work in Torrance and his years at Kwandwe. Does his path seem like a straight line to you?"

"Far from it."

"Yet his time as a tracker gave him every afternoon free to be with you and with God."

"And to spend time in the Word." Ntombi stared at her father, wishing for a moment he was still a tracker and she still his little girl. "He spent hours in study and prayer each day."

Ntombi wiped a lone tear moving slowly down her cheek. She moved toward the image of her father without thought of the rooftop ledge. Suddenly, she felt herself falling. She jerked and found herself sitting straight up in bed.

TWENTY-TWO

Bill-san Make Plan

The Pacific Ocean was eerily calm. Mandlenkosi stood at his porthole and looked up through the seven-inch gap between his container and the girls' container. He was thankful to be on top of the stack and watched a tiny white puff of cloud drift by.

Over the days, and sped by the urgency of the situation, the two groups of girls had melded. Bill-san was clearly the captain of this ship with Annika second in command. They had quickly decided to share all they had. Two girls still had their backpacks. Supplies.

Mandlenkosi blinked twice and adjusted his eyes so he could see into the girls' container. He watched as their impromptu dance lesson settled into the morning chores. It was nice to see the girls relaxed, doing something that girls do. Even better was the bond that had formed between them and across the lines of language and culture.

He turned from the activities in the next container to put the finishing touches on his escape plan. It was time to teach the girls the plans. Plans A and B were straightforward and all about escape—but Plan C...

Mandlenkosi climbed into his hammock and pushed lightly against the back wall to make it swing. He looked up at the ceiling with his arms crossed over his chest and thought of how to teach Plan C. It would only be executed if A and B failed. Still, it was a survival plan.

How could he teach the girls to survive the unthinkable? How could he not teach them?

If he told them what their captors intended, fear might overwhelm them. They may not even understand since they were so young. How could he do it? How could he prepare girls so young and innocent for something so evil and vile?

Mandlenkosi placed both hands over his face with only his nose and part of his mouth peeking through. "God, what do I do?"

The still small voice came: Prepare their souls.

Mandlenkosi removed his hands from his face and opened his eyes. "Their souls?"

Again, the voice. Prepare their souls.

"How do I do that?"

A word settled into Mandlenkosi's spirit. It came with peace, and Mandlenkosi wondered if he had heard it, or if it was somehow gifted without voice: Songs.

Mandlenkosi sat up and wiggled his way to the edge of the hammock. His feet touched the floor as the hammock bounced with his weight. Another word surfaced like something just plopped in his mind: Scripture.

Mandlenkosi displayed his wide, gap-toothed smile, giving him a boyish look. He rushed to the porthole and called the girls to gather round and have a seat on the floor. And he began to sing.

He started with "Amazing Grace," singing softly at first but gradually intensifying as the words took root in his soul. One by one, the girls' small voices joined in, melding in holy chorus. They didn't know all the lines, but it didn't matter. They each sang what they knew.

Mandlenkosi imagined their praise as a sweet aroma permeating the gates of heaven.

When one song ended, he moved on to the next, and the next, until he ran out of songs that he knew well and had to hum his way through parts of those he didn't.

When he'd run out completely, he moved onto scripture, reciting anything he could think of. Annika added a few, and Jasmine added some in Spanish. Collectively, it was only a dozen or so verses.

Another word had surfaced in his mind. Mandlenkosi heard it clearly this time, and responded. "Right—I mean, write. Or right, I'll write." He smiled at the rhythm in his head and the idea. He turned from the porthole. As he did, Annika jumped to her feet and climbed onto the crate to watch. Mandlenkosi inventoried the number of pages remaining in his tiny notebook and then shouted to Annika, "Quick, Annika. We must write them down. The songs and the Bible verses. And use the name Jesus as much as possible. There is power in the name. I'll write them in English, and then you girls write them in Japanese and Spanish. Write small. We'll make a copy for each of you. Hide them in your socks."

Mandlenkosi took on the task of the English manuscript. All the songs and verses he knew fit on three pages, front and back. He shared his copy with Annika, and she quickly transcribed his words into Japanese. Manuela could read some English and quickly created similar pages in Spanish.

Not knowing exactly what to do or how, Mandlenkosi decided they should pray as a group. He asked the girls to kneel, and he dropped to his uninjured knee, looking like a footballer resting on the sideline. Strong, tall and just a bit too thin to be a footballer. He prayed loud enough for the girls to hear. Each girl took a turn after him, and words soon mixed with sobs. Mandlenkosi didn't need language skills to know their agony. The words mother and father can be felt in any language.

Their prayer meeting reached its natural end. Mandlenkosi knew their souls were growing stronger and that they would need strong souls. Strong bodies would not be enough. They would have to fight evil with good. But even as he thought about the word good, it somehow sounded weaker than evil.

No! God was good, and God was greater than evil.

Mandlenkosi made their worship time part of their morning routine. In the afternoons, they had a talent show. He wanted the girls to feel good about themselves before evil made them question their value.

Mandlenkosi also spent hours sharpening the old vent slats into knives. The rough edges of his porthole served as a slow but effective knife sharpener. As he sharpened, he thought of each girl and their individual gifts. A couple were fighters; the rest were not.

He gave the sharpest knives to the strongest girls and taught everyone how to use their new weapons. He emphasized how to fight back as a group and even included information about the more vulnerable parts of the human anatomy.

After dagger training, Mandlenkosi removed the diamonds from the velvet bag and made a tiny pouch out of carefully removed shipping labels. He then took his suit jacket down from the makeshift hook and slid his hand in the breast pocket. In doing so, he discovered a hole in the bottom of the pocket.

He crossed the container to the porthole. "Annika, you have a sewing kit, right? Can you mend the pocket lining in my jacket?"

"Yes, Bill-san. I sew very well."

"Good." He passed the jacket through to her.

Mandlenkosi returned to his work, but Annika reappeared moments later.

"Bill-san, come quick. Look what we find!"

"Find? Where?"

"In hem of coat. When there's hole, always look for what fall through." Annika handed him a small brown-and-white photo of two children, about age twelve.

"Bill-san, it look like you on right. But who is girl?"

Mandlenkosi took the photo and stared at it in curious awe. He couldn't tell her anything about the picture. "I don't know." He stepped back from the porthole and found a seat atop a bag of macadamia nuts.

The girl was beautiful. Her black, curly hair glistened in a soft cascade over her shoulders. He thought it odd for an African girl, but it was beautiful. In the photo, his head was pressed against hers as the pair playfully posed for the camera. Mandlenkosi recognized it as one square of those photo-booth strips. But who was the girl?

He softly traced the outline of her face with his index finger. Her skin was dark but not as dark as his. He didn't know her name, but he knew her. Or at least he'd known her. And she knew him. At the moment, that was enough.

He stood and found a label partly peeled back from a box and tore off a tiny corner. He used it to carefully hang the photo beside his hammock. He then took the diamonds and slid them into the pouch he'd made out of labels. He squeezed it into a hole that had formed in the fabric of his sneaker. The layers of canvas and mesh had created a pocket. Those things done, he dusted his hands together and sat down again to think and pray.

Seeing the photo had given Mandlenkosi a sense of who he was. Knowing the diamonds were among the cargo had given him knowledge of their captors. They would no doubt be waiting at the docks. He suspected they might have only moments before the captors reached them and tried to drug and move them. Mandlenkosi was just about to ask Annika to instruct the others on her bite and spit method of drug avoidance when she called him from the porthole.

"Bill-san?"

"Yes, Annika."

"We draw you. In case you lost. So we find you."

Mandlenkosi heart was warmed. He smiled at his little friend and accepted her kind gesture. She was learning to make a plan of her own, and Mandlenkosi thought it a good sign. "Well, all right then."

"What is Bill-san real name?"

"Mandlenkosi."

"Too hard. You write name."

Soon his portrait was finished, and all he knew of himself was written on the back of it. More memory returned with each day. Soon, he could see his father's face, knew he worked for a South African winery—high up, like an official or something. He could picture his mother's face and knew he had sisters. No names yet, other than his own. He hoped they would come in time and wondered if the drugs he was given would cause permanent damage. He laughed to himself when he realized that it's hard to miss your mind.

The girls were homesick too. But they knew well each thing that they missed. He didn't know what or who to miss. In a way, he was protected. For now.

At day's end, Mandlenkosi stretched out in his makeshift hammock. He thought of the pungent mix of evil captors and the glorious beauty in the girls. He wondered if this was what God saw. Was it all mixed up when he looked to earth?

He knew the ship would dock soon and wondered if the girls were ready. They'd made progress. Good progress. And now he had the photo, and all were filled with faith, hope, and love for each other.

And swords—of both the Spirit and the steel variety.

TWENTY-THREE

The Basement

The next night, after some late hours in the library, Ntombi walked the streets of Charleston, somewhat unaware of her surroundings. Was it her thoughts or the growing familiarity keeping her from noticing the damp stone beneath her feet, the soft, humid air, the tourists walking and laughing arm in arm, and a soup of smells wafting from open-doored restaurants.

Awaking from her internal world, Ntombi looked down at her watch and then up at the street sign on the corner. It was nearly ten. She turned quickly as if somehow compelled to see if Daniel was still at the coffee shop. With the thought of the coffee shop, the sense of the married man's lips whispering in her ear entered her mind. She pushed the thought away and wondered how it had so quickly invaded her consciousness. Ntombi rubbed her ear as if doing so would erase the memory.

The Corner Coffee came in to view. Daniel was standing out front. He greeted her as if he'd been expecting her. "Everyone is gone. I'll lock up once we're inside."

"Lock up? Inside?"

The old wood-and-glass door opened in, making the lock seem more of a suggestion than any sort of protection. As Daniel turned it, an unexpected peace came into the room. Daniel took Ntombi by the hand. "Follow me. We can talk, but low voices will be best."

Daniel went first. He stepped right through the wine cooler as if it weren't there. Ntombi followed behind. As her hand, then arm, then body passed through the glass and bottles, she felt nothing beyond amazement. A passageway led to another, and then they found themselves atop a long, chiseled-stone staircase. A stench wafted from below, unlike anything Ntombi knew. She quickly put one hand over her nose and mouth. The air was still thick with the smell of decaying souls, but now it was accented by the vanilla citrus handwash she'd used earlier, making for a sickening combination.

The stairs were narrow, barely eighteen inches wide, leaning out into the open space and slick with the sweat of darkness. As her eyes adjusted, Ntombi felt the need to stay close to the cold wall behind her. It too was made of stone and was slimy with cold, damp moss. Yet somehow she took comfort in its presence. With the other hand, she held tightly to Daniel's and descended one stair at a time, feeling each step first with her toe and then her entire foot before trusting her weight to it.

They must have been under the tilted stairs. Were they in the basement? No. There were too many stairs. Her eyes adjusted, revealing that the stairs led into a dark, open room, thirty yards or more beneath them. It was like a pit, inviting one to tumble or slip in.

"Let's sit here."

Ntombi carefully lowered herself, feeling each inch of the cold stone wall beside her as she slowly crouched and sat on a step. She tucked her feet in close, not wanting them to dangle into the space. Daniel did the same, though he seemed far more relaxed.

"In a moment, as your ears adjust, you will hear the voices."

"Voices?"

"Yes. They are legion."

Ntombi and Daniel sat in silence. At first, all Ntombi heard were distant murmurs. As she listened, they grew louder. She became aware of herself, her existence in space, and a seemingly inappropriate peace, like the gravity she needed to hold fast to the stairs.

"Do not be afraid."

Ntombi tried moving her hand from her face, but the stench was too strong. "The smell. Do you ever get used to the smell?"

"It's not one you want to get used to."

The white of Ntombi's eyes was probably the only light in the cavern-like space. Soon, Ntombi could make out images below. People—or what looked like people—were seated at tables like those upstairs. It was a coffee shop of sorts. Soon the voices inside their heads became distinguishable.

"You must hurry, you will be late. You know you were late the last time. You're always late."

"You shouldn't be drinking that. It probably has a thousand calories."

"You should join a different group at church. A younger bunch."

The closer Ntombi listened, the more disturbed she became by the voices. At one point she thought of shouting into the pit, "Don't listen to them!" Instead, the voices—the unwelcomed taunts—droned on in the people's minds.

"What are you going to wear? You don't have anything nice."

"You will never make as much money as she does. You deserve better. After all, you are the reason she is successful."

"He doesn't love you."

"There you go feeling guilty again. You know guilt is bad. Live a little. Everyone else is doing it."

"You deserve to be happy. It's just dinner, what could it hurt?"

"You have so much to do today. You will never get it all done."

"You can't do that. What if no one shows up?"

"You don't have the credentials, and, besides, look at your past."

"He took advantage of you, as if…as if you didn't know where the property line was. He'll get his."

The noise swarmed like bumblebees in flight. Incessant. Ntombi wished it would stop. Without thinking, she loosened her grip on Daniel and pressed her hands over her ears. "What are we hearing?"

"You're hearing the voices in people's heads—the enemy's prompting. What word do you hear most frequently?"

Ntombi lowered her hands just a bit, resting them on both sides of her neck. She listened for a moment before replying, "'You.' There are lots of 'you' statements. Even 'you' questions."

"Yes. The enemy never says us."

"Why is that?"

"He doesn't abide with most people, just becomes more and more influential."

"How's that?"

"They listen and let him take up rent-free residence in their heads."

Ntombi looked first at Daniel and then into the dark room below. She lowered her hands to her lap. "It's all about the voice, which voice we listen to."

"Yes, and distinguishing between them."

Ntombi wrinkled her forehead, looked into the darkness, then back at Daniel. "But how do we know the difference?"

"If it's true—wholly, completely, purely true—it's a voice from the Light. God cannot lie. Always ask yourself if what you're hearing is true."

"Does the enemy ever use truth?"

"Twisted truth. He takes something that may be factual and twists it like a corkscrew. Remember his objective is ultimately to destroy—you, your purpose."

Ntombi slowly nodded in agreement, brought the back of her right hand to her mouth, exhaled, and lowered her hand, allowing Daniel's words to permeate the deep crevices. Those hidden places where the truth about Truth abides.

Without any idea as to why she wanted to hear more, Ntombi asked, "Can we listen a while longer?"

"Yes, of course."

"Do they know we are here?"

"No."

Ntombi tuned her ears to eavesdrop a while longer. They obviously weren't all-knowing. The accusations and suggestions seemed disproportionate to the number of people in the room.

Daniel interrupted her thoughts. "Would you like to hear what they say to each other?"

Ntombi offered Daniel a look of surprise. "Minion to minion? Beelzebub to Lucifer?"

"Something like that."

"Sure."

"Take my hand."

As she placed her hand in his, she was aware she couldn't actually feel his hand, yet that peculiar peace came over her again. She looked down and could see his hand in hers, but it was as if her sense of touch had disappeared. Was it gone? No, she could feel the wall against her shoulder and the cold dampness of chiseled stone with that icky moss. It was just Daniel's hand she couldn't feel.

Ntombi returned her attention to the room below and narrowed her eyes in a futile attempt to see the source of the voices.

"You can't see them," Daniel explained. "Rather, most people don't. Just listen."

In an instant, she was hearing different voices—less pleasant, less guarded, and yet cautious in a different way. The more she listened, the more she became aware of a pecking order in the room. Some outranked others. Some gave advice.

"One of our best weapons is hurry. Keep him busy, running from one activity to the next. And, get this. You can even convince him he looks important if he's constantly checking his phone for messages. Whatever you do, don't let him have any quiet time. Fill the spaces on his calendar."

"And if he does get an hour to himself, I'll make him feel guilty about it."

With that, the two shared a snicker.

"Yeah, we've worked that one so well, they've forgotten they're human beings."

"Right. Now they think they're human doings."

Another snicker.

"They even think they're equal with the animals. That they came from animals. Planting that cockamamie idea is how Beelzebub got his promotion."

"What works best with his kind, though, are feelings of inadequacy. Work on that. Tell him his strength is waning and he is weak. Get him to spend hours in the gym. Body worship is an easy sell."

"Yep. Anything in creation but never the Creator."

"Fear. You must create and sustain fear."

"But she really doesn't have anything to fear."

"That doesn't matter. Most of them don't, but they don't know that. Work with the fear that she will never marry."

"She is thinking she wants to start back to church."

"That's fine. Just steer her to a cool church with cute guys.

Whatever you do, don't let her go to one where they actually worship."

"They all worship, don't they?"

"Yes, but pay attention. Listen closely. Some are actually worshipping themselves. We like those kinds of churches."

"Ah. I know just the type. Lots of 'I' phrases in the songs and their self-help style of sermons."

Ntombi heard an icy cackle.

"Yeah. I wrote some of those. You can't let them sing about the enemy, but praise of their praise seems to work nicely.

"Indeed. It's even okay to let them have some of what they call experiences. Just make sure those experiences are of our making."

"Ah."

"And we have done great things by distorting the phrase 'God is love.'"

"And horizontal. Make sure the teaching is horizontal. You know this world and its problems. Oh, and one of my favorites is how they focus so much on what the Enemy can do for them like he's a cosmic vending machine. You know—cause and effect."

Ntombi stared in utter amazement. She had never before considered one's choice of church could be influenced by the enemy. They were, after all, churches. Or were they? Sensing she might miss something, she shook her head and drew her attention back to the voices.

"What else will work with her?"

"Popularity. That seems to be…well, popular. She likes Facebook, doesn't she?"

"Yes."

"Perfect. Keep her busy posting pictures of herself. Then you can have her worry about whether people like her pictures."

Daniel interrupted Ntombi's concentration. "What do you hear? And, better yet, what do you see?"

"They are plotting and strategizing, and it seems to be working. It's like people are deciding things, choosing a path, even things like where they will go to church, without knowing how, or, rather, who has directed them."

"Exactly. Let's listen some more."

Ntombi again turned her attention to the fallen creatures.

"He is a difficult case."

"No. Not difficult—just different."

"He goes to church—one of those churches. One of the Enemy's churches. Reads his Bible daily; prays occasionally.

"Does he belong to the Enemy?"

"Yeah. I'm thinking I should move on. Get a new assignment."

"Never. Never give up. This may be your biggest assignment yet. There's much to lose at this stage. If we don't stop him now, he could take others with him."

"I see."

"With his type, you have to use different tactics. It takes even more skill. For example, fear of death won't work, but fear of failure will. Oh, and the little things. Frustrate him with appliances that break and red lights when no one is coming the other way. And his time. You must distract him. Keep him focused on his body and created things, anything but the Creator. And numb him. Gradually numb him to our tactics."

"How do I do that?"

"It's remarkable. They created it themselves. It's called desensitization. Gradually introduce more abhorrent things. Over time they will cease to disgust him, and he will become desensitized. What shocked him ten years ago becomes entertainment today. Oh, and pleasure. Make sure he pursues pleasures."

"Pleasures? But he won't go to a strip club."

"Not needed. What are his weaknesses?"

"Fear of the future."

"You can do a lot with that. Always enter at the weak point. One of my favorites is to put a horrible thought in his mind."

"Like what?"

"Suicide. Adultery. The trick is to make him think it's his thought, then make him feel guilty for having had the thought."

Ntombi realized she had forgotten to breathe but wasn't sure she wanted any more of the rancid air in her lungs.

Daniel turned and looked at her. "I think that's enough. Let's get out of here." He rose, then grabbed her hand to help her to her feet. He quickly turned and climbed in the direction they'd come from. They passed back through the cooler, through the coffee shop, the front door, and out onto the sidewalk.

Once on the street, Ntombi released Daniel's hand but then feared he would disappear. She didn't ask who or what he was. Instead, she walked down the sidewalk with him at her side, wondering how they looked to passersby. Then she realized how odd it was that such a silly fear had crept in so quickly. When they turned a corner, a park came into view. Ntombi noticed the fog swirling against the backdrop of an old, gas-lit lamppost. Beneath it sat a decorative, wood-slatted, iron bench covered with layers of blackish-green paint. They went over to it and sat together in silence. Ntombi had lots of questions but chose them slowly and carefully.

"So, the battle is for the mind."

"No. The battle is for the soul. The mind is merely the porch."

"And the doorway?"

"Eyes and ears."

Ntombi tucked her hands under her thighs, crossed her feet

at the ankles, and looked out into the night air. "And the enemy directs us toward bad things?"

"If he can, he uses bad to keep us from good."

Ntombi puzzled over that a bit. "And if he can't steer us toward bad?"

"With Christ, people learn to discern good from bad."

"Then what?"

"He uses good things to keep people from their highest good—God and their call."

Ntombi thought about that, and what it meant, but before she could form her next question, Daniel disappeared into the salt-laden fog of the dark night.

Twenty-four

Land, Ho!

Only Mandlenkosi and Keiko were awake. Mandlenkosi watched across the girl's container as Keiko was on watch out her porthole. Her little elbows were planted in the lower corners of the porthole and her chin in her hands. Mandlenkosi watched her watching. He could see only tiny glimpses of the changing horizon on both sides of her head. He created the rest of the scene in his mind's eye. The deep, cobalt-blue of the Pacific lay cold black in the wee hours of the morning, providing the perfect canvas for reflected light. Only glimpses of the amber-lit shoreline made it to Mandlenkosi, but he delighted in the newness of shrouded mystery in the early hour.

Keiko's hair seemed the same color as the ocean beyond. Both were shiny and black, but hers was starting to lose its luster. The light from the shore surrounded her head and turned from amber to white, to a mix of amber and white, as the port came into view. A brief linear view of the port brought a clearer glimpse of the lights on the shore. They seemed to extend for miles.

The ship turned ever slightly, revealing glimpses of what at first appeared to be a manmade mass of metal. In the foreground, Mandlenkosi could see what looked like a massive herd of giant metal cranes. Bright lights behind their giraffe-like necks displayed shipping containers stacked like long Christmas packages, some red or rusty orange, others a dirty white accented by the occasional green.

Just then, Keiko jumped, and Mandlenkosi jumped with her. "What do you see?"

"Something moving."

"What does it look like?"

As Keiko described what she saw, a picture unfolded in Mandlenkosi's mind. A long string of railcars was moving slowly toward the dock. She described others moving in opposite directions and drew her own conclusion. "Train."

At home, Mandlenkosi had learned to tell the hour of the night by the stars and the sounds of the bush. These sounds were all new. He heard only the slow idle of the ship's engine and a muffled, distant hum.

Suddenly, the ship came to a stop. All this time at sea, and it just stopped moving. No fanfare. Not even a bump. Mandlenkosi wondered how something so large could just stop.

Keiko's head whipped around to look at Mandlenkosi. Her eyes popped open. Mandlenkosi smiled gently and nodded. Keiko jumped from her perch and went person to person, waking the others.

Mandlenkosi began instructing the girls, calmly reviewing the plan. He had them use some of the remaining water to wash up a bit. He did the same.

Just then, a tiny hand reached through the adjoining porthole, waving a bright white T-shirt. Annika called out playfully. "Looky here! Looky here, Bill-san!"

Mandlenkosi laughed as much at the giver as the gift. "Where did you get this?"

"One of girls have in backpack. Dad's T-shirt for sleeping."

It was just what he needed. He quickly put on the shirt, then stood up straight and straightened out the wrinkles.

Annika watched through his porthole with the same interest as one watching a fashion show. "Bill-san, you look good."

Her compliment felt good, even if it was far from true. Then again, compared to how he had looked the day before, maybe he did look good. He patted the top of his unruly hair with both hands and shrugged. He then had the girls gather round for morning prayers. They sat like school children for story time, except there was an eagerness about them. They were more fidgety than usual. Mandlenkosi kept his talk short. He too was anxious to see what was happening beyond their containers.

Mandlenkosi ended their time with a prayer. "Father God, thank you for worship. Thank you that it is not confined as we are."

The girls said their amens in unison and jumped to their feet. Annika was first to reach the outward facing porthole. She peeked out and shouted descriptions of the unfolding scene back at Mandlenkosi. In time, the morning began to drag on, and the newness subsided. Annika lost interest.

Still eager to know what was happening, Mandlenkosi asked Keiko to return as the lookout. She seemed to absorb more. Perhaps, as a musician, her senses were more finely tuned. She heard more, knew more without looking, and could sense when something shifted.

"Bill-san?"

"Yes, Keiko."

"I hear sound like cars. And look." Keiko stepped aside, giving Mandlenkosi a view. Beyond the outer window was a cruise ship. Beside it was another ship, but the second ship looked old and had three pipes on top that were blue on the bottom and a faded red on top. They leaned backward, almost like they were curved backward.

Mandlenkosi's mind searched for answers. The scene looked

like pictures he'd seen of the Queen Mary. How on earth could they be docked near the Queen Mary? Mandlenkosi's eyes grew wide. He remembered! The Queen Mary was dry docked in Long Beach. He took a deep breath and prayed aloud, "Is this Long Beach?"

Yes. Tell them about the fence.

Mandlenkosi first puzzled at the Voice, then stiffened. The fence? What fence? And then it hit him. There would be a fence around the shipyard, but he hadn't yet told the girls about it. Mandlenkosi quickly turned his attention to the girls in the next container and began to instruct them on how to scale the fence or sneak out the gate.

Hours passed with a tediousness about them. It was hard to know when to worry. Suddenly, the sound of a nearby crane engine revved into action. Annika gave the shush command, and the girls stopped what they were doing to look at Mandlenkosi.

"Okay, here we go," he began. "We may not have much time. Check the harness. Pull on it as hard as you can. Make sure it is strong."

Annika gave it a hard yank and then had all the girls pull on it.

"Good," Mandlenkosi whispered, as he turned and stepped away from the porthole. He paced back and forth from one end of his container to the next.

Annika returned quickly to the porthole and gave her answer. "It is strong. Very strong. She small."

Mandlenkosi clasped his hands together behind his back and looked over at Annika. "Is Jasmine ready?"

"She is, and she strong."

Mandlenkosi smiled. She was strong like a tiny gymnast. She had volunteered because she was strong and because she

161

could fit through the opening. Still, he worried. What if she fell or the harness failed? Mandlenkosi returned to his porthole with a new sense of urgency.

Mandlenkosi paused to choose his words. He expected those who had shipped them would want their containers—full of living cargo and diamonds—to unload first. He left out a descriptor of the captor's intent, explaining only, "They'll take your container off first."

Mandlenkosi then sent Annika to be the new lookout. "Tell me what you see. Do you see any rigs? Any trucks with a trailer?"

Annika now had to shout back at him to be heard over the dock noise. "Yes. I see trucks. One, two, three, four…seven. I see seven."

"Are there any other people around?"

"No. No other people. Now Bill-san? Jasmine go now?"

"Not yet. Tell me when the crane starts to move."

Annika placed one hand on her hip and gave Mandlenkosi the thumbs up sign with the other. "Okay," she said, without turning around.

Then they waited.

Mandlenkosi used the time to offer final words of encouragement. "Girls, you are strong. You are a team. God loves you. With his help, we can do this. He will take care of you, but you must fight."

Jasmine was perched on the crate just beneath the outside porthole. She spoke out over the heads of the group. "Yes, Bill-san. We fight." He could see her flinch.

Annika yelled back to him. "It's moving! The crane is moving!"

"Jasmine, are you ready?"

"Ready."

"Vámonos!"

With that, Mandlenkosi watched as two of the girls hoisted her up, and she crawled face up through the small porthole. First her arms, then her head, then one shoulder at a time. She paused.

"Is she okay?" Mandlenkosi said.

Annika turned and shouted back to him. "Yes. She okay. Sunlight new."

Two girls held Jasmine's feet, and two others stood on the crate holding her and waiting on her to make the next move. When she did, they pushed. Then, with the form of a well-practiced cheerleading squad, they gave a final shove. Soon, only Jasmine's feet were visible in the porthole. Then they disappeared, first one and then the other.

"Is she safe?"

"Yes, Bill-san. She on top."

"Then Plan A! Go!"

At his word, the girls screamed with all they had and tossed bottles one by one out the porthole. Most exploded on the dock. A few hit the water.

"Scream fire!" Mandlenkosi yelled, then joined in the planned mayhem by throwing full wine bottles against the dock-facing side of his container.

Annika left her perch and hurried across the container to be heard by Mandlenkosi. "Bill-san. People. Some people watching."

"Go back. Tell me what you see."

Annika returned to the far window, then yelled back. "They get out of truck. Two men get out of big truck."

"Anyone else? What about the other trucks."

"No, Bill-san. They stay in trucks."

Fear crept in. Mandlenkosi fought it back with the words he had often heard his father say: Do the next thing.

163

"Just keep yelling and waving. Be careful not to rock the container."

Suddenly the crane apparatus moved into position over the girls' container. Mandlenkosi clinched the bottom of the porthole and rocked up on his toes. He could picture the crane coming down on Jasmine. "What's happening?"

"The crane. They are—they will hit Jasmine. She can't move. Net hooked."

"Cut her loose! Cut her loose!"

Annika pulled the makeshift knife from her sock and began to saw. Two other girls did the same. Soon, each cord was untied.

Annika stuck her neck and arm out the porthole and waved. "Jasmine. You free. You free."

Mandlenkosi could hear Jasmine struggling, crawling the length of the container. He called out to her from his porthole between the narrow space between their containers. "Jasmine. Move to my container. Quick. On your belly. Crawl. Aqui, Jasmine. Aqui."

Just then, the space between the two containers grew dark, then light again as Jasmine crawled onto Mandlenkosi's container.

Mandlenkosi shouted to the rest of the girls. "Plan B! Plan B! Use C if you need to."

The crane hooks locked into place with a loud clank. Mandlenkosi watched carefully to see if the operators would lift it with a quick jolt or slowly. If they lifted it slowly, surely they knew its contents only held the weight of little girls.

The container lifted slowly and carefully through the air. A sick feeling entered Mandlenkosi's stomach. Soon a sudden streak of sunlight entered his container. As his eyes adjusted, he could see the girls' container rock slightly back and forth, tugging against the tight grasp of the crane's hooks. Muffled screams filled the air.

They had implemented Plan B.

Mandlenkosi watched through the porthole. He could hear Jasmine squirm and scream atop his container. The girls' container turned and then lowered on the waiting trailer. The two men in the cab pulled just out of sight of the other truck drivers and squarely into Mandlenkosi's view. In an instant, they had the back doors of the container open to check their cargo.

The girls pounced like big cats, their makeshift knives cutting like claws. Their captors reached to cover their wounds. This gave the girls the time they needed. They ran in all directions.

Mandlenkosi counted. One, two, three. A fourth struggled. One man held her as another speared her with a syringe, then turned and ran after the fleeing girls. Mandlenkosi watched as the captor ran first in one direction and then the next, uncertain which way to go.

Mandlenkosi turned his attention to the immediate. "Jasmine. Tienes harness?"

"Si. Yo tengo."

"Aqui."

Mandlenkosi reached his hand as high as he could out the porthole. Jasmine's tiny hand dropped a crumpled cord to him. As his hand grasped her net, he realized this was his first fresh air in weeks and only human touch. He received the piece of netting, pulled it into the container and quickly tied it around a rivet.

"More? Tienes mas?"

"No mas!"

A single thread would have to do. As the crane hooks moved closer and locked into position, Mandlenkosi could hear her. He didn't understand her words, but he knew she was praying. He prayed with her. For her. Lifting his head, he realized the crane operator had left room between the lifting contraption and the container. He left room for Jasmine.

The container was lifted high, away from the ship and over the water. Mandlenkosi knew they would need a miracle.

And then—Jasmine jumped!

TWENTY-FIVE

Book Thief

Ntombi felt the night air as she hurried from her car toward the brightly lit airport terminal. She had learned to enjoy the moist, low-country air and was eager to hear about Whitting's Boston trip. It was part of their research. He had met with colleagues and done some digging into original sources about The Great Awakening. She knew their parallel path approach would prevent full disclosure but hoped for a few nuggets. Surely the past was a storehouse of hope for today.

As she approached, the glass doors opened automatically as if to say welcome. Just inside, she caught a glimpse of Whitting riding down the escalator with an overstuffed briefcase in one hand, and the other lifted high above his head, waving eagerly. She looked up at him and returned the childlike wave. Noting his corduroy pants, tweed jacket, knit vest, and madras bowtie, she decided maybe he knew how to dress after all, at least for Boston.

As he neared the bottom of the escalator, Ntombi noticed his grin and his eyes looking up and to one side. It was his cheesier cat look. He stepped off, leaned back on his heels and lifted his arms, briefcase and all, for a hug. Ntombi bent down a bit for the hug, and his short, tweed-wrapped arms encircled her.

"Shoo! What a trip! Thank you so much for picking me up.

My ole Citroën is hard to start when she's parked for a while."

"I'm curious to hear what you learned."

Whitting elbowed her as they walked toward baggage claim. "Oh, so much. It was a whirlwind trip." He stopped, lowered his head a little, glanced around with an air of suspicion, and said in a whisper, "Let's talk in the car. I don't want anyone to over-hear."

Ntombi looked around. There weren't many people. The hour was late, and she doubted the few airport passersby cared much about his research, Boston, or the voice of God for that matter.

After what seemed like a long wait for Whitting's bag and a short walk to the car, the pair drove out of the airport parking lot. Ntombi glanced at Whitting and back at the road. "Okay. First, tell me where all you went."

Whitting kept his focus straight ahead as he spoke. "When in Boston, there are just so many options. It's difficult to focus. But on this trip, I had two missions. First I met with an old friend and fellow professor of church history. He is especially knowledgeable about the Great Awakening. I also wanted some time with Thomas Prince's book collection. I was curious to see what else he read and collected."

"Cool."

"It was so hard not to tell my friend or the library staff about the book you found. But mum's the word."

Ntombi had both hands on the wheel, and her eyes watched the dimly lit road. "So what did y'all talk about?" She looked over at him in time to catch his smirk. "You like that? Apparently, I say y'all now."

"Good on ya, mate."

Ntombi's face softened slightly as her mind encapsulated the moment. It was a first for her. She and Whitting were becoming friends. She glanced over at him and back at the road and nodded. She could think of no one she would rather call mentor and friend.

Whitting continued, still looking forward. "We spoke at length. It was such a delight to see him. He was most helpful in preparing me for the next stop."

"Next stop?"

"I, my dear, gained access to Thomas Prince's private collection."

"You did what? How?"

Whitting described the setting down to the dimly lit room and the carefully controlled temperature. He told of floor-to-ceiling, glass-covered bookcases on four walls and the young woman who sat at a desk in the room. She was the guard. Ntombi listened as the picture formed. She thought of words and their value but had never before considered that some needed guarding. Her mind turned to the Thomas Prince book she had found. "Does that make the book we found less valuable?"

Whitting turned slightly in his seat toward her. "Nooo. I don't think so. Maybe more valuable, actually. Besides, what we care about is what's in it." Whitting turned back to face forward. "There are literally hundreds of books in his collection, but we have one he wrote."

Ntombi's forehead creased, her brow lowered. "Must be hard to sit in the dark all day. Can you touch them? The books, I mean."

Whitting gazed out the passenger's window. "Yeah. I wouldn't want that job. You can touch the books. Well, not with fingers. I was given a velvet stand and a page-turner, and the attendant used gloves. I was able to see two at a time. I spent a whole day there."

Ntombi pushed back from the steering wheel, finding a deeper place in her seat, and imagined what it was like to have someone standing over you as you looked at a book. She decided Prince would want people to read the books. After all, words are eternal—good words at least. You can't really guard words—especially God's words. Her mind then turned to the burning of books, and she wondered if the same books that are now guarded were ever burned. "So what did you learn?"

Whitting laughed. "What I learned is that Prince liked books."

"Do you know what he used them for?"

"Do you know much American history?"

"Honestly, very little. I do know a bit about the Revolutionary War."

"Have you ever heard of the Boston Tea Party?"

"Yeah, something to do with England's taxes, right?"

"You know more than a lot of your American contemporaries."

"Sadly."

"Well, Prince pastored Old South Boston for forty years. Actually, he had it built. Several of the great leaders of the day would have been members of his church. I expect his teaching was instrumental in shaping their understanding of the emerging colony called America and America's place in the world, and, most importantly, her place in God's kingdom on earth."

Before Ntombi could respond, Whitting said, "Look. The HOT NOW sign is on!"

"Hot now?"

Whitting pointed toward a brightly lit building. "Pull in. Here."

Sensing the urgency in Whitting's voice, Ntombi turned quickly and slid into the first parking space. She braked hard, sending both of them forward and then back against their seats. Whitting looked at her and shook his head. "You've never had a Krispy Kreme donut? We've failed in your assimilation. They are, I believe, modern-day manna, minus the food value, of course."

In minutes, the two were seated at a tiny booth with two glasses of cold milk and a wax-covered bag of doughy delight. Ntombi watched as Whitting reached his hand slowly into the bag and gently placed a hot donut on a napkin in front of her. He then did the same for himself.

Ntombi followed Whitting's lead and picked up her donut with both hands like one raising a saucer of milk to her lips. As she took her first bite, the warm, leavened bread, encased in still warm, partly crisp glaze, melted into a sweet party for her taste buds. Ntombi's eyes widened. She offered Whitting a closed-mouth smile. "Oh, my goodness. This is heavenly," she said in a muffled voice.

"Manna, I tell you. Manna."

Whitting finished his donut first, carefully lifted the tiny napkin from his lap, wiped the sugar from his fingers and mouth, replaced the napkin, then dusted his hands together to finish the job. He turned slightly toward his attaché and reached in among a pile of papers. With just a bit of fishing about, he pulled out an old book and plunked it down on the table between them.

"What's this?" Ntombi asked as she continued to chew.

"This, my friend, is a book written in 1746 by Jonathan Edwards."

Ntombi quickly dusted the sugar from her hands and reached for it.

"Careful, it's quite old."

Ntombi held the book in both hands, gently lifted it off the table, and lifted her gaze to meet Whitting's. "Did you take this from the library?"

Whitting merely grinned, tilted his head slightly to one side, and looked up toward the ceiling.

"Did you? Did you lift this from Prince's collection?"

"Let's just say I acquired it. After all, doesn't the end justify the means? We'll make far better use of it."

Ntombi was stunned. Her mind raced. He was right about letting the words out, setting them free. Whitting was doing Kingdom work. Edwards' words might come to a good end through their research. But stealing a book?

Whitting responded to Ntombi's perplexed look in a matter-of-fact tone. "Never mind how I came about the book. Let's talk about your assignment."

Ntombi gently opened the book. She first noticed its size. Hundreds of pages and single spaced. Then the title. *A Treatise Concerning Religious Affections in Three Parts.*

Whitting continued. "Edwards was a contemporary of Prince, a fellow clergyman, and a friend. I found several works by Edwards in Prince's library, some with a preface written partly by Prince, which tells me they knew and respected each other. Anyway, this work was written by Edwards in the aftermath of the Awakening, a few years later after the dust had settled, so to speak."

Ntombi's mind was still on the book theft as Whitting went on. "In writing this, Edwards is providing a way for clergy to discern a genuine work of the Holy Spirit from the counterfeit works in their day. Whenever the Holy One moves, Satan is ready to offer counterfeits. He mimics, providing experiences that outwardly resemble a work of the Spirit but inwardly reek of death."

Ntombi turned some pages and quickly realized the weight of the task in front of her. Edwards' sentence structure was turgid, reminding her of the Apostle Paul's writing—very long sentences.

Whitting raised his brow and gave a quick nod. "Your task is to find words. Essential words."

Ntombi looked up from the book. "Just words?"

"Yes. You will be mining for words—truths of the faith. I want you to boil it down to, say, five words or phrases that are essential. Eternally true."

"What kind of words?"

"Words we can't live without. Words of eternal significance. Perhaps words we have forgotten."

Ntombi continued quietly thumbing through the book, touching it gently, not wanting to harm the stolen property. She assumed it would go better for Whitting if the book were not damaged while in his possession.

Whitting was first to break the silence. "Let's go. We can talk in the car. I know the way. I'll drive if you like."

Ntombi nodded and handed Whitting the keys.

The conversation for the remainder of the drive was mostly one-sided. Ntombi sat with her seatbelt tightly fastened, the book carefully perched in her lap, with one hand to steady the book and the other hanging onto the side of the door as they swerved between lanes and then turned down a narrow tree-lined road. Ntombi glanced at Whitting and once again questioned the sanity of her mentor.

"I like the car. It handles well, not like my Citroën, but good for a Swiss product."

"It belongs to the Bayfields."

"I thought so. It doesn't suit you."

Ntombi decided to enjoy the ride and this heretofore undisclosed side of Whitting. "So what suits me?"

Whitting rolled his thin lips in and glanced over at Ntombi, studying her for what seemed like way too long for the driver of the vehicle. "Hmm. I think riding atop a Kaapse Boerperd on an

English saddle along a Cape ridge with your hair emboldened by the sea mist, bouncing in counter beat with the horse's stride, whilst waves crash below. Oh, and the sun is setting. No. Wait. The sun is rising."

Ntombi shook her head. "So you know South African horses?"

Whitting nodded emphatically. "Whitting knows a little about a lot of things," he said, as he turned into a driveway where the gate opened automatically. Ntombi marveled over the gate's massive ironwork.

"The gate knows me." Whitting looked at Ntombi and winked. "No, actually, the sensor is in my pocket."

The driveway wasn't as long as the Bayfield driveway, but it was far more grand. Even at this late hour, Ntombi couldn't help but notice the precisely kept gardens. After a long sweeping turn threading two rows of ancient mystic oaks, the drive presented a stately, brick antebellum home, graciously lit by the full moon. Whitting brought the car to a stop in the circle drive as Ntombi folded her hands and rested them on top of the book in her lap. She looked up at the old house and then over at Whitting as if to ask, this is where you live?

"What? Oh. It's been in the family for generations. I'm merely caretaker for my stint on earth." Whitting stopped the car in front of the house and put it in park. "Thank you for the ride and for letting me drive. Makes me want a new car." He jumped out on the driver's side and headed around the front of the car. Ntombi, still stunned to learn Whitting lived in a house like this, slowly followed his cue.

Ntombi rounded the car and settled into the driver's seat. She rolled down the passenger window to say goodbye to Whitting. He stopped halfway up the porch stairs, turned and waved. He looked small against the backdrop of the soaring-columned porch and, at the same time, at home.

He stooped just enough to see Ntombi's face under the car roof and spoke loudly enough to be heard through the night air and over the old Volvo engine.

"Oh, one more thing. I bought the book."

TWENTY-SIX

A Thread

"Jasmine! Are you okay?"

"Si, Bill-san. I'm flying."

Mandlenkosi peered out the porthole to see Jasmine swinging over the water. He followed the cargo netting back to the single thread tethering it to the container.

"Don't move. Stay still." Mandlenkosi shouted more loudly than needed, then whispered, "God help us."

Just then, Jasmine yelled. "A school bus!"

Mandlenkosi's ran back to the porthole and, sure enough, a miracle in the form of a big, yellow bus. He lowered his tone and slowed his pace of speech. "Jasmine. Wait until the kids get off the bus."

Mandlenkosi watched as children filed off the bus two by two. He waited until all were gathered with their chaperones and gave the cue. When he did, Jasmine called out to the children below. "Help! Up here! Help! We need your help. Call 911!"

Two children ran toward the ship screaming and pointing up at Jasmine. Adults chased after them. Others dug phones from their backpacks and lifted them to call.

Suddenly, the crane moved slightly and then stopped again, leaving Jasmine swinging. Some of the children below moaned. Others screamed. Still others hid their faces.

A Thread

The three men who were waiting to receive their shipment climbed in the truck and sped off. Mandlenkosi flinched as if to give chase.

Within minutes, television vans, ambulances, and firetrucks arrived. The ladder on one of the firetrucks was long enough to reach Jasmine. Mandlenkosi watched, trying not to be seen, as they cut her down and moved her to a stretcher. He watched as she talked with the ambulance crew and couldn't help but smile as he noticed her excited hand gestures. At one point, he saw her point in his direction, but whatever she was trying to convey went unheeded as her stretcher was hoisted into the back of the ambulance and the doors were slammed shut.

Everything in him wanted to cry out to be rescued. But it wasn't the plan. At least not plan C. Mandlenkosi pulled what was left of his tiny notebook from his pants pocket and flipped it over to Plan C. There he read his own words.

Plan C: If we are scattered, meet at the tallest building on the sunset side at 6 pm. If anyone is taken by the bad men, send out a warning before you go to the police. Contact churches, the media, everyone's parents. Create a stir. Then tell the police. But first, put pressure on them.

He folded the notebook back over and looked across the container. The light from his porthole created a bright, rectangular line. In it danced particles of dust and the realization that bad guys had taken Keiko. She was the youngest, but she knew to fight.

Hours passed. Mandlenkosi watched as the police arrived and dispersed the crowd. The children were ushered back on the bus, and the crane operators were taken away, no doubt for questioning. In time, Mandlenkosi sat to rest a bit. As he did, he heard some commotion. He jumped up and looked out. A new crew arrived, the crane engines cranked and hummed, and soon

177

his container began to move. It was the moment he had longed for, yet the sudden movement lifted his stomach into his chest. In what seemed like only seconds, Mandlenkosi felt the thud of asphalt beneath the container and sense of solid ground beneath his feet.

He could hear voices outside. In the distance, a newscaster was telling about the rescue. Then, he heard an entirely different sound. It was metal scraping metal, and, in an instant, a small sliver of light entered the space, and a breath of freedom filled Mandlenkosi's lungs.

TWENTY-SEVEN

Asleep on the Porch

The sun was just starting to peek through the large trees in the Bayfields' front yard. Ntombi yawned and stretched out on the front porch's wicker sofa, extending her legs over its arm. She slowly opened one eye and saw Whitting standing over her and flinched. She opened the other eye and yawned again. "Sorry, when did you get here."

Whitting grinned. "A few minutes ago."

Ntombi sat up and caught the book that had been resting on her chest before it hit the porch floor.

"Good catch. Been out here all night?"

Ntombi took a deep breath and released it with a smile. She yawned, stretching her arms high above her head. "Looks like it. The bigger question is, where did you come from? Am I dreaming?"

"Ah, a nightmare," Whitting said, as he moved around the small coffee table and sat in one of the wicker chairs. He draped his arms over the arms of the chair, leaned his head back, and looked up at the light-blue paint on the porch's beadboard ceiling. "No. I left my luggage in the trunk of your car. The papers I graded on the trip up are in the pocket." He straightened his neck and looked over at Ntombi. "I need them for my first class."

Ntombi looked about, trying to gain her bearings on time

and space. That's when she noticed the porch lamp had been turned off and a cashmere throw was tucked around her legs. She smiled in knowing Becca had likely tended to her as she slept. "Gee. I hadn't realized we forgot your suitcase."

Whitting glanced at his watch and then crossed his legs. The chair creaked with age and layers of paint. "So. How far did you get?" Whitting asked, gesturing toward the book.

Ntombi opened it and flipped through the pages. "Only two hundred forty pages."

"Two hundred forty pages? That's remarkable! Do you have a word for me yet?"

"Okay, one word. An essential word."

"Perfect. What is it?"

"Well, it came to me that I want to filter for eternal versus temporal words. Lots of words are temporal. Of this world. But I want to mine Edwards' work for eternal truths."

"Cool. Excellent filter. So what's the word?"

"Are you ready?"

"That I am."

"Soul."

"Soul?"

"Yes. Seems to me, Edwards had an understanding of the soul—that part of man that longs for God, even when we don't know it."

"Pascal is often credited with writing about the God-shaped hole in each of us, but . . ."

"Hmm," Ntombi said, looking past Whitting.

"Okay, so what wisdom regarding the soul does Edwards depart?"

Ntombi closed the book in her lap and gently placed her hands atop it as if the feel would somehow more clearly reveal its contents. "Much. Oh, so much!" Then, with a slight glance at

Whitting, she continued. "Ever know something and not know how to explain it?"

"Every day."

"That's where I am, but Edwards writes of the seat of our affections, our heart's desires. A true work of the Spirit, the Holy Spirit, changes one's soul. At the deepest level, the level is so deep it is of another kingdom. A true work of the Holy Spirit changes the very nature of man. It is a soul change, a change of the affections."

Whitting raised his brows, extending his oval eyes upward, revealing the soft morning light glistening against their cold blue. He grinned and shook his head.

Ntombi noticed the counter beat of his double chin as he shook his head and found it endearing. "I told you it wasn't cooked yet."

"No, no. I am just amazed at how your mind works."

"Amazed in a good way?"

He leaned back in his chair and crossed his arms over his chest. "Indeed. You do know you're not normal, don't you?"

Ntombi wrinkled her brow. She hadn't yet learned to discern the subtle difference between a genuine compliment and a roundabout insult.

Whitting smiled at her and answered without being asked. "Normal people don't fall asleep on the front porch after reading two hundred forty pages of Edwards."

"Then I am pleased to be abnormal."

"Can I ask you something else, while we're on the subject of heart's desires?"

Ntombi recognized Whitting's segue but assumed his track was theological and in keeping with Edwards' writing.

"I know we mostly talk about our research, but I want you to know I'm your friend as well."

Ntombi lowered her head slightly and looked up at Whitting. "And I yours."

"Should you ever want to talk about Mandlenkosi, I'm a good listener."

Ntombi slid back on the wicker sofa as if the extra five inches would somehow provide an escape. She placed the book on the table and pulled the throw onto her lap. She turned her head toward the front yard and watched a squirrel run up one of the large oak trees. She thought of Mandlenkosi and wondered where he was. Her chest ached. She didn't want to cry—not in front of Whitting.

Whitting turned his gaze toward the squirrel as well and sat quietly.

After what most Americans would measure an awkward silence, Ntombi turned to Whitting. "I know it is well with his soul. What I don't know is where his body is, or if body and soul are intact."

Whitting pursed his lips, nodded. "Yes. It's good to remember we are a soul with a body versus a body with a soul." He looked straight at her and continued, "What if Mandlenkosi's soul has separated?"

"Then he is with the Lord. Of that I am sure."

Whitting nodded twice. "And you would rather he was yet on earth and with you?"

Ntombi looked over at Whitting and nodded resolutely. "Yes. I want him here with me, but I don't know what is best."

Whitting raised both brows. "Ah, what do you mean by best?"

"What I want most for Mandlenkosi is God's highest good for him."

"And?"

"And I don't know what that is."

"And?"

A tear formed and moved down Ntombi's face. She turned to hide it and then wiped it from her chin with the back of her hand.

Whitting stood and made his way around the coffee table to sit beside her. Ntombi lowered her head and tucked her hands under her legs. Stretching one arm around her shoulders, he placed the other one on her arm. She glanced at him and saw that his eyes too had tears so they sat in tearful silence and wept together. Ntombi for Mandlenkosi, and Whitting perhaps for his friend, and for the general brokenness of this world.

Ntombi's sobbing slowed, and Whitting bowed his head and prayed aloud. As he finished, Ntombi wiped her tears, scooted aside a bit, then looked at her friend with a thankful smile. "Nevertheless, not my will."

Whitting's face softened. "But Thy will be done."

"Come. Let's get your suitcase."

TWENTY-EIGHT

Rapture

N tombi grabbed Emma's hand like a little girl and hurried her toward the front of the church, while Emma pointed behind them and proclaimed, "There are side doors, you know."

"Nope. Not as good."

"Well, okay then. Front door it is."

The walkway was just feet from the high outer walls of the stone sanctuary. Each stone had been carefully chiseled, long and thin, and placed artfully with coved, cream mortar to fix it in place, held fast for centuries. The massive height of the wall made Ntombi feel small. Humbled.

Just before the stone steps, Ntombi stopped mid-stride and whispered to Emma. "Listen."

Emma turned her head a moment to listen. Her face brightened. "Oh, my! Real bells."

"Yeah," Ntombi said, sounding like an all-knowing toddler.

She had been here before. She'd prayed here and listened to beautiful music here. And today she came expecting to worship in spirit and truth.

After stopping to enjoy a dose of the bells, Ntombi and Emma stepped into the entrance and were greeted by a smiling usher. Ntombi took the bulletin from his hand and directed Emma's gaze to the mosaic, saltillo tile floor, worn to a beautiful patina by all the saints who had come before them. No doubt thousands had shuffled past this exact spot, eager to adore their Lord. Today, Emma and Ntombi were among them.

Stepping just inside the sanctuary, Emma touched Ntombi's forearm to stop her. Ntombi watched her gaze about while others moved around them, eager to get a good seat. Perhaps they had seen it so much, they now took the majesty for granted. But Emma looked positively awestruck, and Ntombi was re-struck.

They found a pew near the front and took a seat. People around them spoke in low voices, but Emma and Ntombi sat quietly absorbed, allowing the open space to settle in their souls. Worship happened best when there was space for it.

The bells had been silent but then rang three crisp chimes. Emma glanced at Ntombi with a questioning look. Ntombi offered a closed-mouth grin and then whispered, "Chimes of the Trinity."

The service proceeded. Creeds, hymns, prayers. Ntombi was surprised by Emma's voice when she sang. Great speaking voices and great singing voices rarely inhabited the same chest, and Emma could preach.

The sermon came and went, the offering was collected, then the doxology. The final hymn was "Be Still, My Soul." They stood, and Ntombi mostly listened to Emma's angelic voice. She imagined it reaching the very throne of God and decided not to sing but rather to just be in the moment. When the words "it is well" echoed back for the second time, something glorious happened.

Ntombi bowed her head and prayed, not with words but with excitement. A scene of sorts began to unfold in front of her closed eyes, like it was in her mind's eye or maybe it was on her heart. She saw the ceiling of the cathedral space open, revealing the sky. It was a blue unlike any she had ever seen. Dotted amidst the blue were clouds. Pure, white clouds. Ntombi smiled softly and felt her spirit lifting above the pews. She felt beauty and joy all around and then became aware of angels, or something like angels, on either side of her. She didn't feel their touch, only the sense of being escorted as she floated upward.

She saw the scene above the sanctuary, where the sanctuary meets the sky, yet in some mysterious way, she was still part of the worship below, but it was different. More pure. Effortless.

She noticed beautiful, wispy creatures moving about in all directions. Their movements were graceful, like the gentle hands of a symphony conductor, untethered by gravity. Ntombi became aware of two thrones and knew without looking who was on each. They were the subject of the worship.

A third Person was moving about in the glorious space around the throne. Somehow his movements were different. The wispy figures joined with him but were not of the same substance. His was free, full of authority. He led; they followed. Ntombi watched them all moving together, up, down, over, and through.

She noticed an incomplete circle of saints, each standing as figures of light. They were to her left and also before the thrones but not as close to them as the moving figures. Those who were part of the circle stood talking and smiling. As she looked closer, they paused their conversation and smiled softly, as if to say hello. Ntombi returned the smile and felt a welcoming love unlike any she had known. It seemed to encompass her, making it hard to know where she stopped and where all the heavenlies started.

"It is well, it is well with my soul." As Emma continued to sing the words, Nbombi felt the image fade. Tears streamed down her face as the song ended. The benediction was bestowed and "Lift High the Cross" was sung for the recessional. As others made their way out, Emma and Ntombi took their seats again to listen and enjoy the closing organ solo.

She told Emma that she needed to go to the ladies room and left through the back doors of the sanctuary. She needed to collect her thoughts. Or maybe it was her soul she needed to collect.

Ntombi was pleased to discover the restroom empty. She faced the mirror and leaned against the counter for support. She felt so weak.

She studied her face in the mirror. It was almost as if she needed to relearn it. She looked for signs of what she'd just seen, something others might notice, just in case she needed to explain them. But everything looked the same, besides an added light in her eyes.

She breathed as deeply as she could. The earth's air some-how helped paste her soul, spirit, and body back together.

What had just happened? She knew she couldn't explain it. She didn't even understand it. Yet, on some level, she knew it was worship, heaven's worship, and she had joined in..

TWENTY-NINE

Revelation

Ntombi sat on the floor of her closet with her back against the narrow side wall. Her knees were bent and her prayer journal carefully perched atop them. She sat quietly, pen in hand, ready to push the outside world out and talk with her Maker. She liked closet prayers. Somehow they felt higher up and closer in.

Father God,

You are awesome. I am thankful. Thankful for my new friends, for Dr. Whitting, and even for Steve. I am flattered by his interest. I am grateful for Ben and Becca and their hospitality.

Father, yesterday at church. Thank You for inviting me, for lifting me up in worship, and for gracing me with your presence. May I ask some questions? Who were those people? I understand there is a communion of saints, and, oh, there's that verse, in Hebrews I think. It talks about being surrounded by a cloud of witnesses. They were in a cloud. And that old song? How does it go?

Ntombi looked up from her journal, closed her eyes, and sang what she could remember of the lyrics to "Will the Circle Be Unbroken."

Finishing the song, she returned to writing in her journal.

Sorry, that's all I remember. But, it's like the song. Except the circle was broken. It wasn't complete. Am I the missing link?

She looked for a moment at the hems of her three dresses hanging above her. She reached over and pulled a tiny piece of string off one and returned to her journaling.

Father, how about a word of scripture? Rather, if it's your will and in *your* time, will you reveal to me all I am to learn from what happened?

She looked up again, this time with a bit of surprise, then continued her questions. She rolled her lips in and finished writing in her journal.

Father, I was caught up in watching heavenly worship. I am in awe to have seen it. Will you be with me today? And with Tata? And with Mandlenkosi, wherever he is? Will you keep us from evil and evil from us? In Jesus' name, amen.

That afternoon, Ntombi sat nervously on the same park bench she had enjoyed on her first day in Charleston and for several chats with Daniel. It felt different now. The city was starting to feel a bit more like home. Of course, she still had a lot of questions about Daniel—simple things like, who was he and where did he come from? And where did he go? As for the bench, it felt less holy. Maybe the city was less holy too without Daniel around.

She felt the cool, damp wood with its century-old layers of paint and was glad for the sun in the southern sky. Warmth. She needed warmth. What would he think if she was shivering when he arrived?

Steve approached from behind. "Ntombi, I'm so sorry I'm late."

Ntombi, a bit startled by his arrival, stood and turned to him.

"We had a team meeting, reviewing tapes and all. It went longer than I expected." Steve rounded the bench and took Ntombi's hands, bending to kiss her on the cheek. When he did, she noticed his just-showered scent, the slight dampness of his ringlets, and the smoothness of his cheek against hers. She felt his high cheekbones, hard, without the least bit of pudginess.

"No problem," she said. "Isn't that what y'all say?"

"Most do," he said, still holding her hands and looking at her. "But not me."

Ntombi pulled her hands from his and dropped them to her side but didn't take her gaze from him. "You know, I don't like it either. Especially as a response when someone says thank you."

Steve nodded his agreement. "Right. I prefer you're welcome or my pleasure."

Ntombi patted the seat beside her. "Me too." Instead of sitting, Steve offered her a hand.

"Shall we walk?"

Ntombi smiled softly and took his hand. She rose gracefully from the bench. She was glad to be moving and decided it was okay to enjoy Steve's company. She imagined Mandlenkosi walking with them. He would like Steve. Mandlenkosi liked basketball too but rarely played. He was tall but used to joke that his "leaper" was broken. She had to admit, his stately frame looked far more at home on horseback than in gym shorts.

Steve steered the conversation. "Tell me about you."

Ntombi glanced up at him. She liked the fact that he was taller. "Well, I grew up in South Africa but not in a big city. My mother died when I was five, and my father spent most of his life as a tracker on a game reserve."

"She died when you were five. That must have been hard."

"I don't remember a lot about her, just that she was beautiful and gracious and kind."

Steve glanced at Ntombi with a slight smile. "Tell me about your childhood."

"Well, I had a unique childhood," Ntombi said with a shrug. "I lived and played on a game reserve. Have you ever been to one?"

"No," Steve said, then pulled on her hand and turned her toward him. "I would love to go some time."

"Game reserves are really huge," Ntombi said, ignoring the cue to invite him. "Kwandwe is 22,000 hectares, and it has only dirt roads. It wouldn't seem much like a game reserve with paved roads. Anyway, it's not like you can live in a city and commute there, especially with Tata's job. He needed to be available."

"To track stuff?"

Ntombi laughed a bit. "Actually, yes. The animals are called wild for a reason. They're mostly left alone to roam and hunt and just be. Most of the time Tata's job was to find the animals for the guests on photo safaris. But on rare occasions, there was an urgent need for a tracker."

"Like what?"

"Well, this only became urgent in the last minute, but just a few months back, before I left, I shot a rabid black-backed jackal."

"You shot him? Remind me not to tick you off."

"Good idea," Ntombi said, then winked at him. "Seriously, it wasn't something I normally had to do, but there was no time to get someone else. A little girl was in danger. Tata taught me to shoot when I was nine."

"What about schools? Where did you go?"

"At first on the reserve and then a weekday boarding school. It was an excellent school with lots of international students."

"It shows."

Ntombi turned and smirked.

Steve laughed. "No, seriously. I meant that in a good way. I expect the school was expensive."

"Yeah. I don't know what Tata made, but somehow I always had everything—and went to the best schools." Ntombi threw her hands up and shrugged.

"Maybe you had a secret admirer. That is, in addition to me."

Ntombi released Steve's hand and jabbed him in the side with her elbow. "You're not so secret, though."

Steve grabbed his side in mock pain. "And all this time I thought I was being surreptitious. Or is it obsequious?"

Ntombi crossed her arms and dropped them across her chest. "You are succeeding at neither."

Steve smiled. He placed a hand on the small of her back, gestured forward with the other. "Well, then, I need to try harder."

While they walked on, he kept his hand gently touching her back for a moment. She liked it there. It was something she had noticed with other couples. It felt good like he was protecting her without limiting her.

Their walk and their witty dialogue continued as they stopped for coffee. The Corner Coffee looked different without Daniel. She smiled as she decided it best not to tell Steve about Daniel, the basement, or the rooftop. And certainly not about her married man encounter.

They each ordered a beverage and headed outside to a small café table. The air had warmed to the perfect temperature, almost as if it weren't there. Still, Steve suggested a table in the sun. "It's still February, though you wouldn't know it today," he said as they sat.

"Seems to me the perfect day."

Steve lifted his coffee cup with both hands, then paused, his eyebrows lifting slightly. "The perfect day—in more ways than one."

Ntombi returned his words with a soft smile and took a sip of tea.

They sat for a moment in silence. A small, moss-laden wall fountain was attached to a brick wall beside their table. Ntombi watched the water flow from a lion's mouth and then spread out over and around the moss. The moss seemed to be artfully placed by a master's hand—just the right amount and in just the right places. By the time the water traveled the short distance between the lion's mouth and the basin, it had meandered to soft, tinkling droplets.

Steve looked at Ntombi and then at the fountain. "You seem deep in thought."

"I'm just thinking about all the changes in my life since I left Africa. And I like the fountain."

"Me too." Steve reached over and touched the moss.

Ntombi, for the first time, noticed his reach. He had long, muscular arms. She caught herself just before considering them wrapped around her. Instead, she imagined how good they must be for basketball.

Steve shook some of the water from his hand, wiped the rest on his jeans. "Would you rather walk than sit?"

"Yes, that would be nice."

"I'll get us some paper cups."

As they left the coffee shop, Ntombi noticed how people stared at them. She wondered if they appeared odd but then decided they were likely staring at Steve. He was, after all, a local star.

They walked the last block partly in silence, interrupted only by a few remarks on the various scenic views and historical plaques on old houses. They eventually arrived back at the park where their journey had begun. Children were playing, and tourists were strolling along the harbor. Ntombi noticed the worn paths crisscrossing through the park and decided parks are better when they are well worn. South Africa has well-worn parks, and this one felt like home to her.

Ntombi was headed for the same bench where they started when Steve redirected her path. "Let's park it here for a minute," he said, pointing toward a picnic table. He leaned against it with his legs outstretched and crossed at the ankles in front of him. He reached for Ntombi's forearm to stop her and gently turned her toward him.

Her first thought was that they were at eye level. His look left her speechless. It was deep as if he wanted to do more than look at her—he wanted to behold her. He looked as if he was studying her deeply and enjoying the endeavor.

He pulled her closer, leaving his arm around her waist longer than Ntombi felt comfortable with but also not as long as she wanted. There was something about him. Like a magnetic field that drew her and warned her at the same time. She wondered if others noticed it. She also wondered how many other women he'd looked at in the same way. She decided it was many.

In a softer, more sincere voice than she had heard him use before, he said, "I have a dance I have to attend on Saturday night. Will you go with me? Please?"

Ntombi leaned back a bit and answered without thinking. "That would be lovely."

Steve sat up a bit straighter and smiled. "Great. It's formal. I'll pick you up at six-thirty. Dinner is part of the event." Then he stood, gave her an imaginary tip of the hat, turned and walked to his car.

Ntombi watched him walk away. Why had she said yes? She meant no. Surely she meant to say no.

Steve turned around when he reached his car, smiled and waved. Ntombi returned both. She couldn't help but notice that he looked like an athlete, even moved like one, but he sure didn't sound like one. Then again, how would she know what an athlete was supposed to sound like. It's not as if she'd known one before.

Something told her that soon, she would know this one. Of course, it was how she would get to know him that scared her.

Ntombi decided to end the day with a verse from her Bible. She slipped between the sheets and read by the light of her bedside lamp. It was not a custom of hers to play Bible roulette, but she thought she'd just see what God had to say. She closed her eyes, held her Bible up by the sides, and let it fall open in her lap. She popped open her eyes and looked down at the page. One verse—actually, one phrase in one verse—spoke to her, beckoning her to read it again and again: It is through Isaac. Isaac? What could that mean?

The words ran over and over in her mind like an earworm. Even after she turned off the light and pulled the covers under her chin, they played.

It is through Isaac.

She had so many questions. Who was Isaac? She didn't know anyone named Isaac. But what else could it mean? What was God trying to tell her? She then remembered the context in scripture. Isaac was Abraham's son, and God fulfilled his covenant through Isaac's descendants.

She decided maybe it was just an odd consequence of bad Bible roulette but still couldn't get the phrase out of her head. It was stuck like a skipping record. It is through Isaac, it is through Isaac . . .

As she started to doze off, she remembered a game she and Mandlenkosi used to play with his younger twin sisters. They would bury things in the backyard in a way that the girls could find them—just hard enough so they'd have to search, but not so hard that they would become discouraged and give up. Each day, he and Ntombi would bury something new. When the girls arrived home from school, they would run to the backyard to dig for the hidden treasure.

God was like that. He hid things—great treasures of truth—for us to find.

Maybe that's what this was. The words, it is through Isaac, just might be one of those treasures God wanted her to find.

THIRTY

Green Peacocks

Ntombi stepped just inside the sunroom door and announced her arrival. "Becca, it's me. Am I too early?"

"No, darlin', it's never too early for shopping. I'm comin'."

Becca entered the room with a scarf under one arm, hooking an earring into one ear, the other held between her lips. She removed it and put it in her other ear, all without letting the scarf fall. "Gettin' dressed seems to take longer when it's a sunny winter's day. One doesn't want to don spring attire too early nor burn up mid-afternoon."

Becca finished the earring task and began futzing with her scarf in the sunroom mirror. "Now, let's talk a bit about this event. Do you have a printed invitation?"

"No, ma'am." Ntombi watched Becca in the mirror.

Becca pushed her already perfect bob up. "Well, we will just have to make do. Where is the event?"

"I don't know."

Becca turned toward Ntombi with one hand on her hip. "Lord have mercy. Do you know what time it starts?"

"Yes, ma'am. He is picking me up at six-thirty. Dinner is part of the event and then the dance."

"He did say it was formal? I believe a good starting point is my closet. My dresses will be way too short, but it will give us an opportunity to see what looks best on you. Always, always begin your search in your own closet."

As they entered Becca's closet, Ntombi's eyes grew wider. It was a small room with everything arranged by color. One would never suspect such a treasure trove in what was otherwise an understated plantation. Ntombi thought how she liked the word "plantation" and how it rolled off her tongue.

Becca pointed toward the evening section and left Ntombi to her shopping. She carefully selected a silver, satin sheath dress. Its design was simple, and it fit perfectly, except for the length.

"Come out, darlin'. Which one do you have on?"

Ntombi was unsure of her modeling skills but knew the heart of her one-woman audience. As she exited, she found Becca seated squarely in a wing chair with her arms draped slightly over each arm of the chair. Lifting both hands in the air, she said, "You are lovely. Well, except for the hem, of course." With a flick of both wrists followed by a sweeping motion of her fingers, she added, "We could add a ruffle."

Ntombi looked down at her bony ankles and oversized bare feet. She smiled as she noticed the stark contrast to her upper body. It was as if beauty and grace gave way to strong and ordinary about eight inches from the floor.

"Pick something with bright colors. I want to see you in color. Since it's evening, we can break some of the rules. One must know them to break them. I enjoy pushing the envelope."

Envelope? Ntombi thought for a moment about the fashion envelope as she again surveyed Becca's selection of evening wear. She had never considered a dress and the idea of "pushing the envelope" in the same sentence. She smiled and chose a chiffon gown in a floral print with tiny spaghetti straps. The colors faded from bright yellows to lavenders to greens. It was certainly colorful. The fabric seemed almost as light as the air around it. Ntombi twirled back and forth and watched the counterturn of the fabric. Her mind wandered this time to Cape Town. From inside the closet, she asked, "Becca, was the Silly Walks Man at work when you visited Cape Town?"

"Oh, my goodness, yes! He's hilarious. He followed Ben as we left the café. His rendition of Ben's swagger was a sight to see. I was just so thankful he didn't choose me. I don't want to know what my walk looks like. Do you have anything on yet?"

"Yes. You asked for color." Ntombi stepped from the closet and looked down at herself, running her hands over the fabric as if it needed straightening.

Becca instructed her. "Stand up straight." She eyed Ntombi up and down. "Now that's color! In a good way. You can carry it. I am afraid it wears me, but you, my dear, can pull it off. Way too summa for this time of year, though, but the chiffon is nice. We will look for a patterned, soft flowing fabric with deeper colors. You must make an entrance, my dear, not that being on Steve's arm isn't enough."

Ntombi looked down at the dress again. "I'm not sure I want to stand out. I'm afraid people are already talking about me."

"Of course they are. Goodness, child, you want them talking about you. As Granny Bert used to say, 'If they ain't talkin' about you, you ain't shit.'"

With wide eyes, Ntombi laughed and quickly covered her mouth with her hand. Becca returned the laugh, then motioned Ntombi back into the closet with a flick of her hand. Ntombi marveled at how Becca could direct with a hand gesture and teach with an unseemly word.

On the drive to town, Becca outlined the plan of action. She tended to think out loud and listed seven or eight stores before narrowing it to three. As they drove, Ntombi thought about how much fun this was. It was new to her. Shopping at home was more of a chore, one Tata never seemed to like. This was an event, a day with Becca. She decided to enjoy it.

The first store yielded nothing, but in Becca's words, they had learned a lot.

"What did we learn?"

"Not to bother with that store."

As they walked down the street, Ntombi marveled at how Becca could stream seemingly unrelated thoughts together with confidence.

"I'm sorry I keep changing the subject. Ben calls it whirligigging. Anyway, about your eyes. I'm thinking it would be marvelous if we could find something with shades of deep blue-green, almost teal to bring out the blues and greens in your eyes."

Her eyes? She had never thought of her eyes as deep or blue-green. She had always just thought them odd. All of her friends had lovely brown or nearly black eyes. Ntombi thought of her mother and remembered her eyes. She had nice eyes— dark, soft, friendly, and loving.

"We may have made this search more difficult."

We? Ntombi was just along for the ride.

"Oh, there's Caplands. Let's go in. They are way overpriced and rather snobbish, but it's good to occasionally reset one's palette."

As they entered the store, Ntombi noticed a pair of cowhide pants. The big brown spots caught her eye. She wondered who in their right mind would wear such a thing. The price tag seemed equally absurd at just under sixteen hundred dollars.

Ntombi stood holding the tag in her hand as Becca made her way over. A well-dressed gentleman emerged from a back room. Without even a hello, Becca turned to him and said, "Lord, Sloan, what have y'all taken to buying?"

"They are for the nouveau riche, my dear."

"I would say so. We eat them but wouldn't be caught dead

wearing them." With that, she smiled at him and turned for the door. "Thank you, Sloan," she said over her shoulder. "Good to see you. Tell Kara I said hello." Then, with an added smile and a backward wave, she said, "We'll be back when you have something for the likes of us."

Ntombi wondered what "the likes of us" looked like. One old money Charlestonian flanked by a tall Xhosan girl in search of a blue-green evening gown with enough hem to let out for a dance at who knows where with a young man she hardly knew.

Out on the sidewalk, the smell of roasted coffee beans infused the air. Ntombi realized they were near The Corner Coffee.

"Let's stop up there for coffee and a scone," Becca said, pointing in the direction of the coffee shop. "It's best not to shop on an empty stomach."

Ntombi thought of Daniel and how he would enjoy this shopping day. He had an uncommon eye for beauty. She wondered if he were off on another assignment. Had he changed his appearance? Surely he had. The dreadlocks and Blues Brother's clothes wouldn't work just anywhere.

When it was Ntombi's turn to order, she suddenly felt the urge to ask for him. "Is Daniel working today?"

"Daniel? We don't have anyone by that name."

"Oh, I must have gotten the name wrong."

Ntombi wondered if it was okay to lie about an angel, or even to ask. Did asking for him show a lack of faith, a lack of appreciation? Thankfully, Becca hadn't heard her question, or if she had, she didn't inquire.

Once their coffee and pastries were served, they chose a wooden table with comfy chairs. As they settled in, Becca said, "So tell me about Mandlenkosi. How did you meet?"

Ntombi took a careful sip from her steaming cup before

answering. "We grew up together. I have known him since primary school. It was the year I started to school and also the year my mother died. I remember her death like it was yesterday. The children in my class didn't quite know what to do, except for Mandlenkosi. My first day back to school, he brought me a flower, one he had found. He gave it to me and said, 'You need a friend. I will be your friend.'"

"Wow. At five?"

Ntombi nodded. "Yes. He was strong and kind, even then. We sometimes had a tumultuous friendship but always loving. We competed at sport and games until he was clearly out of my league. Then we competed at schoolwork. I could hold my own there. And he was always trying to trick me. I learned to read his face eventually and know when he was up to something. I never told him how I knew." Ntombi took a sip of her tea and looked over the top of the cup at Becca. "To tell him how I knew would be to give up my edge."

Ntombi continued, telling Becca about the first time she realized she had feelings for Mandlenkosi and the awkwardness of moving from long-time friends to the first kiss. Time passed as she talked and Becca listened. Then, with a slight shake of her head and a deliberate turn of her gaze back toward Becca, Ntombi took a deep breath and exhaled. "Well, I guess we had best get busy shopping."

"Good idea. I've thought of just the place to go. They'll only have a few dresses for such an event, but I expect one of them will be just what we're looking for."

Becca was right, as usual. When the deep-green, patterned dress fell from Ntombi's shoulders over her waist and to the floor, she knew it was the one. A closer look revealed the delicate display of pattern on chiffon—muted and artfully arranged peacock feathers. Beautiful blues and greens mixed with warm browns.

"Are you coming out? I want to see it."

Ntombi, possibly for the first time ever, looked in the mirror and said, "I like it."

"Well then let me see."

Ntombi strolled from the dressing room with her head held high, her shoulders back, and her torso erect, resisting the urge to twirl.

"Oh my. That is it. You are stunning. Absolutely stunning. Turn around."

With the command, Ntombi twirled with one hand outstretched and a slight lift of the dress in the other.

"It's perfect. Didn't it have a belt? Let's see it with the belt."

Not knowing quite what to do with a five-inch-wide, rhinestone belt atop a chiffon halter gown, the sales clerk was called to assist.

Becca stepped back for the full view. "Either way. I like it either way. You'll need shoes. You can even wear heels with that."

Ntombi smiled as she realized her height was not a problem—with the dress or with her date.

"Take it off. Let's bag it up and go shoe shopping. Shoes are important, you know."

Ntombi wondered about heels. Kwandwe hadn't afforded much opportunity for heels. She was most at home in her bush boots. Heels and chiffon were perhaps an acquired taste.

Ntombi retired to the dressing room, removed the dress, and sat holding it in her arms. It even smelled good. The entire store smelled good. She supposed other girls had days like this all the time, special days, days spent with their mothers. She wondered if they took days like this for granted. Suddenly a deep sense of longing settled in her chest.

Becca's voice in the distance drew Ntombi's thoughts back

to the moment. She stood and carefully hung her special dress on the hanger, thinking how thankful she was for it and for Becca, her mother for the day.

THIRTY-ONE

Open Door

Ntombi stared up at two massive heart pine doors. She pushed the right door—it opened easier than she expected—and stepped into a narthex with a ceiling that soared high above the room. She looked up and then down at the well-worn stone slabs beneath her feet that hosted a tattered Oriental rug. Both spoke to the lives that had passed through this space. It felt to her like a holy space.

A second set of doors on the far wall framed the space. They were made of dark mahogany and held leaded glass inserts.

The left door opened, and Whitting's voice interrupted Ntombi's touring thoughts. "Hey, you?"

Ntombi smiled big. "Whitting? I didn't know you were already here."

"It's a good place to arrive early."

"Ah."

"Thank you for meeting me here," he said. "Let's sit. How about pew forty-seven?"

The front of the sanctuary was adorned with a massive stained-glass window. "Is that Michael?" Ntombi asked, pointing at the image.

"Good eye. He is slaying evil."

"Some days I wish he'd hurry up and git-er-done."

"Git-er-done? Where did you pick that up?

"TV. Like it?"

"Suffice it to say, it doesn't suit you."

"Thank you, sir," she said, with a slight bow of her head.

Whitting grinned and returned her gesture. "My pleasure."

It seemed okay to Ntombi to laugh in this sanctuary. Some sanctuaries don't like laughter. Here, it seemed right at home. Or maybe this was laughter's home, where it began. It had to begin somewhere.

The eighteenth-century architecture had a softness to it as if the rough edges had been honed with time. Marble memorial plaques lined the walls; the honorable somebody, and a Mr. Deas, and a young man named Parsons.

Pew forty-seven was one of many family boxes, no doubt originally intended to corral the children as the family gathered to worship with like-hearted folks. Whitting turned the wooden toggle, pulled open the small, hinged door, and extended an arm, inviting Ntombi in. She nodded, stepped up, and noticed the narrow space between the pew and the box in front of it. As she sat, the cool of the mahogany beneath her made the holy place feel more real.

Whitting had a certain jolliness about him today as if he were up to something. But before any mischief could begin, or maybe as a way to suppress it, Whitting pulled a blue, leather kneeler from beneath the pew and knelt on it. He made the sign of the cross from his forehead to his heart and across his chest, then folded his hands and bowed his head.

Ntombi found another kneeler and knelt beside him. There was so much for which to give thanks. They prayed in silence together and in a flood of words to their Maker. This was a place accustomed to prayer. One would have to try hard not to pray.

After a few minutes, Whitting settled back on the pew, and

Ntombi followed suit. She liked pew forty-seven. Whitting turned slightly to face her, and she did the same.

"What are you learning from Prince's words?" she asked.

"Much. It helps to have his handwritten thoughts to parallel the published articles. Of particular interest is how the Awakening spread—oh, and the long-term effects. All of which can wait. How are the interviews coming?"

"Quite well," Ntombi said, knowing her short, simple answer wouldn't be acceptable.

"Anything becoming clear?"

"The voice. There is as much to learn about the call as the Caller. To discern call, one must distinguish God's voice from competing voices."

"Or even counterfeit voices. The pastors during the Awakening searched for ways to discern and communicate the true words of God from the counterfeit."

"Edwards certainly shines a bright light."

"Indeed he does. What else is coming clear?"

Ntombi thought for a moment, not sure how much she should say. She grabbed a ringlet of curls and twisted them. As she did, Becca's motherly voice surfaced in her mind: Don't play with your hair. She smiled and placed her hand back in her lap. "Do you believe in the communion of saints?"

Whitting nodded. "One need only walk into this space to know we are surrounded by a cloud of witnesses."

There it was again. That cloud thing. As if Whitting somehow knew about the circle in the cloud.

"Can I tell you about a dream I had?" Whitting asked.

Ntombi nodded an emphatic yes.

Whitting's face became animated as he told his dream. Ntombi had come to enjoy his expressions, especially when he was in his element. This was his kind of space. He was like a soul born at the wrong time, one put here to teach us about the past and those who had come before us. As he talked, Ntombi noticed a ray of light softly filtering through the stained glass, giving Whitting a distinct glow about his plump cheeks and large unkempt eyebrows, all of which added flair to his story-telling.

"In the dream, I was climbing a long staircase, a really long staircase. I remember light all around. Everything was bright white. I also remember the clothing—it was white. I was robed in white, and the people at the top of the stairs were in white. What stood out to me was their conversation. Those at the top of the stairs were seated around a table and were in deep conversation. Their dialogue was intense—joyfully intense—and truly interesting. I don't remember any of their words. I was just a bystander. Oh, and the clothes are important."

Ntombi cocked her chin down a bit. "The clothes? How so?"

"In other dreams, I am missing clothing. Not sure the psychological implications of that."

Ntombi laughed and shook her head at her friend, noticing he had done a good job of dressing himself today.

Whitting went on, "To me, it was a glimpse of the communion of the saints."

Ntombi placed both hands on the pew and lifted herself up slightly. "Cool. Do we participate? Now, I mean? Before heaven?"

Whitting raised a bushy eyebrow. "Hmm. Seems we do, and maybe we are at this moment."

With that Ntombi turned to face the front of the church and allowed the present communion to continue without words. Minutes passed as the two sat in silence. Then, bells, beautifully melodic, chimed three o'clock and broke the silence. They seemed familiar, like the ones Ntombi had enjoyed on her first day in the city.

Whitting followed their cue. "I have something to ask you. Or, rather, to ask of you."

Ntombi's voice softened. "Okay, but may I ask something first?"

"Fire away."

"You are welcome not to answer this question or even to put it off till later."

"But?"

Ntombi lowered her head and looked over at her friend. "What happened to your wife?"

As soon as Ntombi asked the question, Whitting slid as far away as he could in the cubicle and pulled one leg up under the other. He leaned back against the dividing panel and looked at Ntombi. As she waited for him to respond, he fidgeted a bit and turned to face the front. Ntombi could see a tear welling. Maybe she'd been wrong to ask.

"It was an early, cold winter. Elizabeth and I were at my parent's mountain house for Thanksgiving. The house was built on the hillside and had three stories above the garage. On the Friday after Thanksgiving, my father went to the store to get some mustard for turkey sandwiches. When he came home, he parked in the garage beneath the house and accidentally left the engine running. None of us heard it. Three died that night—my wife, my mother, and my father."

Whitting sat quietly for a moment, and Ntombi watched him, not knowing what to say.

"I'd had a lingering cough, so sometime during the night, I went to an empty bedroom on the top floor to keep from waking Elizabeth. I opened a window, thinking the mountain air would be good for me."

Ntombi watched her friend and felt his grief flow like a molten river from his soul to hers. It was a thick river, the kind that made it hard to move.

The tear in Whitting's eye, slowly formed and made its way down his face. He turned to look at Ntombi, wiped the tear from his neck. "They would never wake again on this side of eternity," he said, then took a deep breath. "My parents were on up in years, but Elizabeth was only thirty-nine."

The pair turned again to face the altar and sat for a moment in silence as Whitting wiped tears from beneath each eye with his forefinger. Composure came for each of them, then Whitting turned to face her and changed the subject.

"Now for my question, or, rather, my request of you."

"Sure," Ntombi said, as she felt a yes welling up even before he could ask.

"I brought you here to St. Michael's because of what is happening here the weekend after next. The college and St. Michael's are co-hosting a conference."

Ntombi listened intently, ready to accept what she assumed would be an invitation to attend.

Whitting continued. "I am one of the speakers and, well, another has had to cancel."

Ntombi turned in the pew slightly and knocked a stack of Bibles over. As she bent to pick them up, she asked, "Goodness, what will they do on such short notice?"

"I would like you to fill his spot."

Ntombi sat up quickly, only one Bible retrieved. "With what?"

THIRTY-TWO

The Dance

Ntombi stood facing the antique, full-length mirror with Becca by her side. Becca studied a belt with large, quartz-like stones. "Let's just try it," she said, before carefully placing it around Ntombi's waist. She tied the three satin spaghetti ribbons in the back, commenting as she did. "Oh yes, yes." Then, backing away and folding her arms as an artist steps away from his easel, said, "The belt draws the eye to the small of your back, and your back is exquisite."

Ntombi's eyes were wide, her head slightly tilted, and her brow way too serious for the occasion. She glanced at Becca in the mirror. She never before had thought of her back, much less how it looked with a rhinestone sash.

"Let me look at you. Turn," Becca said, twirling her finger in the air.

Ntombi raised her arms to each side, like a ballerina going into a pirouette, and turned slowly, gracefully across the floor. Becca, now ten feet away, smiled and shook her head.

"What?"

"You are absolutely beautiful. Inside and out." Becca wiped a tear with the back of her hand. "Go, my child, and have the time of your life."

As if on cue, the doorbell rang. Ntombi felt her heartbeat quicken and looked to Becca for help. Becca patted the air with one hand. "Wait. Just wait. A lady never rushes in. Ben will get the door. He has some questions for Steve anyway."

After what seemed like too long, Becca made her way down the hall. Ntombi listened through the half-open door as Becca introduced herself.

Ntombi took a deep breath. She walked to the door but stopped in front of it. Then she pulled her shoulders back and down, opened the door, and stepped through.

Becca moved to one side as Ntombi entered the room. Steve stopped mid-sentence and stood in silence, lips parted. As Ntombi continued toward Steve, Ben crossed the room to Becca and placed an arm around her shoulders.

Ntombi's eyes never left Steve's. She finished her thirty-foot approach with a slight curtsy and a soft smile. He gently took each of her hands, stepped back a bit, smiled, then bowed, bringing her right hand to his mouth for a delicate kiss.

Ben broke the over-the-top formality, providing a smooth segue to reality and a less than awkward exit by opening the front door and announcing, "Well. Looks like your chariot awaits."

Ntombi caught sight of the Bentley and the chauffeur standing at attention and hurried through the door like a little girl toward a pony.

She stopped in the doorway and turned back toward Steve. "What a surprise!"

"Oh, the car? No, that's only part of the surprise. The real surprise is inside."

They walked to the car, and the chauffeur opened the back door. As soon as he did, Emma's voice escaped from the cavernous back seat. "Hey, girl. Wanna dance?"

"Emma!" Immediately Ntombi's angst for the evening vanished. She jumped into the car and plopped herself beside her new best friend, taking a moment to rearrange her dual-layered chiffon dress.

Next to Emma sat a man. Emma gestured toward him. "Meet my husband. This is Doc. Well, his real name is Xavier, but everyone calls him Doc."

"It is so good to meet you finally," Ntombi said, giving Doc a one-pump handshake.

As the night progressed, Ntombi found she was enjoying herself. She had never been to a ball and certainly never been on the arm of a star. When people approached Steve, it was as if they had rehearsed what they would say and do. Each had a little phrase, like a script they had practiced beforehand. They sounded so awkward, but it was still kind of funny to watch.

When she and Steve finally caught a rare moment alone, Steve turned and leaned in toward Ntombi. "The music will start soon, and we'll have some time to ourselves," he said. "Perhaps, I should have warned you about these events."

"Not at all. It is all new to me and quite interesting."

"You're too kind. If we manage to have one genuine conversation tonight, other than with each other, it will be a miracle."

"I believe in miracles," Ntombi said and winked.

As promised, the lights soon dimmed, and the music began. Ntombi had not anticipated a full orchestra. The dance steps she had rehearsed in her mind were not at all what was needed here.

Steve bowed slightly and extended a hand. "My lady, may I have the honor of this dance?" Ntombi's hand rested atop Steve's as they made their way to the dance floor. Without a word, they began waltzing and twirling.

All of Ntombi's attention was on Steve. The dance seemed to flow as if coming from somewhere unbeknownst to her. Some of the crowd eventually cleared the dance floor and became spectators, watching Ntombi and Steve move gracefully over the floor. They danced as if immersed in the joy of all creation and each other.

Just then, Becca's words came to Ntombi: Just be. A smile spread across her face, and her head drifted back and to the left just a bit more as they twirled.

Soon the song ended, and gentle applause erupted. Steve, as if sensing Ntombi's discomfort, placed his right hand on the small of her back and gently guided her off the dance floor and through the massive, paned doors to the balcony. They made their way to the edge of the terrace and looked across the expanse at the manicured English gardens. Ntombi felt what she didn't want to feel. It was almost like an ache but a good ache.

Steve slipped his hands low around her waist, turned her, and pulled her toward him. She turned her head, placing it on his chest, avoiding his gaze.

He loosened his grip. Ntombi's hands slid up to his shoulders to put space between them. Slowly, she moved away and turned her back to the gardens. Steve did the same, and they both leaned against the balcony's stone balustrade wall and stared over the gala-lit ballroom.

Steve interrupted the silence. "How about some punch?"

Ntombi breathed deeply and released it. "Punch would be good."

"Do you even like punch?"

"Hate it. Let's get some."

As they passed their assigned table, Ntombi grabbed Emma and whisked her off to the ladies room. On the way, Emma looked up at her and shook her head. "Wow. I didn't know you could dance like that."

"Neither did I. Must be a private school thing. They made us practice."

Emma locked her arm through Ntombi's. "That, my dear, was more than a private school dance lesson. Beautiful. Absolutely beautiful. Of course, the two of you eating ribs would be a thing of beauty."

Inside the ladies room, they both made a beeline for the mirrors. As if on cue, both extended their lips to reapply some lip color. Following Emma's lead, Ntombi rolled her lips together and side to side, then asked, "Will you be ready to leave soon?"

"We're here for you. Just give us the word."

"It was thoughtful of Steve to invite you. I am not sure where I would be now if it weren't for you."

About a half hour later, the four of them were back inside the car. Steve had planned the return trip. The chauffeur's first stop was Ntombi's cottage. She was somewhat relieved as she realized their goodnight wouldn't be private. Steve walked her to the door and gently placed a welcomed kiss just to the side of her mouth. Ntombi expressed her thanks, first glancing into his eyes, then away, as she spoke.

"The pleasure is mine," he said.

Ntombi opened her cottage door. She chose not to turn around to watch Steve get in the car. The thought of Emma's all-knowing eyes was enough to keep her focused straight ahead.

Once inside, Ntombi leaned back against the door. As the sound of the Bentley diminished down the drive, Ntombi stepped forward, stretched both arms overhead, lowered them, forming a half circle, and twirled.

Just then, Ntombi noticed her bed was turned down. She smiled. That was Becca—thinking of every detail. Yet, something was amiss. The large room was lit only by the exterior lights, but there, on her bed, she saw a package. The cardboard exterior told of its long journey. The layers of tape gave evidence to its having been opened and closed many times. The stamps were South African.

With box in hand, she made her way to the other side of the room. The large window facing the garden offered just enough light from the lamppost to see the sender's address. It was from Mandlenkosi's mother, penned in her own hand. Ntombi knew it well. His mother was a gifted writer and had a knack for words of encouragement. Perhaps this was a care package from home.

Ntombi settled into a chair and placed the package on her lap. With more careful study, she could tell the box had traveled many miles, even before making its way to Mandlenkosi's mother and then to her. Angst oozed into every part of Ntombi's body as she realized this was not a gift. It was ominous.

Ntombi began peeling off the layers of tape. She considered the scissors but wanted to touch each inch, unwind each strand. It took little effort to release the flaps from the heat dried layers of tape, some old, yellowed, and crackly, some new and sticky.

She sat alone in near darkness, too aware of her quickened heartbeat and shaky fingers. She lifted the flaps of the box. There, atop the contents, was a note from Mandlenkosi's mother. Beneath it was a shoe. Just one. A man's dress shoe.

Fear entered Ntombi's chest like a dollop of molten lead. She could feel it move to her arms and legs. She sat, heavy, as she lifted the shoe from the box and brought it closer to her face. It was Mandlenkosi's shoe, his dress shoe, the left one. It was missing its shoestring.

Her mind raced to collect the many possible meanings. Did this mean he was alive or was he found dead with only one shoe on?

The note. She hadn't read the note. Fear rose within her as she slowly unfolded the sheet of paper.

Our dearest Ntombi,

We hope you are well and enjoying your time in America. It is with love and a sense of what is right that I send this to you. I struggled between not wanting to hurt you and knowing you need the truth, even if it is not yet complete.

This shoe was found nearly a kilometer from the site of the wreck. It was alone, a single shoe. The detectives do not know what it means other than they suspect Mandlenkosi was alive after the crash and walked some distance. The other explanation is that the shoe was stolen, but they do not believe anyone would take just one shoe and then drop it.

This is but one more piece of the truth. My hope and prayers are that it is like one of the few raindrops just before a downpour, and the downpour of revelation will come soon.

Ntombi carefully refolded the letter and set it to the side. She lifted the shoe and examined it as a surgeon would look at a tumor before placing it in a specimen jar. At first, she inspected it without emotion, almost certain she would see something the detectives had missed. Crossing the room, she quickly found the bank of light switches. In an instant, the carriage house was lit like a landing strip. She reached for the antique, horn-handled magnifying glass atop the desk, realizing then that it wasn't just for looks.

She inspected the shoe from top to bottom, looking inside and smelling it. The magnification revealed traces of sandy soil. Tiny remnants. She wondered if they had analyzed it and quickly decided that surely they had.

Blood. She would look for blood on the shoe. With spyglass in hand, she carefully inspected it, looking specifically for blood this time. It was so hard to tell. Everything had dried into a caked, flaky mess.

At that point, the voice entered. Just look at you. The lights are probably waking people for miles. You should turn them off. After all, you're still in the dark. You may as well sit in the dark. And besides, what good is one shoe? Why did she even send it?

Ntombi felt a painful ache in her chest. She sighed, turned the lights off, and walked across the room carrying the shoe, and grabbed a pillow from the bed on her way. The openness of the room was somehow too much for her. She needed a corner, a closed space. She made her way to the tiny kitchen where she slumped to the floor in the spot the cabinets make their sharp turn. As she did, the lead in her chest gave way to gasping tears.

The voice returned, and with it, a wave of fear. It nagged at her: You should have gone to the closet. You only have protection on two sides.

Ntombi looked at the doorway and wanted a door to close. She curled up in the corner, trying to be as small as she could. Hugging the pillow and the shoe, she tucked her dress around her bare feet and ankles.

The voice subsided then. Perhaps the tears had pushed it out, or maybe it only rested victorious. She lay curled in the corner, trying to pray. Joy had given way to fear, and fear to grief, and, eventually, grief to hard-floor sleep.

THIRTY-THREE

Whitting's Office

Ntombi turned the corner and found Whitting leaning against the side of his old mahogany desk, his arms crossed. He welcomed her with a big smile. "Ntombi. Glad you're here."

On a mission and unswayed by Whitting's chipper mood, Ntombi jumped right in. "Thank you. And about the speaking engagement."

Whitting gestured for Ntombi to take a seat. "Glad you brought it up. Yes, isn't it amazing the way the opportunity just opened up." Whitting waited on Ntombi to sit and then pulled up the second chair. "What a great way for you to decide if seminary is right for you."

Ntombi folded her hands and dropped them in her lap. She lowered her chin and looked up at him. "Seminary?" She pursed her lips. "Well, I was thinking—"

"Me too." Whitting put his hands on his knees and leaned toward Ntombi. "I'm thinking your subject matter should be the evangelizing of your country." He brought a fist to his mouth, glanced away, and then back at Ntombi. He quickly lowered his fist, as if pounding the air with enthusiasm. "Yes, evangelizing. And include your father's story. Seems there is already interest building. You know, buzz."

Ntombi straightened. "Buzz? About me speaking?"

"Yeah, I hope you don't mind. I put out an e-flyer noting the change."

219

Ntombi's eyes widened. "Oh my. What are they expecting?"

"I'm not sure, and it doesn't matter."

"Doesn't matter?"

"Not really. You are to play to an audience of One."

"Who's that?"

"God."

Ntombi sat with her hands in her lap and what she knew was a look of shock on her face. When she didn't respond, Whitting continued. "Okay, it's like this. The way I look at it, our absolute best is merely refrigerator art."

Ntombi scrunched her forehead. "Refrigerator art?"

Whitting leaned back. "Yeah, don't people do that back at home? You know, put up their children's art?"

"Well, yes, of course," Ntombi said with a slight shrug, "but not everyone has a refrigerator."

Ignoring the detail, Whitting continued, "Is their children's art anywhere near museum quality?"

"Well, no, it's usually pretty bad."

Whitting leaned back, grinned, and crossed his arms. "Well then, why do people put it up?"

"Because they love the child who created the art?"

"Precisely. Even our very best, lifelong work is merely refrigerator art to God. Yet he hangs it on his refrigerator because he loves us and the fact we made art—for him."

Ntombi smiled.

They finished discussing the talk. Ntombi left with a pile of books and Dr. Whitting's words in her head. His final words of counsel were, "You can do it." She wanted to believe she could do "it," but had to wonder what "it" was.

The following day, Ntombi made her way to the library with a stack of books. She found a quiet table next to the window. The sun filtered in, adding unique shadows and a sense of mystery to her new corner of the world.

Before opening the first book, she imagined an audience and saw herself climbing the stairs to the raised podium. The voice of fear resumed.

You don't even know what they're expecting. They've seen Andrew's art. They know it. They don't know you.

Ntombi wondered how the voice had gotten in but felt powerless to stop it once it got going.

What are you going to say? To all those people? You know how sarcastic students can be. And what about the others? You don't even know who's coming. You'd best get busy inviting your friends. You know, stack the deck. It's really late notice. Most of them will probably have other plans. What if Steve comes? He doesn't know this religious side of you. Kinda hard to give a talk for the Religion Department and not come across as religious. What about the non-Christians in the audience? Have you even thought about them? You don't want to offend anyone. How on earth are you going to read all these books in time?

Ntombi tried to fight the voice. I will not listen to you. Dr. Whitting is right, it is refrigerator art to God.

Easy for him to say, he has tenure. And that voice. Have you noticed his voice? Of course, people listen to him. You, on the other hand…

As the voice pricked her thoughts, a large Palmetto bug with all its cockroach ugliness made its way across the table, then up and over her stack of books. She hated them but didn't want to squash it—she also hated the crunchy sound and the oozing, creamy mess they made. She grabbed the top book, then slung it quickly to keep the bug from running up her arm. She watched as he bounced off the wall, landed in the corner, and scurried off.

Ntombi had just sat back down when she heard footsteps approaching in long, sure strides. From where she sat behind her tower of books, she couldn't see who it was, but she heard a thud of books landing on a nearby table and the sound of a man clearing his throat. Ntombi tried to ignore his presence but soon found herself peeking around the end of the stack. There, stretched out and completely engrossed in an organic chemistry book, was Steve. From her vantage point, Ntombi could see only the side of his head. She pulled her head back behind the books, moving like she was guilty of something, hoping not to be seen. She told herself she didn't want to disturb his studies but found her studies near impossible with the thought of him just twenty feet away.

Just then she heard the click, click, click of heels across the old pine floors and a familiar voice.

"Oh. Hi, Steve. I didn't know you studied here."

Ntombi listened as Steve pushed his chair back and stood. "And you are?"

"Dominique. People call me Dom. We met at a party once. I'm a good friend of Ntombi's."

"Ah, you know Ntombi?"

"We grew up together."

"Forgive me. You're South African. Ntombi mentioned she knew someone from home. I'm pleased to meet you." Ntombi pictured him shaking Dom's tiny hand before he continued. "Would you like to join me? That is, if you are a quiet studier."

Ntombi froze. She was trapped. It was impossible not to listen in, and the only way out was past their table.

"I am quiet. Stealthy quiet."

Ntombi imagined Steve gesturing for Dom to have a seat and Dom settling in.

In a moment, Ntombi heard Dom suppress a screech, then Steve asked, "Do you want me to get that?"

"No need. I suppose they need to live too."

"Ya think?" Steve said, laughing.

Taking advantage of the distraction the Palmetto bug had created, Ntombi reached up and removed two books from the shelf to create a small peek hole between them. She could see Dominique smile and tilt her head slightly. She was looking at Steve.

"Sorry to be so fidgety. Excuse me, I'll be right back," she said and demonstrated an added swing to her hips on her way to the ladies room.

Ntombi thought about announcing herself but decided it was too late. She had listened for too long. Surely he would think her some kind of stalker if she spoke up now.

Soon, Dom returned, with the top button of her blouse loosened, presenting an unapologetic display of the best features she had to offer. Ntombi fixed on them as they jiggled toward her. Dom then lowered herself to the wooden library chair with a slight bounce, creating an impossible to ignore, counter bounce. She then folded her hands and placed them between her knees, leaned forward and rested her chest on the table as one of a more normal stature would rest their elbows.

A sinking feeling settled in. Ntombi didn't breathe.

Dom began again. "Ntombi is a delight, isn't she?"

"That she is."

"I suppose I know her better than most. At least longer." Dom leaned back against her chair and tilted her head from side to side for emphasis. Ntombi watched and listened with her mouth slightly gaping and her brow furrowed.

Steve hesitated for a moment, then leaned forward and said, "Will you tell me about Ntombi? Growing up I mean?"

"Okay. She was as lovely then as she is now. I think that's the mystery."

"Mystery?"

Dom gave Steve a pursed-lip grin, turned her head to one side, and looked at him with one eye. "Surely you've noticed."

Just then, a library assistant pushed a cart full of books toward them. The wheels screeched as they passed by. The cart driver stopped, looked straight at Ntombi, and flashed her a disapproving look. Ntombi raised a finger to her lips in the universal sign for quiet. The library assistant heeded her warning and began pushing her cart again.

Ntombi went back to eavesdropping. She could see only Dom but imagined Steve smiling, as he leaned back in his chair and stretched the length of his legs out under the table, crossing them at the ankles. Surely, they reached Dom's side of the table.

Steve replied, "Of course I've noticed. They're gorgeous."

Ntombi wrinkled her forehead and so wanted to ask, What? What's gorgeous? She immediately started to inventory everything she had more than one of.

Dom reached down and playfully slapped Steve's foot, which was now right beside her chair. She smiled over at him and added, "I am not one to gossip, but with looks like that . . . I'm just saying, folks like to talk."

Dom softened slightly and leaned back from the table. "I'm sorry. You said you wanted to study, and here I am reminiscing. I'll be quiet." She then scooted her chair back and forth, as if trying to get it just right.

Ntombi again used the momentary noise as a foil to give her just enough time to pull her backpack across the wood table and unzip the small outside pocket. She flipped it up and leaned in to see the small narrow strip of a mirror. She looked at her eyes. Then, like the thorns of a porcupine unfurling, a childhood playground taunt surfaced in her mind. "Ntombi, Ntombi, eyes of green. Oh so skinny, like a long string bean."

Dom broke Ntombi's train of thought. "I guess I'll head home," she said.

Steve reacted as if on cue. "Wait, it's really late. I should walk with you."

"Oh, I'll be fine," Dom said in an unusually sweet voice.

"No, I insist."

Ntombi waited for them to leave and followed just out of sight.

From the library steps, she watched them move down the sidewalk. Dom's tiny stride seemed to slow Steve's usual pace. They chatted as they walked, and Ntombi knew she was likely the topic. Then, she worried she wasn't.

Suddenly, there was a loud bang as a dump truck hit a storm grate. Dom jumped and turned toward Ntombi. Ntombi quickly backed out of the light and into the shadow of the building. Readjusting her eyes, Ntombi saw Dom grab Steve's forearm and pull it toward her, cradling it against her chest. Steve jerked slightly, but Dom held tight. Dom then motioned with one curling index finger for him to bend down.

Ntombi shuddered in disgust as Steve obliged.

THIRTY-FOUR

Stormin' the Gates

By Friday night, Ntombi had abandoned her academic pursuit of an outline for her talk. The voice had returned.

> It's tomorrow. You haven't written a thing. Have you even thought about what you're going to wear? You'll be in that raised pulpit. Everyone will notice. Have you ever used a microphone? You should have practiced. You should practice your speech. You know what they say about practice. Steve might be there. What about Dr. Whitting? Have you told him your plans for the talk? He may want to approve the content.

Ntombi stood on bare feet wearing only her nightgown, the voice still droning in her head. She made her way to the Bayfields' back door and let herself in.

She called out."Becca? It's me."

Mae came around the corner from the library, putting both hands on her hips. "Ain't you the sight?"

"Good sight or bad?"

Mae winked at her. "Good to see you. I'll get Becca."

"Wait. Mae? I'm glad you're here. I was wondering if you, I mean y'all, would pray with me."

Mae glanced back. "Lord, child. We thought you'd never ask."

Turning and making her way through the library, Mae

called out. "Miss Becca, Ntombi's here. She's asking us if we'll pray."

Soon, Mae reappeared with Becca. Both had their jackets on, and Becca was holding a third.

"Here, put this on. We're going to the shed."

"The shed?" Ntombi asked, as she slipped into Ben's over-sized field jacket and wrapped it around herself. It smelled like Ben, kind of a mix between sandalwood and the outdoors. At that moment, his jacket felt like a bullet-proof cloak.

"Y'all go ahead," Becca told them. "I'll get the light switch."

Mae took Ntombi by the hand and led her down a narrow rut of a garden path. Ntombi could feel the grass on either side of her legs and the cool, damp sand beneath her feet.

Suddenly, the path was lit by a scalloped string of round bulbs, like Christmas bulbs, only bigger and round. The added light made the evening fog appear thicker with swirls. Each light had a personal halo fading to a soft, grayish mist. Mae stopped for just a moment as Ntombi breathed some of the night into her lungs. Her eyes quickly adjusted and followed the scalloped strand of lights. There, at the end of the path, was a brightly lit view of what Ntombi had thought was the potting shed.

One entire wall was lined with small, leaded-glass windows. The light from within was a bluish white. Becca soon caught up with them and insisted she walk in front. Ntombi and Mae stepped up and slightly off the path as Becca moved past them. Mae took the rear-flank position. Ntombi, at this moment in her life, could think of no other place she'd rather be than with Becca in front of her, setting the pace, and Mae protecting her back.

The trio reached the shed. The door was secured with a long, iron lever jammed into a C-hook of the same material but of a newer era. Less rusted. Neither served as much protection for the shed's contents.

Becca pushed on the door a bit, grabbed the small knob on the lever, and yanked it up. "This door swells when it's humid like this."

Becca opened the door in and motioned for Ntombi to enter first. Stepping just inside the door, Ntombi noticed the raw, wide-plank floors. Each board was nearly twelve inches wide, and some didn't quite meet, leaving mysterious jagged black lines and access from below. One small, simply patterned, Oriental rug lay in the center of the room.

On the far wall was a potting bench and beside it a shelf with pots hosting layers of dust and masses of cobwebs. Around the center of the small room sat a collection of old upholstered pieces, one a light-green swivel rocker, and beside it was an off-white, vinyl beanbag chair. In one corner was a carved-wood kneeling bench, like the kind used for weddings, and on it sat a cushion with worn, ornate needlepoint images.

The walls were unfinished; merely the other side of the exterior shiplap walls. Covering all four walls and even some of the windows were pieces of scrap paper with handwritten notes, each hung with a push pin, nail, or one of an array of tapes.

Ntombi walked to the back wall to examine them and saw they were scriptures and thank you notes to God for answered prayers. Some were written by Becca or Mae and others by names Ntombi didn't know.

Ntombi continued her exploration with the potting bench. On it was an open Bible with a few black droppings beside it. Having grown up on a game reserve, Ntombi knew scat when she saw it. She examined it and looked over at Becca.

Becca came over and blew the droppings off the Bible. "Field mice. I think they get in here at night and read the Scriptures, but they've never chewed the pages."

Ntombi looked around. "What is this room?"

"Command central," Mae said. "This is our prayer shed."

Becca smiled over at Mae. "And, it's a thin place."

"Thin place?" Ntombi asked.

"Yes." Becca rubbed the fingers of one hand together. "Where the divide between heaven and earth is worn threadbare by all the prayers."

Ntombi breathed in, released it, lowered her head a bit, and folded her hands. "Thank you so much for agreeing to pray. It has been really hard preparing."

Mae looked over at Ntombi and spoke without a hint of judgment in her voice. "We know. That's one way you know you on the right path. Child, if Satan ain't nippin' at your heels, you ain't a sheep."

Ntombi offered a sideways smile. "Well, he's been nipping—more than nipping."

Mae rolled her lips in and over her teeth and nodded. "Yes, and you don't know how to fight. It's a war. I learned a long time ago, when revival is about to start, the first one to get revived is the ole devil himself. He's sure enough working on you. Must be revival a-comin'."

Mae motioned for Ntombi to sit in the swivel rocker as she grabbed a cushion, placed it beside the rocker and fell to her knees on it. Becca landed in the bean bag and laid back with her legs outstretched. Before Ntombi had time to settle in, Mae and Becca started praying at the same time. Aloud. They sounded like little girls. There was an innocence, a joy to their voices. Each spoke directly to God, telling him how much they adored him and delighted in him. Yes, it was delight that flowed from their mouths. Then smiles crept across their faces as words of thanksgiving began to flow in no particular order.

Ntombi just watched and listened. Mae had her eyes closed,

and her head tilted to one side. "Now, Father," she said. "You knows Ntombi is one of Your special ones. She is chosen for special use, and You is workin' on her, in her, and I expect through her. We know that, and we're thankful for all you done for her. And thank you for bringing her to us. You know mine and Becca's babies are with you, so you up and sent her here so we have somebody to love on. Now about this talk she's givin'. Just seems to me that you arranged it. I mean with how it came up sudden and all. Like you just opened the door wide open. And I'm expecting there will be people there who just come for the show and who don't know you. Now, they may know something about you, but they don't know you. Some of them may not even know they don't know you."

While Mae prayed, Becca sat up straighter in the beanbag and crisscrossed her legs at the ankles. She sat with her eyes still closed, her head facing forward, and the occasional tear streaming past a soft smile. Occasionally she'd nod and add a "Yes, Lord."

Mae paused, for a moment and looked as if she was listening for something before continuing. "Um...I see...yes, Lord." She paused again, then smiled a bit. "Sure enough." Again, she sat silent for a moment. "About this talk. Well, I guess it's your talk, and she's just doing it for you. I'm sure you have something you want to say. Will you please tell her? Thank you, Lord. And the enemy is putting thoughts in her head, and then he make her think they her thoughts, and then he make her feel bad about having those thoughts. Jesus, in your name and by the power of your blood, I bind all of the forces of evil, and I send them to Jesus for you to deal with. Every thought, every disturbance, everything that would try to come against her ability to prepare for and deliver this talk."

Becca reached out her hand and placed it on Mae's arm.

"Thank you, Father, for Mae, and for sending her to me, and for what she knows about prayer. I know she is your favorite. Thank you for letting me hang out all these years with your favorite. Thank you for her biscuits at dinner, for the warmth of this jacket, and for the privilege of prayer."

Mae smiled wide through closed lips, shook her head side to side, then took Becca by the hand. Tears were now streaming down her face. Ntombi bowed her head. After that, it was as if she lost time. There were moments when she was aware of Becca and Mae standing over her chair with arms outstretched. Other times they touched her gently. They prayed, and she prayed. They prayed for things she had not told them about and for things that didn't yet make sense to her—future things.

At some point, Ntombi felt as if she were falling asleep. She tried hard not to, not wanting to appear ungrateful, but it was unlike any sleep she had known. There was a sweet, sweet peace to it. She was aware of her body outstretched on the Oriental rug in the middle of the room, but she was completely unaware of how she got there. With her eyes closed, she saw herself rising from the grave. Her body was filled with light, and she knew it to be the resurrection. She was making her way to Jesus in the sky. Before she reached him, other graves started opening, and other people began to ascend, each a bright light. She then became aware of the earth's sphere. People were rising up, coming up like hundreds of bright lights from all corners of the earth. And there was a message: These are the ones who are to join the kingdom through your calling.

Ntombi was awestruck. She wanted to ask if there was some mistake. How could she possibly reach all those people? But she couldn't form the words. Instead, she rested in pure, complete joy.

When she opened her eyes, Mae was kneeling on the floor

on one side and Becca on the other. She looked up at them, searching for the right words, but found herself temporarily mute.

In time, they helped her to her feet and over to the swivel rocker, then began walking about the room, continuing to pray. Mae began to sway and sing. "Swing low sweet chariot, coming for to carry me home. Swing low sweet chariot…" Her voice had a depth to it, not necessarily a depth of tone, but like it came from someplace else. Soon, Becca joined in.

The song ended and, without any further words, the three walked in sweet silence along the narrow path toward the house. When they reached the carriage house, Ntombi was first to speak. "I think I can study now. Concentrate."

Mae looked at Becca, then back to Ntombi. "Child, I have a word for you."

Becca grinned and nodded in Mae's direction. She reached an arm around each of them, then excused herself and went in the house. "I'll leave you to it."

Mae and Ntombi took a seat on the Charleston-style, slatted bench just outside the carriage house door. Ntombi sat back and rested one arm against the cold iron. Mae perched on the bench's outer edge so that her feet reached the ground and looked straight ahead.

"A word?" Ntombi asked when Mae didn't say anything.

"Voice."

"Meaning, God's voice?"

"Mmmhmm. Eve's sin was listening to the wrong voice."

"I've been listening to the wrong voice, haven't I?" She looked at Mae. "How do I know the difference?"

Mae took one of Ntombi's hands and cradled it in hers, then patted it a couple times, "First, if it's true what the voice says, it is of God."

Ntombi stared at her hand in Mae's "And that other voice lies."

"And disquiets," Mae added. "Or sometimes he tell you something that is sure enough true, you know, from the past. It happened and all, but it no longer matter 'cause Jesus done forgave it. But Satan brings it up. If it's no longer true on God's books, it's a lie." Mae released Ntombi's hand. "He will also find an old hurt and just pick at it."

Ntombi took a breath, released it, and looked down at her crossed ankles. She uncrossed them and tapped her feet together, dropping a clump or two of wet sand with each tap. "He's sure been picking at me."

Mae glanced over at Ntombi and down at her feet. She stomped them a couple times to shake some sand loose, then rubbed the sand back and forth with one foot till it settled between the patio bricks. "Yeah, the devil will sure enough take up rent-free residence in your head if you let him."

THIRTY-FIVE

Speaking Gig

Ntombi and Dr. Whitting stood peeking around the sacristy door as the sanctuary filled. First were the early folks, who chose to kneel and pray or sit quietly and look about. Soon the cool, silent, holy space changed. It was filled. Somehow having lots of saints in the pews brought transformation. Or was it a flow? It brought fellowship—the fellowship of the saints. Ntombi's face softened as she thought of modern-day saints blending their prayers with the glorified souls in the churchyard. Surely prayer doesn't have a shelf life, and those that have gone before mingle with the new. She imagined the old church walls were there only for effect and certainly not to separate heaven and earth.

Ntombi saw Mae arrive, and raised her brows teasingly, tapping her watch a couple of times. Mid-aisle, Mae stopped to smile and wave with both arms stretched high in the air. Ntombi returned the gesture with a tiny, waist-high wave and a slightly smaller smile, like the middle schooler who is pleased to see mom but doesn't want to let it show.

Steve's entrance was hard to miss. He stood a head taller than the rest and found a seat near the back. As he settled down, Ntombi took in some measured air and uttered a quick prayer of thanks, combined with an apology for having hoped he wouldn't come. Soon after, Ntombi picked Emma out in the crowd as well.

Not wanting to make eye contact with Steve, Ntombi kept her eyes on Mae as she found a pew near the front. The lady beside her was kneeling. Mae simply nodded, found her kneeler, and plopped down. As soon as her knees hit the padding, she began to rock. Ntombi couldn't help but think of how Mae would say, "Lordy, we gonna have church!"

A certain excitement was building in the room. The sanctuary was filled, with dozens more in the balconies. Ntombi thought of fear and wondered why she didn't have more of it. With her eyes still fixed on the audience, she asked Whitting, "Why are all these people here?"

Whitting responded with an accomplished smile. "I think Andrew should be a marketing major. Some are here because they need the boost to their grade; others were recruited by Andrew. He made flyers that read COME SEE THE GIRL IN THE PICTURES.'"

Ntombi's eyes grew wide, and she turned to look at Whitting. "Really?"

Whitting chuckled. "Yes. I thought it was brilliant. I also recognize several St. Michaelites in the crowd."

Ntombi turned slightly toward the door and then back to Whitting. She placed a hand on her hip and looked squarely at him. "So, wait. Really? People are here just to see the 'girl in the pictures'?"

Whitting lifted his bushy brows and grinned. "Oh, yeah. Sounds a bit like carnival barking. But, hey. It worked!"

Ntombi shook her head and then turned again to peek around the door and watch the audience file in. The people seemed to have quieted down a bit, and Ntombi hushed her tone to match. "I'm glad some church folk are here...and Mae."

"Why's that?"

"They know how to forgive."

Whitting continued his study of the audience. "It is a noble virtue. But you, my child, will not need forgiveness. Remember, you are playing to an audience of One."

Whitting straightened up and gently turned Ntombi around to face him. He spoke slowly and directly to her. "Now. You are third to speak. The first is merely emcee stuff and the second a professor just back from a Burundi mission trip." Whitting brought one hand up to his mouth. "Oh, wait. I almost forgot. I was wrong about the time. You have forty-five minutes, not thirty." Ntombi sent him a blank stare as he continued. "I'll be in the audience as part of your fan club."

Ntombi looked down at him with a new look, more like a deer caught in headlights. "Will you pray for me?"

"Now?"

"The whole time."

Whitting gently hugged Ntombi. "Father, bless her as she speaks." He opened the door wide with his left hand, placed a hand in the center of her back, and gently ushered her out. "Remember, gratitude eliminates fear."

Ntombi sat up front in the preacher's pew box. Her chair faced the side, giving her a glimpse of the altar, a full view of the audience, and a straight-up view of the mahogany, double-decker pulpit with its sweepingly carved and painstakingly polished matching canopy. The canopy seemed to her a form of protection. She hoped she wasn't too tall for it, and there was the big hair. What about the hair? Would there be room for the hair?

Ntombi looked at all the people, and with a force of will and with Mae's words playing in her head, began quenching the fiery darts from the enemy's quiver with thanksgiving. She continued to pray even when the voice stopped, thanking God for everything that had led her to this moment and that the words of her mouth would be acceptable to Him. From somewhere within the far reaches of her prayer, she heard another voice:

"Take one of the tapestry cushions at the kneeling rail with you."

Tapestry cushions?

"It represents the veil."

Ntombi leaned over to see around the pulpit. There at the front of the church was a kneeling rail with needlepoint-adorned cushions. Each was a work of art with a lovely background in winter white and blue and uniquely adorned with gold and red symbols of faith. She studied them and decided they were about seven inches deep, some wider than others. Maybe she could take one of the shorter ones.

Are you sure? What if they think I'm defacing the church?

It's my church. Take a cushion. Tell them about the veil.

Ntombi's mind turned to how the veil fit with her planned speech while the last speaker's words wound to a close. He finished, people applauded, and he returned to his seat. Ntombi glanced at the emcee in the lower pulpit and received the nod she expected.

She made her way to the front, paused and knelt at the rail for a short prayer. Her out-of-the-ordinary behavior brought a hush over the room. As she stood, she lifted the kneeling cushion, wrapping an arm around it tightly. She climbed the steep stairs to the upper-deck pulpit and carefully placed the cushion on the ledge where all could see. Then she laid out her notes.

After a long pause, she began. "Father God, we ask, will you show us your glory?"

She lifted the cushion and displayed it like Vanna White would show a placard. As she turned, she saw Ben and Becca quietly enter the south balcony and take a seat.

She spoke. It was in a new voice. Deeper. Calm. More sure. A voice even she had not heard before.

"I am from South Africa, and my people are Xhosan. It came to me that the history of my people could be taught with these thickly woven threads. You see, there was a time when most were shrouded in darkness like a thick heavy woolen veil between my people and the light of glory in Jesus' face."

The audience sat and drank of the gospel through Ntombi's stories of a people and a homeland she loved. As she spoke, soft light flickered on the audience's faces. She thought it oddly beautiful. She turned to make eye contact with the front balcony seats. From this vantage point, she garnered a glimpse of the stained-glass window behind the altar. The image of Michael slaying Satan was bright. At the same time, the image of the fallen Satan grew darker and blurred by contrast. The source of the light was quickly revealed, and without missing a single beat of her speech, Ntombi found the flickering glow a nice touch and silently thanked God for it.

Ntombi's talk came to a close precisely at the forty-five minute mark. She placed the cushion under one arm and turned to descend the stairs. As she did, out the corner of her eye, she saw Andrew stand. He didn't clap. He only stood. Mae, Emma, and Steve followed suit, their stance like pillars in the crowd. Moments later, Ntombi was wrapped in the sound of people all over the sanctuary rising to their feet.

Ntombi carefully replaced the cushion. Nearly the entire room was standing now. Some bowed their heads; others looked straight ahead. Some stood with hands lifted toward heaven. They were resolute as if moved to stand with Ntombi and her people. It was an unplanned, silent praise moment.

Ntombi stopped and stood in front of the crowd, folded her hands, and bowed her head. Those on their feet and those yet seated followed suit. They prayed within the sweet aroma of silence. Hearts were strangely warmed. Steve's heart was among them.

THIRTY-SIX

Corporate Call

The office doors opened, and Ntombi stepped into a land of marble floors, mahogany furniture, Oriental rugs, and fine art. It was a good feel. Behind the reception desk sat a well-coiffed, middle-aged woman. Ntombi approached her and was greeted in a hushed tone. "May I help you?"

Ntombi leaned over slightly and whispered her reply. "Yes, ma'am. I'm here to see Mr. Wilson."

The woman looked down at the list on her desk. "How was your drive?"

"Thank you for asking. It was fine. I left early enough to avoid the traffic."

"I love Charleston. Charlotte traffic has gotten so bad. My husband and I try to escape a few times a year, and Charleston is one of our favorite spots."

Ntombi thought to mention South Africa as a good place for escape but instead smiled and nodded. The receptionist returned the gesture and looked back at her list of names. "You'll find Mr. Wilson's assistant at the end of the hall."

Ntombi walked down the hall and, not finding anyone at the desk, moved around behind it to look out the floor to ceiling windows. Looking down, she realized this was the highest she'd ever been, besides her one transatlantic flight.

"Young lady?"

Ntombi flinched and spun around to see a short, redheaded

lady with glasses perched on her freckled nose. "Yes, ma'am. I'm here to see Mr. Wilson."

The woman shook her head in frustration. "It is beyond me why he…" She took a deep breath. "Oh, never mind," she mumbled to herself. "Take a seat."

Ntombi moved from behind the lady's desk, leaving the view of the city behind, found a chair, and perched on its edge. Her posture was fully erect. Becca would be proud. She watched as people came and went for brief meetings and hoped she was given more than ten minutes. Then she thought it awkward or maybe even rude to have arrived so early.

As she waited, she watched the faces of the people who came and went from Mr. Wilson's office. Some went in smiling and left with a furrowed brow. Others went in burdened and left with a spring in their step. Ntombi imagined Mr. Wilson was like the Wizard of Oz, and people were coming to ask things of the wizard. Some requests were granted; some were not. And the wizard decided quickly.

Just then, the redheaded sentinel lady looked over her glasses at Ntombi and said, "Mr. Wilson will see you now."

"Yes, ma'am." Ntombi bounced up and stood erect. She smiled big and gave the woman an over-the-top thank you.

Ntombi entered Mr. Wilson's office and was taken aback by its size. It was so big, in fact, that, for a moment, she couldn't find him in it. He wasn't behind the desk, where one would expect to see him. In a far corner was a sitting area with a camelback sofa and two wing chairs centered in front of a fireplace and grounded with an Oriental rug. He wasn't there either. On the other side of the room was a meeting table. But he wasn't there.

Then a voice spoke from a window-lined corner of the room. "You must be Ntombi?"

"Yes, sir," Ntombi answered, before finding the voice's source. When she did finally see Mr. Wilson, he was smaller than she'd expected.

He motioned for Ntombi to join him at the windows. "Come look. I enjoy watching the fog lift this time of morning." Ntombi stood beside him as he pointed out the glass. "Look. Buildings are reaching up through the clouds. It amazes me. We seem to reach higher and higher with our structures as if trying to stretch to the heavens."

The two stood for a moment enjoying a downward glimpse of the lower heavens. Ntombi spoke first. "Do you think there are highrises in heaven?"

Wilson shrugged. "God's there. No need to reach."

"Good. I don't think I'd want to be in one there."

"Me neither, and I built this one." Mr. Wilson said, with a sideways grin.

Wilson stepped away from the window and gestured, inviting Ntombi to have a seat at a small table. She approached the table as he pulled a chair out for her to sit.

"Whitting tells me you are a worthy fellow sleuth."

Ntombi sat and allowed Mr. Wilson to help her scoot her chair forward. "You know Whitting?"

"Oh yes. We were at Sewanee together. My only degree but one of his many." He walked around the table and took a seat on the other side of Ntombi.

Ntombi sat erect with her hands neatly folded on the edge of the table. "I expect you have some stories then."

"Indeed."

Ntombi's smile met his as she pivoted the conversation. "Will you tell me about your call?"

Mr. Wilson leaned back in his seat, glanced out the window for a moment, and back again at Ntombi. "I was in my late twenties. For a young man, I had accomplished much, but I was restless. There was a deep discontent. I had more stuff than most my age. I was reared in the church but left most of it behind in college. I didn't reject it. Just stopped doing church things."

Mr. Wilson's chair faced the wall of windows. He stared out them, almost as if he'd flown away for a while. Ntombi decided to quietly await his return.

"One night, I awoke at three a.m. As my eyes opened, I saw arrows, hundreds of arrows, all shooting toward heaven. It was unlike anything I've ever experienced. It was peaceful. I didn't do anything—didn't have to do anything—to make the arrows fly. They just flew. I knew they were traveling to heaven." He smiled and looked straight at Ntombi before continuing. "The next morning, I called my girlfriend and said, 'I am to start a business, and we are to marry.'"

Ntombi looked up from her notepad. "Really? Just like that?"

"Just like that."

"So did you?"

"Yes. Well, of course it didn't all happen the next day. I didn't know how I was to start a business. I had this strong desire to use what I had learned about managing capital to help people. I knew I was to take my eye off building my own wealth and put it on building wealth for others, specifically others who wanted to use it for good."

Ntombi jotted down his words and asked, "Do you know the meaning of the arrows?"

Mr. Wilson scrunched his forehead. "I expected you to ask that, but no. Not clearly. They are still a bit of a puzzle."

With the nearly four-hour drive home, Ntombi had lots of time to ponder the meaning of the arrows. She recalled a passage of scripture that speaks of them. In David's song of praise, there's something about the Lord shooting arrows and scattering his enemies. But that imagery is arrows from heaven to earth; Mr. Wilson's arrows moved upward.

She thought maybe they represented his sin leaving him and piercing the heavens. Or was it all the good, the eternal good, that would result from his work on earth reaching the heavens? Likely sin first, then good.

Ntombi stopped by the library on her way and finally arrived home around nine. Just inside the door, she noticed something out of place. Her bed had been turned down, and there was something on her pillow. It was dark brown. She moved slowly toward it as if it might suddenly leap out at her.

As she got closer, she realized it was Mandlenkosi's shoe. Ntombi's brow furrowed and she shook her head. Ever since his mother had sent it to her, she'd kept it in the closet. Her heart sank. Who would have gone through her things and placed it on the white pillowcase? Was it some sick joke?

She grabbed the shoe but quickly jerked both hands back, dropping it to the floor beside the bed. She stood with her hands still hanging in the air and her mouth wide open staring down at the shoe. It was identical. Except…

It was the other shoe—the right one!

THIRTY-SEVEN

The Answer

"Careful with him. His name is Right Richard."

Ntombi looked up to see Mandlenkosi step from the dark kitchen. He smiled at her as he had thousands of times before. She wanted to run to him, but her feet wouldn't move, and her voice was somehow trapped within her chest. Words whirled in her head, but none came out.

His hair was longer and his skin lighter than she remembered, but the smile... The center gap and mischievous look were the Mandlenkosi she knew. A moment or two passed in silence, then he crossed his arms, tilted his head, and peered across the room at her. He waited like that for a moment, as if giving her time to process. Then he slowly moved toward her and offered his hand. She looked at it first and then placed a shaky hand into it.

Mandlenkosi led Ntombi to the sofa and gently pulled her down beside him. She faced forward with her hand still in his and leaned back.. Mandlenkosi followed her cue and placed his arm around her shoulders, and she leaned her head against his.

And then he spoke. His story flowed out in its entirety. He told of his car accident, the head injury, the drugs, the string of captors, and the girls in the next container. He gave Ntombi their names and ages and a description of each. He told of their escape and Keiko's rescue.

As the details poured from Mandlenkosi, Ntombi, for the first time, turned her gaze from the garden on the other side of the window to the man who had replaced the boy she lost. Releasing his hand, she turned to face him, placing her left foot beneath her thigh. From this vantage point, she could see the side of his face. It was a chiseled form she knew well. Without thinking, she reached over and stroked the line of his jaw with the back of her fingers.

Mandlenkosi kept his gaze forward and continued.

Soon, a question formed, one Ntombi could release. "How did they find Keiko?"

"It was mostly your father."

Ntombi sat up, looked at Mandlenkosi, and dropped her chin. "Tata? You've seen Tata?"

"Yes. He helped the police find Keiko."

"I don't understand." Ntombi glanced toward the house. "Is he with you?"

"No, we are not allowed to travel together."

"Why?"

"He's a witness. A minor one but still. He sends his love, and he sent a package for me to give to you. It's in the house."

"What's in it?"

"He wants you to fly to Boston on your birthday and meet him. He put the airline ticket in the package."

"Boston? Why Boston?"

Mandlenkosi shrugged. "Don't know."

Ntombi leaned back against Mandlenkosi and went silent again. She had so many questions at this point in his story, she didn't know where to begin. She was suddenly exhausted as if the events of the past couple of months had finally settled their weight on her. For the time being, she could only listen and try to process everything and its meaning.

Mandlenkosi picked up his story where he left off. When he finished, she simply stood and stretched, then bent to untie and remove her shoes. He watched her.

Knowing his eyes were still on her, Ntombi moved toward the bed, grabbed a pillow and a throw, and returned to the sofa. She placed the pillow in Mandlenkosi's lap and leaned in close as she patted it a couple of times to get it just right. With her face now inches away, she knew he wanted to kiss her and liked the fact he chose not to.

She stretched her body across the sofa, placed her head on the pillow, and pulled the throw up to her chin. Her feet were sticking out. She could see Mandlenkosi watching as she grabbed it with her toe, pulled it down, and tucked it under.

Carefully, and with a tentative gesture, Mandlenkosi rested his right hand just beneath her ribs. She responded by laying her hand atop his. Mandlenkosi looked into her face, smiled ever so slightly, and began stroking her hair with his free hand. "I know why I'm thin. But why are you?"

"I fasted."

"Fasted?"

Ntombi turned slightly to look up at him. "Yes. I fasted and prayed."

Mandlenkosi lifted his head and looked across the room and out the large, garden-facing window. The night sky was thick, not at all like a South African sky. The mist made it starless. She felt Mandlenkosi draw in a breath and release it.

"I needed your prayers," he said. "I wouldn't have made it through the dark night without them."

Ntombi reached up and gently pulled his head toward hers. She kissed him softly and released him. "You are the answer."

When Mandlenkosi woke, he was stretched out on the sofa with the pillow and the throw Ntombi had fallen asleep with. Ntombi stood across the room looking out the window. The lights from the house created a glow around her. Mandlenkosi stood quietly and moved toward her. As he approached, she said, "There are lights on in the house."

Mandlenkosi came up behind her, and with his body touching hers, reached his arms over and around hers.

"Agents are guarding us and the house."

"Agents? What kind of agents? Are we in danger?"

Mandlenkosi bowed and kissed the top of her head.

"You are safe in my arms, and we are safe in the arms of God. The guards are there for their own sense of security. God has brought me this far. I don't expect he will leave me now."

"No. I expect not."

Ntombi leaned her head back against Mandlenkosi's chest and watched as the guard on duty exited the back door of the main house and paced back and forth talking on his phone. She was glad he was in a suit instead of SWAT gear but wondered if he realized a marine type with a butch haircut would garner suspicion outside an old plantation home at five in the morning.

Ntombi playfully nuzzled in a bit closer. "Why do you have guards?"

"I am a protected witness until the trial."

"What trial? You didn't do anything." She loosened Mandlenkosi's grip and turned around in his arms.

Mandlenkosi looked down into her eyes. "It's not my trial. The trial is for the traffickers. I'm told this cartel has very powerful customers. Killing me would be a small price to protect their business and their clientele. You would be shocked if I shared names."

Ntombi paused the conversation for a moment and finally said, "To get to you, they'd have to go through me."

Mandlenkosi wrapped his arms all the way around Ntombi's shoulders and gave her a playful squeeze. "Good!"

Ntombi pushed him away. "No, you are good."

"Not me. You."

Ntombi stuck one foot out, planted her fist on the other hip, and with a bob of her head, said, "You the man."

Mandlenkosi laughed. Ntombi returned his laugh and reached one hand toward him. He took it, and the two began to dance.

"Wait, let me show you what I learned on the ship. Jasmine taught me some Latin moves." Mandlenkosi backed up and began swaying his hips side to side with an occasional dip on the off-beat. He then demonstrated some cha-cha steps. The wiggle of his taut rear offered little hip action but great comic relief for Ntombi. She laughed.

"That ain't nothin'. If you're good, I'll demo Mae's moves."

Mandlenkosi popped her on the rear and darted out of reach. "Show me!" he said.

She turned, crossed her arms, and shook her head. "Some things never change."

"Like your bum?"

"Like your cheekiness."

THIRTY-EIGHT

Walk Beside

As the morning star faded, replaced by the first rays of the sun, Mandlenkosi and Ntombi walked along her favorite rice plantation road. Mandlenkosi's tone was gentle but matter-of-fact. "I must leave today and travel to an undisclosed place. I will be sequestered until the trial."

"Where?"

"The locations are undisclosed to me as well." He continued as they walked toward the sunrise, "I had some magnificent sunrises on the ship. No sunsets but beautiful sunrises."

Ntombi knew this spirit, the one that finds good in all and everything yet still marveled. With all he'd been through, it was the sunrises he remembered.

Mandlenkosi continued. "I can see why you enjoy this place—the morning mist, the moss hanging from the oaks, and even the smell. It is all so beautiful."

"Isn't it? The sweet smell? Ben says that's tea olive."

"I smell the sand as well. Ever since I got off the ship, it's like I now appreciate dirt."

"And today we feel it between our toes."

Mandlenkosi leaned closer and elbowed her softly. "Yebo yes."

She smiled wide. "Yebo yes," she answered, then planted a playful kiss on his cheek.

Turning quickly back toward the house, Ntombi walked ahead of Mandlenkosi with her arms outstretched and her face to the morning sun. She felt like she was floating weightlessly and knew she was showing off.

He merely smiled a look of delight. After a few turns, she gestured with an outstretched arm, and Mandlenkosi jogged a few steps to catch up. Just then, Mae appeared at the end of the road and called out with both arms waving overhead. Her short, stocky frame was lit by the morning light, giving her dark skin a well-suited, radiant glow.

Ntombi ran ahead a few feet and motioned with a big circular wave, "Come on. Breakfast is ready. Mae is here to meet you—the fruit of her prayers."

They sat that morning around the two-hundred-year-old, wide-plank breakfast table. Ntombi thought of all the meals, all the conversations that had taken place around this one table. She touched the worn edge, what Becca called the patina, and could sense the generations who had eaten here before. Mae and Becca had no doubt prayed here. Though Ntombi was sure this conversation was a first of its kind, considering a few federal agents joined in this feast.

Agent Jones explained the events of the day. The plan was laid out for them to leave midday. Mandlenkosi would be safe but unable to make contact as the investigation progressed and the hearing date was set. Ntombi watched like a spectator of her own life. The chapters seemed to unfold before her without her permission and unlike anything she could have thought or imagined. She wanted to continue in her celebration of Mandlenkosi's return. The sick ache of loss was stuck in her gut. He'd just returned, and he'd be leaving again so soon.

Ntombi decided to fight the fear with thanksgiving. As the breakfast conversation flowed, she prayed silently.

Jones broke through her thoughts, thanking Becca and Mae for the meal, then looked across the table at Mandlenkosi. "I hate to steal you away, but can we talk outside?"

Becca stepped in to direct the flow of things. "Ntombi, you can help Mae and me with the dishes—that way you can keep an eye on Mandlenkosi through the window."

Soon Ntombi stood at the sink swirling soapy water atop a plate before placing it in the dishwasher. She never looked at the plate though. Her gaze stayed on Mandlenkosi as she wondered about his conversation with Jones.

Just then, the sound of shells crushing announced a vehicle's arrival. Ntombi called out to be heard in the next room. "Becca, are we expecting anyone else?"

From the sun room, where she was clearing the last of the dishes from the table, Becca answered. "No, ma'am. Ben's flight doesn't get in until midnight. He hates he's gonna miss seeing Mandlenkosi."

When Ntombi saw the car, she let the plate she was washing slip from her fingers. It hit the side of the sink, shattering, before falling in pieces into the sudsy water.

It was Steve!

Becca ran into the room behind Ntombi and set the dishes she was holding on an empty section of the counter. Ntombi whipped around and looked at her, wide-eyed and frozen. Becca wiped her hands on her apron and hurried to stand by Ntombi's side. Mae joined them. The two women flanked Ntombi on either side, and they stood in a row, staring silently out the large kitchen window.

Steve opened his door and stood to look around. He reached across through the car and pulled his backpack from the passenger's side into driver's, unzipped it, and pulled a pair of high-heeled gold sandals from the backpack's grasp.

Ntombi felt her heart stop and made a quick move toward the door. Becca restrained her with a gentle yet firm side hug. "Wait. Just wait. Let them sort it out."

Ntombi looked at Becca, her face full of confusion and panic. Then she returned her gaze to the scene unfolding in front of her. Steve pulled his shoulders back and walked squarely toward Mandlenkosi.

Jones backed away, and Steve offered Mandlenkosi his hand. Mandlenkosi took it and gave it one quick, firm shake. Steve lifted Ntombi's sandals in the air, then lowered them to his side. A conversation ensued. Steve mostly talked, and Mandlenkosi nodded his head in acknowledgment. Then, like one receiving a communion wafer, Mandlenkosi raised both hands. Steve, in a somewhat exaggerated gesture, dropped the shoes in Mandlenkosi's hands. Mandlenkosi caught them.

Ntombi still couldn't feel her heart. Surely it had stopped. She wanted to run out and explain, but who would she explain to? Surely they both had the wrong idea—or the right idea, but who didn't she want to offend? Who didn't she want to lose? She wasn't ready to make that decision.

Becca reached a hand around Ntombi's waist and pulled her toward her. "It's okay. It will all be okay."

Ntombi doubted Becca's words; she didn't even know what okay looked like anymore. She watched as Steve's car motored back down the drive. Mandlenkosi walked through the back door holding the shoes with the same loose dangling grip as Steve had. Becca, Ntombi, and Mae turned in unison to face him. Mandlenkosi dangled the shoes from two fingers. "Seems you left these in the Bentley."

Then Mae, in perfect form, planted one fist on her hip. "Lordy, I wondered where I left those. I didn't think to look in the Bentley."

THIRTY-NINE

A Good Bye

Mandlenkosi turned to watch out the rear window of the black Escalade as they motored through the treelined drive. He watched Ntombi wave to him, with Becca on one side and Mae on the other, all waving. He waved back, yet doubted they could see anything through the dark glass.

Mandlenkosi reached for the button to roll down the window. Without turning around, Jones corrected him. "Those don't work. Here." Jones rolled down his front seat window.

Mandlenkosi reached up and stuck one hand out to wave. He blew a kiss, hoping Ntombi could interpret it with only his hand visible, then turned around and planted his knees in his seat to get the final glimpse. Soon, all sight of Ntombi was gone. Still, he stayed with crossed arms on the back of the seat, looking backward. He longed, instead, to be by her side, waving goodbye to the Escalade with Jones and company on board.

"Mandlenkosi?"

He breathed in and out before responding. "Yes, sir?"

"I would like to go over the day's events with you."

Mandlenkosi, turned around and settled into his seat, then looked at the back of Jones's head. "Thank you for allowing the visit."

"My pleasure. It was worth the trip to watch the shoe exchange. Now put your seatbelt on. I'd hate to lose you in a crash."

Mandlenkosi fastened his seatbelt, watched out the window, and listened halfheartedly as the plans were discussed. He knew he would be guided and guarded. He marveled at how he was just weeks ago guarded by the bad guys, and now he was being guarded by the good guys. He expected another flight. Instead, it was a long drive. A few hours later, sleep came over him. There hadn't been much of it in recent weeks. The hum of the tires and the sense of being cradled by protectors brought sleep—deep, deep sleep.

In that space, somewhere between sleep and waking, Mandlenkosi saw a black rosebud. As it began to open, light came from between the petals. Each petal was brittle and struggled to break free without shattering. It was like the light was trapped by the hardness. He reached his hand toward the rosebud. As he did, the petals became stronger, more supple. One by one, they opened, releasing a bead of light. Tiny glistening beads of light floated about and then ascended toward the heavens.

For a moment, Mandlenkosi wondered if his hand was actually moving and withdrew it. As he did, the rose stopped opening. A petal fell to the ground, taking the beads of light with it. When each petal touched the soil, it became black and oozed, releasing a stench like the smell of rotting flesh. Mandlenkosi extended his hand again, this time in earnest, and the rose opened as a mountain climber would stretch his arms upward and outward, atop the highest peak. The rose petals slowly softened to a velvety pink, each again releasing tiny beads of glistening light. Soon, the beads of light were all around, floating, glistening. As they touched things in their path, they sparked light and color. Each bead floated along on its own unique way but always upward.

"Mandlenkosi?"

Mandlenkosi shook his head, blinked a couple times. Jones was watching him from the front seat. "Uh, yes."

"Are you awake."

"No," Mandlenkosi said with a yawn, as he stretched both arms up and back, touching the headliner.

"You will need to put this on for the next few miles of the trip."

Jones handed him a dark shroud of a hood. Mandlenkosi looked at it and then at the guard. "Ah. No man! I can't breathe when I feel trapped. I'm okay as long as I have light. The container. I think it was the weeks in the container."

"Okay. Just put your head in your lap, and we'll lay it over you. It's for your protection. You can't know where you are so you don't accidentally tell someone."

It all seemed strange, over-the-top, to Mandlenkosi. But he quickly folded over, placing his head in his lap to receive his shroud. As it fell over him, he thought of the image of the black rose. What could it mean? It was so vivid. Etched in his mind like a film watched a hundred times over. And the tiny beads. What were they?

Or, rather, who?

In what felt like half an hour, the car came to a stop.

"You can get up now."

Mandlenkosi unfolded as all four car doors opened, revealing a massive, old, English-looking home. Its brick walls rose high in front of them.

"This is my hideout?" Mandlenkosi joked.

"Yes. It's on loan. The owner is out of the country. She despises trafficking and likes to help out when she can."

A butler stood erect at Mandlenkosi's door. "I will get your bags."

Mandlenkosi wondered if his two grocery bags of belongings counted as bags as the butler continued, "You have guests in the drawing room."

Inside, they rounded a corner that led to the drawing room. Mandlenkosi stopped in the doorway. There amid the drawing room's towering ceilings and opulent furnishings was a couple seated on a velvet sofa. They stood in unison and joined hands when Mandlenkosi entered the room.

His thoughts ricocheted, landing quickly on the right memory. "Father. Mother."

Mandlenkosi walked the last thirty feet of what had been a very long journey home. He slowly knelt before his parents, bowed his head, felt his father's hand on his right shoulder and his mother's in the center of his back.

"Welcome home, son. Welcome home."

FORTY

In the Whirlwind

Whitting had all the windows down in his Citroën as he turned down the Bayfield's long drive. The morning shadows reached forward from each massive oak. The air smelled delightfully pungent as it wafted from the distant marsh. He was eager to hear Ntombi's progress with her side of the research and maybe some specifics about Mandlenkosi's miraculous return. He thought the two subjects were well suited. Each provided an answer to an eternal question.

On the porch, Whitting noticed the door open and only the screen door remained between him and the front room. The furniture had been pushed aside, and Ntombi was seated on the floor with books, papers, reports, photos, sheet music, and sticky notes, all strewn about in two semi-circles, one in front of her and one behind, obscuring the center medallion of the rug. He let himself in.

"Oh, hi, Whit. Glad you're here," Ntombi said, keeping her gaze on the pile in front of her. "I'm close. So close. There are patterns."

Whitting stood over her as she explained each pile of papers. The grouping in front was from the twelve students who collected and analyzed data from churches throughout the country. Behind her, she explained, was the culmination of her interviews on calling and numerous books on the subject. She spoke in disjointed thoughts, almost as if to herself.

"I tried arranging by denomination, but that didn't tell me anything. Wait, what if we arranged this stack in chronological order . . ."

Whitting stood over her and watched in amazement as her hands moved bits and pieces about, formed a more linear pattern with the books and reports, then arranged the pieces of sheet music first in a row below and then above, all the while explaining the new possibilities. He decided it best not to interrupt.

"Thanks for the craft supplies. They came in handy."

Whitting noticed them still in their jumbled state, piled just to her left. As ideas flooded, she would reach in for a sticky note, sometimes adding a little extra blue painter's tape to help it stick to the rug. Realizing the limitations of his knees, Whitting pulled a wing chair over, perched on its edge, and leaned over to watch.

Ntombi began to explain the various piles in front of her, starting with the now linear arrangement of church research. "You see, this is the big picture. Well, not the really big picture, merely what is happening in the church in America. It's a snapshot, you know. The last twenty years. Here are books describing practices. The student researchers—wow. They must've really gotten into this. They have reviewed thousands of church websites, newsletters, bulletin inserts, scores and scores of music, done word searches . . . Isn't technology grand?"

"If you say so." Whitting chuckled, then forced himself to make the switch from an interest in Ntombi's revelatory frenzy to an interest in her actual findings.

"You see the pattern forming? It's more about what's missing than what's here, though I can't seem to get at the crux of it. Wait!" She glanced up at him and then back at the piles in front of her. "What if I pull out the outliers?"

Ntombi began extracting pieces one at a time and placing them in a separate pile. "Amazing, there is a pattern. Well maybe not yet a pattern, but a momentum, a movement of sorts."

"Which pile?"

"The small pile."

"Good. Tell me about the big pile first. What do you see?"

Ntombi hovered one hand a few inches above the pile. "Activity. Lots of activity. The recent two to three decades have been a flurry of activity in churches. They put the local community center to shame. There's something for everyone. Lots of programs, groups, fitness centers, yoga."

"With what focus?"

She looked up at Whitting. "That's easy. Self." She paused and added, "Now, don't get me wrong, they're solving problems. You know, life problems: depression, grief, alcoholism, oh, and lots about the family."

"That's a good thing, isn't it?"

Ntombi looked back at the data. "Oh, of course. How to raise adolescents, the terrible twos, Christian style, lots of good stuff."

"Okay, so what's missing?"

"Well," Ntombi said, as she looked at the piles, then back at Whitting, "God is missing."

"God?" Whitting said, with a hint of surprise in his voice.

"At least in our word search, we found very little about God. His name doesn't seem to come up much. There's lot's of psychology but not theology. Just look at this pile. These are materials for study groups. At best it is group therapy, not Bible study." She glanced at Whitting again, this time with a blank stare and then back at another one of the piles. "This stack is sociology, lot's of social justice initiatives. Again, no theology. We are focused on the wrong 'ology.'"

Whitting's brows lowered as he waited on Ntombi's next revelation. Then he continued, "Well. What about Jesus?"

"Nope. Rarely mentioned. And then there are contemporary books. Seems people want something from God, but rebirth and transformation are not happening. I guess then they need more and more programs and self-help books—kinda like trying to cobble someone into Christlikeness. It is very different than what Edwards described in the book you gave me."

Whitting nodded, somewhat wishing he had read the more recent books. Then again, in his view, a copyright date in the last century generally yielded little of import. Now equally as interested in his research assistant's transformation as he was in her findings, he simply added, "Go on."

"I'm not sure I can. Wait. One more thing. While new methods are being tried, in rare instances there is also a reinstatement of old methods, like silence and Bible study."

"Both good things."

"Not just good—essential. But I'm still missing something, like the key that will open the treasure chest."

"It'll come to you." He pointed to the collection of papers behind her. "What about those?"

She turned around. "This is a different lot altogether. Again, denomination doesn't tell you anything."

"How so?"

Ntombi wrapped her arms around her raised knee. "May I share what I found in my interviews first? Somehow I think it all fits together." She pivoted on her single planted foot with the speed of a whirling dervish. "In this comparison, I think it's less important what each person is called to do or how but more important the why. It's clear, thousands, possibly hundreds of thousands or more, maybe millions are being called. I don't know if the numbers are unprecedented, but it's like an army is in training, and some are already in formation. The One is calling all sorts of people to all kinds of work. And they are being trained, many not by their local church, but individually, directly. And they don't know why either.

Looking up at Whitting, she continued, "Some are being called to move to a new place and wait there. They don't know why, but the Spirit is strong, and they move. It's like they're in a formation awaiting their next order."

Ntombi glanced back at the pile and gently touched the top piece of paper, and stared straight ahead. "There's a rhythm. Some are marching in unison and are being spiritually gathered, yet they are physically dispersed throughout what we call the Church. For many, it's not the rhythm of their church. It's a different drummer. And there's a longing, a powerful longing." Ntombi lifted her hand from the stack and sat back. She looked up at Whitting. "Like the music in their heads is different than what others are hearing."

Ntombi again pointed at the small stack of outliers, sat back, and brought one folded hand to her mouth. Whitting watched as a ray of low, morning light filtered through the oaks and the front window to light her face. The scene reminded him of Rembrandt's painting of the Apostle Paul.

"Now for this group. Some of those called out are finding their way to these churches and organizations. Not all of these are churches; some are gathering outside the formal structure."

Whitting prodded. "Tell me about them. What's different?"

"It's not so much what they're doing—though that differs as well—but why. They're all about God and eternal things."

"Go on."

"Well, I think a good way to understand the difference is the cross." Ntombi grabbed a piece of paper and drew a cross. "This outlier group is all about the vertical line, the link between heaven and earth. You know, 'thy kingdom come' stuff."

"And the larger group?"

"They are working really hard but on the wrong things and without the power."

"The power?"

"Without the vertical relationship, there is no power."

Whitting sat in amazement as his heart was again warmed by her words and the realization that others were hearing the same music. In his mind's eye, he could see the vision of others who were one by one joining the formation, hearing the music, obeying without knowing why or how they fit into the battle plan. He smiled as he recalled the passage in Revelation and imagined a scene with the armies of heaven camped about and Jesus standing beside the milky-white horse, reins in hand, brushing her coat.

Ntombi sat in silence, half studying her work. It seemed the flow of revelation had waned, and the reality of little sleep was setting in. Whitting watched and wondered if this was what the Apostle John looked like after a big day on the Isle of Patmos.

"Would it help if I show you my graphic from our newly found historical sources? A look at the history may help us to understand how, or at least when, the church went afield."

Ntombi inhaled deeply and looked up at Whitting as if she just realized he was in the room. She exhaled. "Yes. Now would be a good time."

"Good then. I'll get it."

Whitting went to fetch it from the car and returned, eager to show Ntombi what he had discovered. Just then, Becca stuck her head through the doorway and offered a cup of tea. Both accepted her kind and timely offer and the opportunity to return to the earthly realm for a moment before traveling back in time.

Whitting carefully pulled the graphic from its tube and unrolled it across the dining room table. His creative whirlwind had settled into what was at least discernible, if not revelatory.

He looked at Ntombi and explained, "I've gone back and reread the sermons of Whitefield and Edwards. It would be very telling to do a word search on them."

"How so?"

"It would reveal God to be the subject—not what he can do for us, but who he is, his characteristics, power, authority. And in the middle of the sermons, the Awakening just happened. It is said that on one occasion, mid-sermon, so many people were on their faces praying for forgiveness, Edwards put a mark next to that part in his sermon notes."

Ntombi looked straight into Whitting's eyes. "That's it. Not the marked page, but God as the subject." She turned back toward the timeline and pointed, moving her hand back and forth. "When did we change our focus?"

Whitting turned and touched the timeline, moving his hand from the Great Awakening toward the Second Great Awakening. He stopped midway between the two. "Somewhere in here, the very meaning of the faith changed." He crossed his arms, then brought one folded hand to his lips. "I almost forgot to include it. In the Great Awakening, there was a keen sense of death to sin and rebirth. By the Second Awakening, something quite different happened."

"What was different?"

Whitting looked at her and then back at the timeline. "No death and rebirth. It became being saved instead of being reborn."

"Aren't they the same thing?"

"Not at all. Some theologians believe it began with the Enlightenment, which, by the way, is very wrongly named."

"What about rebirth versus being saved?"

Whitting paused and turned from the chart to face Ntombi. "The approach became to add salvation to one's life. Edwards and Whitefield preached rebirth. Well, mostly they preached about God and, by the thousands, people were transformed. They didn't just get a ticket to heaven—they were new creatures. The so-called enlightenment also resulted in a macro shift, a shift in our view of God. It was a dumbing down of sorts. We ceased believing in a supernatural God who interacts with His creation. He became smaller." Whitting took a deep breathe and let it out. "Why, just yesterday, while watching snippets of news and weather, I heard three references to Mother Nature. Edwards and Whitefield believed Father God used lightening and disasters to get our attention. Now such a statement would garner laughter, even from many pulpits."

FORTY-ONE

More Truth

The next day, Whitting arrived early to finish their research merger. Ntombi was different today—more settled, like getting some of it out the day before had brought clarity. They stood in the dining room with Witting's timeline banner stretched across the front window. The morning sun lit the middle section from behind. They stood nearly shoulder to shoulder in front of it, although Ntombi's were higher. They looked like a pair of art connoisseurs in a gallery—pointing, commenting.

After some discussion of the timeline, Ntombi said, "Have you read much about the Shroud of Turin?"

Whitting backed up to look at Ntombi and cocked his head to one side. "Yes. Interesting you ask. I actually saw it once and have been reading about it recently." He turned back to the chart and folded his arms over his chest. "Why do you ask?"

"Do you think it was Jesus' burial cloth?"

"What I know is that researchers are sure the image on the cloth was created by a sudden burst of light and all of twenty-first-century technology is unable to recreate the image. They can come close with UV directional radiation, but it isn't intense enough or quick enough. They believe the image was created by some form of electromagnetic energy, like a flash of light on a short wavelength. They've tried to create a forgery and cannot, thus, I doubt an eighteenth-century forger could either."

Ntombi nudged him lightly with her elbow. "But, what do you believe?"

Whitting turned to her. "I believe it is the burial cloth of Jesus and the flash of light was created the moment his resurrected life re-entered his body."

Ntombi smiled. "Kinda like the egg at conception."

"The egg?" Whitting asked, with a sideways turn of his head.

Ntombi turned and headed into the living room. "Yeah, I have the article," she called out and returned with it in hand. "Researchers have discovered a bright flash of light at the moment of conception."

"Really?"

Ntombi flipped the pages of the article and handed Whitting the photo page. There before him was a perfectly formed human egg, photographed the instant it was fertilized. All around it was a bright halo of yellow light.

Ntombi pointed to bits of the article. "The research is amazing, but I had never thought about the connection to the shroud. It's all about the light."

"Amazing science. And an even more amazing parallel." Whitting placed the article on the table and began pointing out the state of the church at the time of the Great Awakening. "It had fallen away and was barren."

Ntombi dropped to the edge of a velvet cushioned, carved, mahogany dining chair, stretched her legs out, and leaned back. "So what else are we missing?"

Whitting turned a chair backward and straddled it. He glanced at the banner and back at Ntombi. "You hit on the crux, as you called it last night. The end is God Himself, not what He can or will do for us. The beauty, the goodness, the truth we long for is in Him and through Him."

Ntombi tilted her head a bit. "Did people know that then? I mean, before the Awakening?"

"I believe they knew more, at least from a quality standpoint. People in that time used more exact language. We have lost much of the language of the church."

Ntombi cocked her head. "Like what?"

"The word "soul." It is trivialized, used in movie titles even, but no longer spoken of in the church."

Ntombi's eyes widened. "Oh, that reminds me. I went to one of your local, big-chain bookstores. I went first to the Christian section and couldn't find anything about God, so I went to the desk and asked. She looked on the computer and nothing. So I asked for books on the glory of God. Again, nothing. I decided to expand my list, so I asked what they had on the soul. She looked and said, 'Oh yes, we have several on the soul.'"

"Were they any good?"

Ntombi smiled. "Wait for it. She gave me instructions on where to find them. Well, I went there, and guess what? They were in the Wicca section."

"Wicca? The books on the soul are now in the witchcraft section?"

"Yes! All the works on the soul were in the Wicca section."

Whitting dropped his head.

"And without a sense of the soul and the spirit, our connection point to God is lost, or at least forgotten."

Whitting shook his lowered head. "We have given over the word soul."

"Looks like it."

Whitting sighed. "We have also completely lost the meaning of glory."

"What do you mean?"

"The word is now used to describe fame, worldly adoration,

when, in fact, the Hebrew and Greek words paint a much different picture."

"What should our picture be?"

"We will never fully fathom God's glory, maybe not even on the other side of eternity, but I believe we are never to stop trying. Read Arthur Michael Ramsey some time. And Edwards has a work on it too. The short answer is that when scripture refers to glory, it means the full character of God, his weight—who he is."

Ntombi made a note of both authors' names on a sticky note and put it on the doorframe of the dining room.

Whitting smiled as his young friend returned to her seat, knowing she would actually read Ramsey and more Edwards and enjoy them.

"What other words did you find missing from the document scan?"

Ntombi leaned back against her chair, crossed her arms, and answered Whitting with a decisive nod. "Sin."

"Oh, my goodness, it wasn't in there?"

"Nope. The word searches did not turn up the word sin. Not even once."

Whitting turned slightly to look at his banner on the wall and spoke slowly, deliberately. "What happened during the Great Awakening was an overwhelming sense of sin. Conviction is an almost indescribable sense of disgust and raw anguish over what one has done against God. Much has been written about the visible manifestations during the Awakening. Onlookers, for instance, focused on the outward signs."

"In the book you gave me, Edwards describes the outward signs and—"

"Yes, Edwards describes tremors, crying, speaking aloud." Whitting grabbed a marker from the table and walked to the banner. "What people were witnessing were the outward signs of conviction and, in many cases, the moment of death to sin." He touched the timeline, moving his hand softly across the 1700s. "The soul was dying to self and being reborn. Of course, the body responded."

"Like the flash of light as Jesus' resurrected life re-entered his body."

Whitting turned back toward Ntombi and fidgeted with the marker as he spoke. "In true rebirth, the heart's desires are transformed."

Ntombi quickly scribbled Whitting's words on another sticky note, stood, and stuck it to the wall. She turned to Whitting. "This is good stuff. What else?"

Whitting looked at the timeline banner, and in a voice full of breath and deeper than before, said, "I believe it is coming. The army you talked about. Those who are loving God and secretly enjoying Him are being planted, called out for such a time."

Ntombi turned and looked through the doorway to her research piles in the next room. "Even with the work the researchers did, we saw only a tiny fraction of it." She looked back at Whitting. "If what we saw is merely representative, it is a massive army."

Whitting had a new light in his eyes. He closed his lips and smiled.

Ntombi matched his look and said, "And their training is intensifying. Maybe this is going to be big."

Ntombi paused, took a breath. "But what is the army preparing for?"

Whitting glanced down at the floor. His head popped back up. "An awakening! God isn't done with us yet. There will be another awakening as to who God is and who we are in his sight. The chasm between."

Ntombi's eyes widened, and Whitting continued, "Maybe millions. People will experience a transformation—dying to self and rebirth to the pure love of God. Then all else changes."

"Has it begun?"

Whitting turned his chair to face Ntombi and took a breath. "Yes. I think so, but maybe it's different than before."

Ntombi let his words settle in. "In the last days, God says, 'I will pour out my Spirit, and your sons and daughters will prophesy.'"

"And your young men shall see visions and your old men shall dream dreams."

"Peter's words in Acts," Ntombi said with a slight sense of pride in knowing.

"And the prophet Joel's."

Just then, Becca appeared in the doorway with a tea tray in hand and leaned against the doorframe. "It's like this," she said. "What is an awakening but a supernatural work of the Holy Spirit?"

"Well, yes, and on a big scale," Whitting said.

"Right. Well, look at the two of you."

Whitting and Ntombi looked at each other and then back up at Becca.

"You don't think y'all are normal, do you? If it weren't for the Holy Spirit, how on earth would a sixty-something professor and a twenty-something South African girl who grew up on a game reserve come together to sleuth around Charleston, trying to figure out what God is up to?" She grinned, then walked over and placed the tea service on the table.

Whitting flipped both palms up and out in an exaggerated gesture. "Well, there you have it."

Ntombi laughed. "Sounds like confirmation to me. Becca, will you join us?"

Becca headed toward the door shaking her head and flicked a backward wave. "Y'all enjoy."

The odd pair of God sleuths sat pondering all their research. Finally, with a sigh of accomplishment, Ntombi spoke. "We've had several revelations but seems there's something we've missed. Maybe some truth the church once held dear that has been lost amidst the hurried activity or the loss of language."

Whitting motioned for Ntombi to face the table as he moved to the other side and sat down across from her. Her curiosity was piqued. With the same care as one who had planned a proposal, Whitting reached into his jacket pocket and pulled out a small, clear, acrylic case. Ntombi sat with her hands folded on the table, and her eyes fixed on the object. A pure and peculiar peace settled into the room.

Or was it a breath?

Whitting slid the encased object toward her. In it was a tiny, gossamer-thin piece of woven linen.

Ntombi studied it. The tiny sliver of cloth was barely intact. Time had gradually worn it threadbare. It was stained, and its edges were frayed. But there was something about the stain.

"What is it?"

"It is believed to be from the Shroud of Turin."

"Seriously? From the shroud? How did you . . . I mean, when did you . . . the Shroud?"

Whitting's eyes sparkled. He was enjoying the moment.

"Do you remember the shopkeeper?"

"The brother who owns the books? Of course. Who could forget him?"

"He called last week and asked me to pay him a visit. Asked that I come alone. When I got there, he gave it to me. He said he's treasured it for years. It was acquired as part of the same collection as the book."

"And he just gave it to you?"

"He said he was dying, and he wanted to ensure it ended up with someone who would cherish it. Three days later, his obituary appeared in the paper."

Ntombi's head snapped up. "He died? The shopkeeper gave you this, and then he died?"

Whitting nodded.

Ntombi lifted her hands to cover her mouth. "Oh, my goodness." She lowered her hands and looked at Whitting. "I really liked him." She lifted the case to look more closely at the stain.

"Perhaps a fraction of a drop of Christ's blood."

Ntombi looked at Whitting, suddenly beyond all words and all reason.

Whitting continued. "You asked what else we are missing? I believe the answer is in that tiny stain."

She placed the case back on the table and looked questioningly across the table at Whitting.

"I'll explain. When you parallel the gospel accounts of Jesus' words on the cross and create a chronological list, a power-filled truth emerges—one often overlooked." Whitting stroked his brow, and turned and dug through his attaché, bringing out a crumpled copy of a painting. He smoothed out the creases and turned it toward Ntombi. "This is Andrei Rublev's fourteenth-century depiction of the Trinity."

Ntombi pulled it close and studied it.

"What do you see in the painting?" he asked her.

"I see three ethereal-looking figures around a table." She glanced up at Whitting and back at the picture. Pointing to each, she said, "You can tell who is who. Father God is in the center, the Holy Spirit is on my right, his left. And Jesus is seated at the Father's right hand."

"What do you see on the table?"

"It's a cup. Looks like a chalice of wine. And their attention is on the cup."

"Yes. To me it depicts the cup of salvation. If you recall, Jesus prayed in the Garden of Gethsemane and asked, 'If it is your will, let this cup pass from me.'"

Ntombi nodded.

"Okay, now fast forward to what happened on the cross. Jesus continued to minister to others after he was on the cross."

"Yes, his mother, Mary, and John, who were at his feet, and the thief beside him."

"He also prayed for those who were crucifying him."

"But there is a point where he stops. He says, 'I thirst,' and the guard gave him soured wine on a hyssop branch." Whitting leaned toward Ntombi. "So do you know what the hyssop was used for in ancient Israel?"

Ntombi scrunched her forehead. "Uh, something to do with the sacrifice."

"Yes, the scapegoat. The scapegoat received the sins of the people, was slain, and then his blood, filled with the sin of the people, was sprinkled on the altar—wait for it—using a hyssop branch! When Jesus received the soured wine on the hyssop . . ."

"He received the sins of the world!"

"Precisely. I believe it was the moment he received the cup. And then, immediately afterward, he said, 'It is finished,' and breathed his last breath."

Ntombi sat back in her chair and placed both hands on the table in front of the shroud. She glanced at it and then at the painting. "And in the cup, the sins of the world."

"Yes." Whitting brought the fingers of one hand up and together. He took his empty porcelain teacup and placed it atop the perch of his fingers. "You see, the cup now contains pure wine. The soured wine of sin is gone. It has been cleansed through the body of Christ."

Ntombi looked at Whitting's makeshift chalice. "And it's still a cup. He offers it, but it's up to us to receive the cup of rebirth." Ntombi looked down at the picture. "It's just sitting on the table, offered."

Whitting placed the cup back on the saucer and was quiet. In the sweetness of silence, a new revelation began to surface.

Whitting turned to look beyond the room and out the adjacent window and Ntombi did the same. It framed part of a massive live oak. Sun rays streaked through the limbs and gave the hanging moss an added gray-green glow. Ntombi heard a soulful voice rise from the other side of the table.

"There is pow'r, pow'r, wonder-working power in the blood of the lamb," he sang.

Whitting smiled over at Ntombi. "My friend, what we are missing—what we have forgotten—is the wonder-working power of the blood."

FORTY-TWO

Boston and the Cape

The early flight and a day of touring the city brought Ntombi a sense of fullness. She leaned against the inside of the limo door and stretched her legs out on the back seat with her feet toward Tata. " What a day!" she said, tucking her arms behind her head. "It was a good birthday. Thank you, Tata."

Tata patted her feet. "I've missed my girl."

She brought both hands to her mouth and blew him a kiss, then leaned her head against the seat and dozed. When she woke, she didn't know exactly where they were. The ocean had moved. Before she'd closed her eyes, it was on the left. Now it was on the right.

Tata was asleep. Ntombi sat quietly so as not to wake him. She studied the side of his head and thought the way his mouth hung slightly open was cute. Her heart was full. This man who had so loved and cared for her all these years had helped bring Mandlenkosi back to her. Tata was her hero.

Night was settling in around them, and a mist descended as the black limousine turned toward the national seashore. Ntombi had no idea where she was going, yet she rode without fear. Calling was like that. You take each step, not knowing where it will lead. You simply trust the guide. Ntombi smiled softly. Tata was guiding her steps now.

The limo turned onto a narrow seashell-paved path, winding through the sea-stunted trees to reveal a small, weathered cedar-shake home built in a Cape Cod style. The porch light was on, and a lamp in the window seemed to welcome them.

Once inside, Ntombi sank onto the cotton, pillow-ticking couch, then turned and knelt on the sofa to look out the large bay window at the front of the house. She called out to Tata in the next room. "Tata, the driver. He's leaving?"

"Yes. We'll take it from here. We have keys to the car and bicycles."

"Wonderful. I assume both are for tomorrow."

Ntombi was awake before Tata the next morning and thankful they were on their own. She made coffee, and with a cup depicting Cape Cod lighthouses in hand, explored the house and the sandy path outside around it. It was a peaceful land. She wondered where she was on the map. Never before had she traveled without at least knowing where she was going.

"Lily?" came Tata's voice from the doorway, calling her by her once-familiar English name.

"Yes, Father."

"Get dressed. We're going for a bike ride."

"This early?"

"Yes, early is best."

In no time, they were winding along tree-lined paths. All the nearby houses had a similar look, each in the same weathered gray as if to quietly nod acceptance to the other and show homage to their Puritan past. Ntombi liked their simplicity.

"Let's park the bikes here," Tata said. "We'll take this path."

Ntombi was reminded of her time on Kwandwe. Tata knew where he was going. There would no doubt be a surprise at the end of the path. But this time, it wouldn't be an elusive white rhino or, one of her favorites, the aardvark. As they walked along, she smiled a knowing smile and exaggerated her steps and the swing of her arms. The last few meters were uphill. As they topped the hill, Tata said, "Look."

Ntombi could see the ocean in front of her and a bay to her right. She breathed in the air, unlike any she had known. She breathed in beauty and majesty and glory and peace unlike that of home but still oddly familiar like an ancient memory.

They descended just a bit from the knoll through a narrow path lined with wildflowers, piercing the tree canopy like thread through a needle. As they rounded a small bend, Ntombi lifted her eyes to a magnificent display of God's handiwork. The forest clearing presented a meadow of lupine that descended to the sea on one side and a cliff that led to the grass-lined harbor on the other. Birds played in the bearberry thicket on the cliffside as small wooden boats bobbed in the harbor. The boat colors of red or blue, or the occasional deep, glossy green, seemed carefully chosen by an artist's hand.

Ntombi dropped to her knees and then sat cross-legged in the grass. Tata followed suit, though a bit more carefully.

"This spot is called Fort Hill," he said.

After a due time of silence, Ntombi spoke. "Did you know sailors must consider two points: where they have been and where they are going?"

"A good principle for calling."

"It is, isn't it? The past isn't ignored but rather transformed. Even sin. Jesus said something about those who are forgiven much, love much. The past is a part of the call."

"A humbling part," Tata said.

Ntombi looked at her father, then back over the scenery. She pondered the idea of Tata and sin. She couldn't imagine he had ever needed forgiveness. They sat a bit longer in silence as they had so often done, peering across the vast horizons of Kwandwe. They were content just to be and to marvel at God revealing himself through his handiwork.

Tata pointed south-southeast. "Look. What's that way?"

Ntombi smiled. "South Africa is that way."

"I think she's waving at us."

Ntombi waved and nudged Tata to do the same. He did, and they shared a laugh. Ntombi stood and dusted the grass from her clothes. Tata smiled and rose to his feet, repeating her grass-removal technique.

"Tata, thank you for bringing me here. It's a special place."

Tata grabbed her hand and squeezed it. Ntombi looked him in the eyes. It was if he wanted to say something more but didn't. Instead, he turned and led her back down the path and to their bikes.

Back at the cottage that afternoon, Ntombi settled in on the sofa with a book she'd found on the shelf. Before she could make it through the first page, she heard the sound of tires crunching along the crushed gravel drive. She looked out the window. "Father, the limo is here. Are we going somewhere?"

"No, my dear. We have a visitor."

"A visitor? Way out here?"

"Yes. A special visitor. She's a long-time friend of mine. Her name is Lucille."

Tata opened the inside door, leaving, for a moment, the storm door between them. On the other side stood an older, white woman. She stood erect but was only about five feet tall. Tata pushed the storm door open, and Lucille stepped through.

Ntombi smiled at Lucille. She noticed her hair was completely white. To Ntombi, it looked like finely spun silk, and her first instinct was to touch it. She resisted, but somehow she seemed familiar, like a memory from Kwandwe. She wondered if she had been a guest before but saved the comment.

Tata was quite formal in his introduction. "Lucille, please meet Ntombi. Ntombi this is Mrs. Lucille—"

"Just call me Lucille." The woman extended a tiny hand to Ntombi.

Ntombi smiled and shook her hand. "Pleased to meet you." Her hand felt frail like mostly just skin and bones. Ntombi held it gently. As she did, Lucille brought her other hand up and cradled Ntombi's, looked up at her, and said, "It is indeed a pleasure to meet you. Of course, Tata has told me so much."

Ntombi looked into Lucille's icy-blue eyes and decided she liked her. "Thank you, ma'am. Would you like some tea?"

"Yes, please. Tea would be delightful."

Ntombi listened from the kitchen as Tata and Lucille exchanged pleasantries. They didn't sound like long-time friends to her. There was an awkwardness, like something fragile in the room.

Ntombi placed the tray of teapot and cups on the coffee table and began to pour. Lucille graciously accepted her cup and quickly complimented Ntombi on her bush tea.

Tata explained, "Lucille's family foundation supports my mission in Torrance."

Ntombi took a sip of her tea and replaced it on the saucer. "Really? That's wonderful. The mission does amazing work." Glancing over at Tata, she added, "And Tata seems to enjoy it. I think he's the perfect mentor for the men."

There was a moment of silence, and Ntombi felt the need to fill it. "So how did the two of you come to know each other?"

Lucille looked at Tata and smiled softly. "My husband and our family used to visit Kwandwe."

"Oh, my goodness. I thought you looked familiar."

"It's been a few years since we've been there. My husband passed away two years ago."

"Oh, I'm so sorry. I'm sure you miss him."

"Very much. He was a wonderful, godly man."

Ntombi took another sip of her tea. Lucille and Tata did the same.

"This is excellent Roibos," Lucille told her. "Hard to find good Roibos here."

"Yes, ma'am; we've learned to travel with tea leaves."

"It's good to be prepared." Lucille took another sip of her tea and placed her cup on her saucer and the saucer on the coffee table. She looked at Tata. "We have prepared for this conversation for years, and now here we are."

Ntombi's graceful form stiffened slightly, and she looked at Tata. Her mind searched their faces for understanding. "What conversation?"

Lucille gave another quick glance to Tata. Tata reached one hand over, and Ntombi scooted closer and took it.

"We have prepared for this conversation about you and your beautiful past."

Ntombi's kept her eyes focused on Tata. "My past? How could you tell me about my past? I lived my past."

Tata filled in the gap. "Yes, but as the sailor needs a fixed point behind in order to navigate forward, we love you and want you to know more of your fixed point behind."

Ntombi wrinkled her brow. Tata took a breath. "Sweetheart, I love you very much and always will . . ."

"But?"

"And, Umama and I adopted you."

Ntombi's hand dropped from Tata's. She felt her eyes grow wide and her lips draw tight. She stared at Tata, and he didn't look away. She turned to look at Lucille.

"Yes, dear one. I am your grandmother."

Ntombi looked back to Tata, expecting he'd correct her. Instead, he continued to look at her silently.

Ntombi looked back at Lucille. "But, you're . . ."

"White?" Lucille forced a sideways smile. "Very much so. Even the crown of my head these days."

"I mean, you are a beautiful lady and all, but . . ."

"As are you."

Ntombi stood and went into the kitchen. She leaned over the sink and looked out the window. After a moment, she returned to the living room. "How did this—I mean, how did I happen? You're saying you're not my father?"

Tata answered her quickly. "I am and always will be your father. But I am not your biological father."

"My son, Clarkson, is your biological father."

Ntombi stared at Tata. Pain entered her chest. It was like the pain she felt the night Mandlenkosi disappeared, only stronger. It made breathing hard.

Tata motioned for Ntombi to have a seat on the sofa. She obliged. He leaned toward her and continued with a practiced voice. "Your mother's name was Nombeko. She was Umama's niece. There were complications when she had you, and she knew she was dying. She knew we couldn't have children, and she asked if we would take you. We promised her we would love you as our own. She also made us promise we would not tell you. It was a mistake to make that promise. I know that now. But she was dying. And we loved her. We loved you."

Ntombi began to cry and soon had difficulty catching her breath. She tried to sort through her thoughts but could only think that everything was a lie. Every thought and memory she'd ever had was no longer real, because they were all based on a lie.

"Why tell me now?" she asked.

Tata placed his elbows on his knees and lowered his head. With a shake of his head, he said, "We couldn't tell you before your birthday—for reasons that will become apparent. We wanted you to know before the wedding, but then Mandlenkosi went missing." Tata's words trailed off and turned to sobs. For the first time in her life, Ntombi saw her father cry. Lucille was still perched on the edge of the sofa, posture erect, feet together, but a tear now welled like liquid crystal over her milky eyes. Ntombi fixed on the tear as it traveled along her nearly transparent skin.

Ntombi kept trying to wrap her mind around it. A lie, lived for a lifetime, was now revealed. She had thousands of questions but again found no voice. For the second time in her life, when she opened her mouth, nothing came out.

So they sat in silence. The truth was now in the room. It hurt, but the truth always sets people free.

FORTY-THREE

Black Roses and a Tiny White Box

The cottage was oddly peaceful. Ntombi had watched Tata's limo disappear out of sight. Even the limo was a symbol of control and ownership. Ntombi hated the fact that she'd been "kept" all these years. Part of her wished her "real" father—this man they called Clarkson—had just disappeared forever. Really. Why money and things without any contact? It was time that mattered, not all the stuff.

Tata had answered each of Ntombi's questions as they surfaced. He'd stayed a couple more days, then at her request, he let her be. But he'd left behind a box of old photos. The box's top and base were hewn out of wood, likely acacia, and wicker adorned all four sides. It contained pictures of her mothers—both of them. Tata had kept it all these years.

Ntombi had taken only one or two photos out of the box a day. With each one, a new picture of who she was began to form in her mind. She could see herself in each of the photos. Her cheekbones were from Nombeko, and her ears were clearly Umama's. She wondered how that could be.

A knock on the door surprised her. Surely it wasn't him. She wasn't ready yet. What would she do it if was him?

Ntombi moved slowly to one of the front windows to peek out. She didn't see a car.

There was a second knock. This time, someone spoke.

"Ntombi, I know you're in there."

Mandlenkosi's voice brought unexpected excitement. Forgetting her grief for the moment, Ntombi swung open the door.

Mandlenkosi stepped through the door and exaggerated his inspection of her, looking her up and down. "My, my, my, look at you. We've got work to do."

"It's good to see you too."

"How long have you been holed up in here?"

"Days, I think."

Mandlenkosi took in the room. "Great cottage."

Ntombi shrugged and lifted both palms up and out. "How'd you get here?"

He returned the shrug. "They have to move me every few weeks. I convinced them no one would find me here."

"Who won't find you?"

"All I know is the trail has led to people high up. Very high up, apparently." Mandlenkosi placed both hands on the top of her arms, dropped his head slightly, and looked directly in her eyes. "Never mind all that. You get in the shower. I'll work on straightening up around here. And see what you can do with that hair. It's bigger than I've ever seen it."

As Ntombi turned to head down the hall, Mandlenkosi popped her on the rear with the back of his hand. "Run along now."

She turned back toward him and planted a hand on her hip. "Stop it! You can't do that now. We're not children."

"Seems one of us is acting like one."

⁓

Later that day, they rode in the rag-top Jeep that came with the house, bumping along the sandy road. Mandlenkosi watched

Ntombi almost as much as he watched the road. Everything about her seemed new to him yet still somehow familiar. He watched as she dug a barrette and some bobby-pins from her backpack, gathered her damp hair up, and piled it loosely atop her head. When she noticed him watching, she tilted her head slightly and preened a bit longer. Then, with a bobby pin in her mouth, she asked, "Where's your bodyguard?"

"I don't know. Maybe in the house across the street from yours or maybe behind us."

Ntombi turned around in the seat and rose to her knees to see. "Gee, is he following us?"

"I'm not sure. Likely."

Ntombi turned back and sat with her back against the Jeep door, facing Mandlenkosi.

At breakfast, they talked over recent events: Mandlenkosi's first safe house, the reunion with his parents, and the progression of the case.

"Why all the moves?"

"They've apprehended some of the ring. A major sting went down last week. There are others, but I'm told some of the mid-level players were arrested. The top guy is still out there. Thirty-three women and children were freed just last week. One woman was kept in a cage for years in a suburban house outside Atlanta. Men would line up to rape her, sometimes as many as thirty a day. Others were rescued from a small island."

Ntombi zipped her sweatshirt the rest of the way up and crossed her arms in front as if to protect herself from the evil of the world. She bowed her head and prayed aloud for the captives, for their healing, and for the capture of the other bad guys. She prayed for Mandlenkosi's protection and for Tata's. She gave thanks for Mandlenkosi's return and for the part he played in setting the captives free.

As she prayed, Mandlenkosi watched her. He too was thankful—thankful for her innocent beauty, both inside and out.

Later that afternoon, they sat on the sofa in the living room at the cottage, facing each other with legs outstretched and overlapping. Ntombi did most of the talking, explaining without any hesitation all she had learned of her mystery sponsor family.

"What was your real—I mean, biological—mother's name?"

"Nombeko."

Mandlenkosi was quiet for a moment before speaking again. "You had two mothers die."

Ntombi pursed her lips and nodded. She looked out the window and spoke softly. "She worked at Kwandwe with Tata and Umama. I think she was Umama's niece or something."

"What about your biological father?"

She turned back to look at Mandlenkosi. "His name is Clarkson. He married my mother. Well, kinda."

"What do you mean?"

"Let me back up. He and his parents were at Kwandwe during his Christmas break. He had been there the summer before and had met my mother. They fell in love, but he was a student at Oxford and a guest at Kwandwe. She was a maid. Anyway, he convinced the family to return during Christmas break, and, well, that's when they made me."

"Go on."

"When Nombeko found out she was pregnant, she didn't want Clarkson to know. She knew he would come, and it would upset his studies and disgrace his family."

"So how did he find out?"

"Someone from Kwandwe called him. We still don't know who."

Mandlenkosi smiled softly. Ntombi's use of the word "we" was a good sign. "Go on," he said again.

"Clarkson arrived the day before I was born and insisted they marry. Tata performed the ceremony. They had one night together, and my mother gave birth the next day. She died later that night. On her deathbed, she asked Tata and Umama to take me and love me as their own and not to tell me until I was out of college."

"Then why extend the wait?"

"Well, you went missing, and Tata said there's some legal reason. I don't know all of it."

"Amazing. Have you met Clarkson yet?"

"No."

"Well, do you plan to?"

"Sorta."

"Sorta?"

"He's staying on the Cape. Has a home here. I'm not sure where. Each day he goes to this place called Fort Hill. He's there from three till four."

"To meet you?"

"Yes, but only if I want to. He sent word that he will go there every day. I'm to go when I'm ready."

"But you haven't yet?"

Ntombi sat up and turned forward, placed both feet on the floor, and rubbed her hands back and forth atop her thighs. "I'm not ready."

"I see."

Ntombi took a deep breath and stood. "I have something I need to return to you." She walked down the hall and, after what seemed like a bit too long to Mandlenkosi, returned from her room with a tiny, white box. Mandlenkosi's eyes widened, and he stood to face her.

"It was found in the wreckage, under the car, and was given

to me by the inspector. I don't know what's inside. I haven't opened it."

Mandlenkosi looked into Ntombi's eyes and raised a hand to receive the box. "I was on my way to propose, wasn't I?"

"Only you would know," Ntombi said. She held Mandlenkosi's upturned hands in her left palm and placed the box in them with her right.

Mandlenkosi looked at the box. "You haven't opened it?"

Ntombi folded Mandlenkosi's hand around it. "It isn't mine to open. I was merely entrusted with it." Then, with an abrupt change, she took a seat on the sofa and patted the cushion beside her. Mandlenkosi sat, leaving no space between them. He leaned forward and placed his elbows on his knees, fidgeting with the bow on the package.

Ntombi placed a hand on his back. "What happens next with the case?"

Mandlenkosi sat quietly for a moment. "Once the trial is over, I'll be placed in a witness protection program, given a new identity and a new occupation."

"Just when you were beginning to remember the old one." She leaned forward, placed her elbows on her knees, and leaned her shoulder against his. "Do you get to choose where you go? Can you return to South Africa?"

"I can influence the decision, even decide the country, within reason of course."

Ntombi curled her toes under against the rug, "What do you plan to do?"

"I don't know yet." Mandlenkosi sat up and back on the sofa, turning to face her. "Can I tell you about a dream I had? Somehow I think it's linked. Oh, and I want to tell you about the conversation I had with Steve."

Ntombi sat up straight and faced Mandlenkosi. "Oh?"

He grinned. "Yes. I saw you watching through the window. I expect you want to know what we talked about."

Ntombi's only response was raised brows.

"Well, first off, I hate to say it, but I can see why you would like him. Anyway, we decided to do the brave thing."

"Brave thing?"

"Yeah. Man up." Mandlenkosi paused, then added, "Man up and love you, even though you will break one or possibly both our hearts."

Ntombi cocked her head to one side. She crossed her arms in an exaggerated gesture. "So you had a may-the-best-man-win conversation?"

Mandlenkosi met her look with a closed-mouth grin. "Something like that."

Ntombi smiled at him. "Glad I get a say in the matter."

"We thought so."

Ntombi widened her smile and shook her head. "Let's hear about the dream."

Mandlenkosi told of the black rose and the vivid memory of the dream. It had not faded. If anything, it had grown clearer in his mind. He told of the brittle petals that seemed to soften and open as he reached for them, and their crackling recoil as he withdrew his hand. His eyes brightened as he told of the tiny beads of light and the way they danced about before drifting to heaven. "It was the most bizarre imagery."

Ntombi reached over and took one of Mandlenkosi's hands. "It's not bizarre at all. The black rose represents each child held captive. Your hand frees the light within them. The light is what they were created to be, what God had in mind when he made them. Your hand allows the light to shine on earth, to dance about as was intended before it returns to the Father above."

Mandlenkosi lowered his chin slightly and looked at her

from under his brows. How had she so quickly provided the meaning he craved, and yet was afraid to hear? Ntombi scooted back against the arm of the sofa, drew her knees up, wrapped her arms around them, and looked down at her feet.

She knew. He knew. He was to rescue the enslaved. His call was clear. The question was—did his call include her?

FORTY-FOUR

Abba

The sun lit Fort Hill gently from behind. The small bay had only whispers of waves, leaving the colorful, wooden boats lightly bobbing against their moorings. Each vessel cast a short shadow from stern and rope alike. Ntombi watched them and wondered if fishermen used them, or if they were placed merely for beauty's sake. She imagined herself in one of the boats, drifting out to sea, drifting toward South Africa.

Ntombi stood holding a hand-picked bouquet of wildflowers. She saw his feet first, approaching from behind. Then they were beside her, and she could see the faded canvas of his topsiders and wondered if he sailed. He had a familiar smell, like a mixture of water from the crystal sea, a familiar musk, and a flower that only grows in heaven. She knew it but at first couldn't place it.

Then he spoke as if they had known each other from eternity past. "Would you like to sit for a while?"

Ntombi turned and was oddly surprised by his height. She handed him the flowers. "Here. These are for you."

Clarkson took the flowers, looked at them, then at Ntombi. He smiled. "Thank you."

Ntombi smiled too, tilted her head, then turned and sat on a nearby bench. Clarkson followed.

They sat facing forward. Clarkson gently rubbed a flower

petal between his fingers and then brought the bouquet up to smell it before placing it beside him on the bench. Ntombi loosely folded her hands in her lap. She spoke first.

"You were on the flight from South Africa."

"Yes. I decided at your birth, I would be there for life's big transitions." He paused, then added, "I chose times when Father God would be by your side and joined him."

Ntombi looked down. "And the flight to America was one of those times?"

"Yes. After Mandlenkosi went missing…" Clarkson looked out over the sea. "Suffice it to say, I tried to help the detectives. When their efforts and my resources turned up nothing, I decided to help you transition."

Ntombi paused and nodded an inkling of understanding. "This is a beautiful place."

"I've always loved it. I have a house just up the road."

Ntombi turned around. "Really?"

She stayed turned for a moment, but Clarkson didn't point it out.

Clarkson continued, "There is indeed something special about this spot. It's the land of our ancestors."

"Really?"

Clarkson grinned, and Ntombi noticed the dimple in his chin, and the one on his right cheek that came and went when he smiled.

He nodded. "Yes, nearly four hundred years ago, a grandfather known as the Reverend Elder John sailed across that ocean as a very young man." Clarkson looked at Ntombi. "He was in search of pure worship." Looking back at the sea, he added, "He left the comforts of home, his studies at Oxford, and came to a new land to worship in Spirit and in truth."

"Oxford? What was he studying at Oxford?"

"He was studying to be an Anglican priest when he was called to this place. America was still a distant wilderness. Nonetheless, he obeyed the still, small voice and came."

"Was it a one-way boat?"

"Pretty much. At least it was for him. His uncle had arrived ten years earlier. He stayed with his uncle and worked for him until he could repay him for his voyage."

"What year did he come?"

"1633."

Ntombi scratched the side of her head and then, with both hands, pulled her hair back and twisted it to retrieve it from the seaside breeze. As she did, she noticed Clarkson's nearly black, curly hair. His too was unkempt and a bit too long.

He responded to her preening with, "Mine is usually a bit tidier, but I didn't want to risk a cut on the Cape. Not everyone can cut curly hair. Yours is beautiful."

"Thank you. Not for the hair, for the compliment."

Clarkson chuckled. "You're welcome for both."

She leaned toward him and bumped his shoulder with her own. "Tell me more about the land."

"That's a great story. Our great-times-ten grandfather's uncle bought it from the Indians. He had a house," he pointed to the highest point overlooking the bay, "right there. In fact, his house was the first built on the Cape."

Ntombi's eyes grew wide as she looked at the majestic spot overlooking the sea. "Oh, my goodness. I would choose that spot."

"Me too. I got as close as I could."

Ntombi turned forward, stretched her long legs, tucked both hands under them, and bounced her knees up and down a couple of times. "Tell me more about the Reverend Elder John."

Clarkson stretched out as well and crossed his legs at the

ankles. He leaned against the back of the bench and folded his arms in front of him. "He was a fisherman and a preacher. He pastored a church in a small town called Hull." He paused and pointed in Hull's direction.

Ntombi turned her gaze in the direction he pointed. "Why was he called the Reverend Elder John?"

"He preferred Elder, actually, because he didn't finish at Oxford and wasn't ordained."

"Why didn't he finish?"

"Persecution." Clarkson sat up and turned sideways on the bench, tucked one leg up, and faced Ntombi. As he did, she leaned back against the back of the bench and kept her gaze on the ocean. "A few years earlier, those who were part of the Reformation were burned at the stake in Oxford."

Ntombi's eyes again grew wide. "Really?" She paused. "You went to Oxford. Did you finish what he started?"

Clarkson smiled softly. "No, ma'am. I studied global economics."

Ntombi nodded. "I see."

Clarkson turned to face forward. "It's for another to finish what he started."

Ntombi breathed in some of the salt air and chose not to ask who.

The two sat together looking out over the vista. Ntombi thought backward, trying to reconnect the dots of her past and erase a myriad of dots that no longer held true.

In time, Clarkson broke the silence. "I have something for you. It belonged to the Reverend Elder John." He removed a carved, wooden box from the large patch pocket of his sailor's jacket and placed it on Ntombi's lap. She noticed the intricacy of the carving and a clumsily tied white satin ribbon, which didn't seem to go with the box.

Clarkson grinned, and a tiny flicker of sun reflected from one corner of his deep, blue-green eyes. "Do you want to open it? Now?"

Ntombi studied his face, then glanced down at the box. "May I wait till later?"

Clarkson looked at her, revealing, then hiding his disappointment. "Well, may I tell you something about it? John gifted it to Thomas, his grandson, who kept it and—"

"Now don't spoil the surprise!"

Clarkson folded his hands like one caught in the cookie jar. "Okay. I put a note inside."

"Good. Tell me about Thomas. Was he also a grandfather? I mean, our grandfather?"

"No. You see, the Reverend Elder John had seven sons—"

Ntombi removed a hand from the box and touched Clarkson's arm, stopping him mid-sentence. "One of his sons was named Isaac."

Clarkson glanced at her with genuine puzzlement on his face. "Yes. And it is through Isaac..."

FORTY-FIVE

Flight

Ntombi lifted the shade and peered out the porthole, hoping to see Clarkson looking back at her. Through the seven a.m. Boston fog and across a short span of tarmac stood a tall man with black, curly hair. He stood erect with squared shoulders and his arms crossed. He likely could see only the plane. She could see him, though. It was her turn to watch him without his knowing.

For twenty-two years he had watched her and known her from afar, without her even knowing he existed. At this moment, she watched him, longing to know more of who he was, and at the same time, wanting to hug Tata's neck and make sure he was okay. It was all a tangled mess. But, then again, love was like that. It gets all stirred up into a porridge of joy with lumps of hurt, sometimes big ones of joy and sometimes a porridge of mostly hurt with little lumps of joy.

Ntombi waved at her father, knowing he couldn't see her but needing to do something. The plane began to taxi, and she lost sight of Clarkson. She settled back into her seat, took a deep breath, leaned her head against the headrest, and thought of Whitting's words. He had once shared a wise friend's definition of love, "My steady intention toward another's highest good." She thought of Tata and Clarkson, Steve and Mandlenkosi. She wanted the highest good for each of them.

"Saying goodbye to someone?"

Ntombi turned. She hadn't even noticed her seatmate until now. She was a little lady, at least seventy, with soft, silver curls on her head. Her face was round and her skin barely wrinkled. The first-class seat left her feet dangling about five inches from the floor and her arms reaching out for the armrests like a child.

"I'm sorry," the lady said. "I didn't mean to interrupt your thoughts. I'm headed to Charleston. My daughter lives there."

"Yes, ma'am. I'm headed to Charleston too. I was waving goodbye to my newly found father."

"Has he been lost?"

Ntombi smiled down at her seatmate. "I just found out I was adopted. Or, is it that I am adopted?"

The little lady looked at the seatback in front of her and bounced her feet a couple times. "I think I'd say I have a bonus father."

"I like that."

Soon the bustle of preparing the cabin interrupted their tête-à-tête, and the plane lifted off. As Ntombi watched the ground grow smaller, she thought of how much had changed since her first flight. She thought of Chip and Carly and wondered if they were back in Africa by now. She could recall Carly's sweet face, strawberry hair, and freckled skin, and Chip's calloused hands and jolly nature. She thought of connecting the dots of how they crossed oceans to minister to Zambians and Tata ministered to the homeless and addicts in Torrance who prayed for Mandlenkosi—all just part of the communion.

As the seatbelt sign faded, Ntombi reached for her backpack and placed it beside her. She noticed how it fit nicely in the large, first-class seat. She retrieved the wooden box Clarkson had given her and put it in her lap. It was tied up loosely, like a bundle, with a wide satin ribbon. Ntombi pulled one end of the white ribbon. She moved her fingers across the top of the box, noticing the intricate carving. She imagined the craftsman who had spent years honing his craft and possibly weeks carving this one box. Careful inspection revealed three initials carved in the top. They were slightly off-center. Ntombi smiled as it came to her that they represented her first name and both of her last names—Tata's and Umama's, Clarkson's and Nombeko's, and then a blank space. With upturned lips and new light in her eyes, Ntombi touched the blank space and looked up at the seat back in front of her. He had left room for a future last name—a married name.

Ntombi sat for a minute, oblivious to the roar of jet engines and competing chatter all around her. She held her gift and realized the box was more precious than anything she had ever owned. She thought of the time Clarkson invested in having it made. Ntombi touched both hinges on the back and noticed the pendulum clasp on the front. It was tightly closed and took some finagling to loosen.

Finally, she opened the lid, revealing a velvet lining and a folded note. She lifted the note and beneath it was a small, black, leather-bound book nesting in the box's green velvet lining. The book was without outward markings but was clearly quite old.

Ntombi sat the note beside her on the seat, gently extracted the book from its velvet nest and opened its front cover. The paper lining was patterned with scallops in various shades of maroon and gold. And there was a sticker which read THOMAS PRINCE LIBRARY.

Ntombi's mouth fell open. Her heart began to race. How had he known? With shaking hands, Ntombi fumbled for the note and opened it.

My dearest Lily,

I have had this for months, eagerly waiting to give it to you. I passed my time by carving this box for it. For you. If you are reading this, we have met. I want you to know how proud I am of you. This book is considered rare and precious. I chose it for you because you are far more rare and precious.

Tata has told me of your research. He's a fine man and a proud father. With his blessing, I bought this for you as a token of my love and a reminder that we all have many fathers. This book once belonged to The Reverend Elder John. He gave it to his grandson, Thomas, to start his book collection.

Ntombi didn't finish reading the note. Instead, she folded it over and tucked it beside her right leg, then looked up and took a deep breath. She could smell the pages. They smelled old—the good kind of old. She gently opened the cover of the book again. Turning just a couple of pages, she found the cover page. THE WHOLE BOOK OF PSALMES, FAITHFULLY TRANSLATED INTO ENGLISH METRE. At the bottom of the page was the date: 1640.

She was holding an original Olde Bay Psalm Book!

Without thinking of its age or dollar value, Ntombi tenderly felt the pages. Generations had passed since her grandfather had held this book, preached from this book, sung from this book. Tears welled in her eyes, providing a kaleidoscoping view of the pages. Ntombi blinked to clear them and quickly wiped her cheeks with the back of her hand, lest a tear fall to the page. A smile came across her face, and her heart was strangely warmed as she thought of her tears mingling on the page with those of John and Thomas and even David. Surely David cried when he penned the psalms. Ntombi again picked up Clarkson's note.

> Scripture teaches us that many are called, but few are chosen. John and Thomas were among the chosen—as are you. I gift this to you as a token of my love for you and my admiration of your obedience.

Ntombi looked up from the note. He saw her as called, chosen. Even obedient. With a full and humbled heart, she continued to read.

> As our grandfather of ten generations past crossed the Atlantic, not knowing why he was going, only that he was called to go, you, my child, had the courage to do the same. May his example of obedience go with you through this, his book of Psalms, and may you grow into all God had in mind when He created you and placed you among so great a cloud of witnesses.

Ntombi's eyes again filled with tears and she turned to look out the window. There before her were puffy clouds set in a blue sky. Her mouth parted as she remembered the imagery of a circle that morning at church. It was her cloud of witnesses. John was there and Thomas and Nombeko.

Ntombi gently touched the glass porthole as if wanting to touch the clouds beyond. Just then her seatmate interrupted her thoughts. "Is that a book of Psalms?"

Ntombi turned slightly toward her then down at the book. "Yes, ma'am. A very old copy."

"They were written thousands of years ago, and yet they speak truth for today."

Ntombi looked again at her seatmate, who was now bouncing one foot. The woman turned slightly and extended a hand. "I'm sorry, I haven't introduced myself. I'm Pearl."

Returning the offered handshake and noting the tiny frailty of her hand, Ntombi said, "I am Ntombi, but you can call me Lily."

"Which do you prefer?"

"I don't know yet."

With that, Pearl turned and sized her up. "Goodness, they both fit. Ntombi is strong and bold, and Lily is a beautiful form and fragrant. You are both names. Best to wait and decide." She turned back around in her seat with a sense of surety and crossed her arms. "Tell me about your newly discovered father."

Ntombi recanted the story, ending with, "It's just such a shock to find out I have another father."

"Well, now that I think about it, you have three." Pearl nodded decisively.

Ntombi gave her new friend a look of playful surprise. "Three?"

"Yep. First Father God, then Clarkson, then Tata, who did the heavy lifting." She paused for a minute as if choosing her words and then added, "And, actually, you've always had three Fathers. What has changed is that the delusion is gone. Before, you didn't know them, and now you do. Of course, many don't even know their first father, Father God."

"That's true. We long for him. Do you think on some level I longed for Clarkson and missed him without really knowing what was wrong?"

"Of course. We miss Father God that way. And you miss Nombeko." Pearl glanced over at the book cradled in Ntombi's hands and then up at her. "Would you like to read a Psalm?"

Ntombi looked at her seatmate. She hadn't thought of actually reading it. Does one actually read a book that sold at auction for fourteen million dollars?

Ntombi shrugged. "Sure. Do you have a favorite?"

"Psalm 37:4."

Ntombi carefully turned the pages. Finding the psalm, she read. "Delight thyself in the Lord, and He shall give thee the desires of thine heart."

Pearl turned in her seat to face Ntombi and folded her hands around her plump midsection. "So what are they? The desires of your heart?"

"I'm not sure yet."

"I'll help. What are the options?"

Ntombi laughed and shook her head. She told Pearl all about Mandlenkosi and Steve, Whitting and the research. It was a long story for a long flight. She ended it with, "and then, yesterday, Clarkson and I met with this lawyer in downtown Boston. The building was amazing. Anyway, turns out, Clarkson's father, my grandfather that I didn't even know I had, left me one hundred and sixty-two million dollars. Something to do with taxes—some generation skip thing. Anyway, it's in a trust."

Pearl, who was still listening intently, took a deep breath and exhaled. "You have a greater trust than the money. Paul wrote about those entrusted with the secret things of God. God has entrusted you with secret things and revealed to you things others do not understand. And, as one given a trust, you must prove faithful."

Ntombi looked at the woman, unsure of how she knew so much. "How do I do that?"

"Ah, my child. That too is in the verse. You see, the first, last, and middle steps are to *delight*."

"Myself in the Lord?"

"Precisely. Every day. Then, and only then, will *His* desires become *your* desires—then He gives them to you."

Ntombi carefully tucked the note and the psalm book back

into the box and paused once again to notice the engraving on the top. Pearl was right. It was time to delight.

Ntombi placed the wooden box carefully in her backpack and retrieved a journal, a pen, and a pencil. For the first time, first class made sense. Lucille had been paying her way all these years. Providing was her way of showing love.

Pearl reclined her seat, crossed her arms, and closed her eyes. Ntombi dug her seat tray from the armrest and began to doodle in her journal. As she did, her focus returned with a new earnestness. She drew clouds and, inside each, placed a delight-filled descriptor of Father God with words such as Creator, Mighty, Giver of Life, Ancient of Days, All-knowing, On His Throne, Big, On Time. Words flowed onto the page and then they stopped. She'd run out of words.

She closed her journal, reclined her seat, closed her eyes, and began to pray. But, it was a different prayer. First her spirit sang the words of a hymn. *Holy, Holy, Holy. Lord God Almighty...God in three persons, blessed Trinity.* The few words of the song melded into sleep and an image. She became aware of herself in the picture with the lightness of heaven all around. In her dream, she had her notebook open to the doodled names of God. As she glanced down at it, she became aware of a presence and fell slap forward like a stiff plank except she didn't feel the ground. She was prostrate on what she thought should be ground, but it felt soft. A hand began to write on the notebook, finishing the list.

Suddenly, the plane dropped, jerking Ntombi. She fought to stay in the dream and heard a voice, a thundering voice. The words were, "Tell them about Me. They don't know what they're—"

The plane dropped again. This time jarring Ntombi from her sleep. At that moment, she didn't know if the plane had hit turbulence, or she'd fallen from her heavenly vantage point.

"Father? Your last word, what was it? *Missing*, right? They don't know what they're *missing*?"

With eyes partly open, she looked at the back of the seat in front of her, grabbed her armrests, and pushed herself back in her seat. She spoke aloud.

It is You we long for. We don't know what we're missing.

FORTY-SIX

Glory Landing

It had rained overnight, leaving the early morning July air bearable. Becca and Mae sat in the Corner Coffee courtyard sipping coffee. As was the custom in Charleston, the slight change in the weather warranted comment.

Without being asked, Becca pulled a folded, salmon-colored newspaper from her summer-sized handbag and handed it to Mae who fanned herself with it.

"Not too hot yet," she said.

"The rain cooled it off for now, but it'll get there."

"You is right there." Mae paused, crossed her arms and looked past Becca's head. "Lordy, look who just come through the door."

Becca swung around and saw Dom at the side door looking about the courtyard for a good table. She saw Becca, smiled big, and made a beeline for their table.

"Hi, Becca. It's Dom. Dominique. Ntombi's friend from home?"

Becca decided not to stand and answered Dom somewhat through her teeth. "Of course, Dom. Are you alone? Why don't you join us?"

"Are you sure? I don't want to interrupt."

"Not at all. Dom," Becca said, turning slightly and gesturing toward Mae. "This is Mae, a long-time friend of mine."

"Pleased to meet you," Mae said as she stood halfway and extended a hand. Dom shook it and lowered herself into the metal café chair.

"So what are you up to this summer, Dom?" Becca asked. "Have you been home?"

"Home? Oh no, too much to do. This is home now anyway."

"I see." Becca raised her coffee mug to her lips with both hands and blew in it. Steam rose in front of her. "What are you working on?" she asked, before taking a sip.

Dom gently set her coffee on the cast-iron tabletop and folded her hands in her lap. "I'm taking a couple classes this summer to get a head start on the semester."

Becca nodded.

Dom turned to Mae. "Mae, how is it you know Becca?"

Mae smirked, tilted her head and looked over at Becca. "Actually, we're sisters. Becca don't like having to explain."

Becca had to cover her mouth with her hand to stifle the laugh and keep any coffee from escaping. A grin stretched across Mae's face, and she lifted her cup in the air for a self-commending toast.

"We're closer than most sisters," Becca explained. "I never had a sister. I chose Mae!" She looked at Mae. "Mae has three, so I'm not actually sure—"

"No, no. They helped me know what to look for in a sister. And what not to look for. And I chose you." Looking over at Dom she added, "Besides, we's sisters in Christ."

"Indeed." Becca winked across the table at Mae. She straightened in her chair and shifted her attention to Dom to continue her query. "So, Dom, you and Ntombi are friends?"

"Yeah, we go way back. Primary school. I've been meaning to call her and get together. Every time I see Steve, he asks about her. I know she'd want to know."

Becca glanced over at Mae. She looked like the cat that ate the canary. Becca corrected her with a swift kick under the table and returned her eyes to Dom. Becca heightened her Southern accent ever so slightly. "Oh my, you haven't heard?"

Dom sat back in her chair and sputtered, "Well, yes, of course, I know about her being adopted. Actually, I've known quite some time—"

"Oh, honey." Becca swatted her hand in the air. "Everybody knows that."

Dom lowered her head. "Oh, well, I suppose I don't know then. You know we run in different circles," she said, in a weak attempt at recovery.

Becca paused, then took a sip of her coffee, glancing over at Mae. Mae sat up straight with her hands in her lap, leaning slightly forward like a child at the circus waiting on the next act.

Dom waited and sipped foam off the top of her latte, leaving just a tad on her top lip.

"Well, honey, that's why we're here this early on a Saturday. We took Ntombi and her team to the airport this morning."

"Her team?"

"Yes, she and Whitting left with the others for a six-week tour of Europe."

Dom set her coffee mug back on the table, lifted the napkin from her lap, and wiped the foam from the side of her mouth. "A six-week vacation? Must be nice."

Becca turned slightly to face Dom and better ignore Mae's promptings, then rested her left hand on the table and began tapping her diamond-clad ring finger. "Not exactly. They're visiting thin places around Europe as the first step in their next research project."

"Thin places?"

Becca stopped tapping. "Yes. Places where the veil between

heaven and earth is thin. Power-filled places. Holy places. Mostly places with a long history of fervent prayer. Places where people go to listen and where God frequently speaks."

Dom again placed her cup down and this time her pretense aside. "Really?"

"Yup," Mae said.

Dom looked at Mae and then at Becca with her brow slightly lowered. "I didn't think the college would pay for such an extravagance."

Becca smiled. "Oh, it is indeed an extravagance. They're going first class the whole way." She felt the side of Mae's foot give her a nudge under the table. She knew it to be a second message of restraint but decided to ignore it.

"Ntombi is funding the research. Or, should I say, her trust is funding the trip."

"Trust?"

Becca tapped her fingers on the table a couple of times before answering. "Well, I'm not supposed to say anything about it, but seeing as you're a close friend . . . Suffice it to say, it's a nine-figure trust." Becca turned to Mae. "I believe she can afford a few trips."

She turned back to Dom and watched as she scrambled to manage her reaction.

"Wow!"

Becca softened. "It's such a blessing. We're just so happy for her. Oh, and I almost forgot the best part."

"It gets better?"

"Well, more interesting."

"How so?"

"First, Tata or, rather, Simon, has taken time off from the Torrance mission and is going with them."

Dom placed a hand on the edge of the table. "That's wonderful. I've worried about him. You know, with the other father coming forward and all."

"Actually, he and Tata have become quite close over the years. They have Ntombi in common. But, the big news . . ."

"There's more?"

Becca put both hands on the arms of her chair, leaned forward, and whispered, "Steve is on the team."

Dom's eyes grew wide and her face pale. "Steve? He's in Europe?"

"Soon will be." She glanced at her watch. "Flight just took off."

Dom slumped slightly in her chair. A long pause settled over the table. It was clearly Dom's turn to talk, but no words formed. Perhaps the air had gone out of her lungs.

Becca watched with surprise at the realization that Dom had feelings for Steve. Had she hit too hard? She prayed silently and knew Mae would be doing likewise.

"I'm so sorry," Becca said.

"Oh, no need to be sorry," Dom said with a short breath. She paused and then added, "I am glad she'll get some time with him." Dom looked back at Becca. "What about Mandlenkosi? I was just thinking, with him back in the picture and all . . ."

"Who knows? Court date is coming up." As the words left her lips, Becca wished she could retrieve them.

"Court date? Is he in some kind of trouble?"

Mae jumped in. "Oh, no, darlin'. He's some kind of expert witness or somethin'. The good news is that he gets to stay in the country."

"Oh."

Thankful for Mae's rescue, Becca added, "Well, anyway, it's a research trip, and there's a group of them. I expect once the trial is over, Mandlenkosi will be on the next plane with a sudden interest in thin places."

Dom looked forward. "Still, it's time with Steve."

"I hate that you didn't get to go but with your studies and all."

Dom looked back at Becca and said with a matter-of-fact tone, "Yes, well, it isn't my field."

Becca recognized the tiny opening, but before she could jump on it, Mae chimed in. "Thin places are everyone's field. Who wouldn't want to hear from God?"

"Me," Dom said, looking squarely at Mae. Mae sat with her hands folded in her lap and a twinkle in her eye. Dom returned her irresistible smile. "At least, I don't seem to ask him many questions. I guess I'm afraid to hear the answers."

Mae kept her eyes on Dom. "His are the only answers not to fear. All others are tainted."

Becca knew she meant present company included but doubted Dom had noticed the inference.

Mae stayed steady on course. "Would you like to visit a thin place?"

"In Europe?"

"Best to start close to home."

"Is there a thin place nearby?"

Mae replied softly. "Several. But I have one in particular in mind."

"Sure. Will y'all go with me?"

Becca and Mae glanced at each other and responded in unison. "Wouldn't miss it."

———

That night, Ntombi watched out the airplane window as the sun set over the Atlantic. It seemed way too early for sunset.

Her mind turned to her first flight and how much had changed since then. Was she different now? Or was this always who she was inside, and God had just let it out? Then, oddly, Dom came to mind. Ntombi prayed for a forgiving heart, one that could forgive Dom and her ways. She prayed for Dom, *Father, will you give her holy guilt that leads to repentance?*

Suddenly, the lights on the wing set against the rapidly darkening sky reminded Ntombi of the string of lights dotting along the path to the potting shed. She smiled softly and envisioned it all lit up with Becca, Mae, and Dom inside. Somehow she knew, this would be the night heaven would come down, and glory would fill her soul.

Soon the skies turned to black and the porthole filled with Ntombi's reflection, yet she didn't notice. Her gaze was fixed on the mystery beyond. She nodded a knowing yes and whispered, "Thy Kingdom Come."

About the Author

L.P. PRINCE is President of PRINCE consulting services, a business consulting firm specializing in transformations. As such, she calls herself a "prophet to the profitable," helping leaders and organizations discern and live out their highest good.

She is invited into organizations around the globe to bring about change. As a result, she has had the privilege of conversation with thousands upon thousands of people from all walks of life on six continents.

All that travel has also afforded her countless early morning hours in scripture and classics of the faith, including a ten-year delve into everything written about the glory of God.

At the very foundation of her work is God-given foresight for *what could be* along with insight into reality—*what is* set before her. Her gifting includes creating a shared vision in organizations and using the power of vision to help businesses, leaders, and associates flourish.

As a speaker, Prince crystalizes the depth and height of a client's situation or even a complex Bible topic into crisp, understandable, and actionable words, while engaging the audience in joy-filled learning.

Her counsel is sought by leaders, especially during challenging times and seemingly impossible situations. She is masterful at discerning a path forward for her clients. In this, her first novel, she offers an array of collected wisdom told the medium of story.

Story has long been a part of her life. It began in the company of Appalachian uncles who would spin a yarn and compete for best tale. Today, she uses it to teach at the highest levels of corporations. It works. Through this medium, she is able to make the complex understandable and impart truth from beyond the ages into the lives and calling of those she serves.

For more information or to engage Prince as a speaker, go to
lpprince.org